Room

Nineteen

Also by Diane Eklund-Āboliņš

The Space in Between
On the Circle
Glänsande vitt på blått

Room

Nineteen

Diane Eklund-Āboliņš

Published by AoE Publishing 2014

First published in Australia in
2014 by
AoE Publishing
Sydney, Australia

ISBN: 978-0-9873473-3-6

Typeset in Times New Roman
Cover design: Annette Abolins
Printed and bound by LSI

Regarding -ize and -ise suffixes,
the OED spelling convention
has been followed.

There exists only the present instant... a Now which always and without end is itself new. There is no yesterday nor any tomorrow, but only Now, as it was a thousand years ago and as it will be a thousand years hence.

Eckhart von Hochheim c. 1260 – c. 1327

Fragment One

She walks down the long corridor, keeping close to the wall on the left-hand side. The walls are a nondescript grey colour, and the corridor itself is narrow; she thinks of intestines winding around in a confined space; she also thinks of the Ghost Ride at the Fun Park where, beyond the entrance, there does not seem to be any kind of exit. Her eyes are fixed on the highly polished, dark timber flooring, and they rarely rise above the ever-changing patterns of shoes and trouser legs and the very occasional long skirt.

She knows that there are many people all around her, ordinary, anonymous people, like those she might see at the train station or in the street, hurrying in different directions. Some of them are well-dressed: she can tell by the shoes. When she very occasionally lifts her eyes from the floor, she sees tailored suits and jogging outfits side by side, young people in Gothic black with facial piercings and hair thick with gel, and trim, well-trained people alongside others who are quite obviously overweight. Almost everyone looks slightly anxious; some appear dazed. No one is talking; she knows that it is forbidden. She looks around quickly: there are no children anywhere.

She can still not understand why no one is refusing to walk along the corridors, nor can she understand why she has not refused. It is the fact that people are doing exactly as they have been told, without question, that worries her the most. She remembers once being intrigued, watching cows and sheep obediently following one another, and she wonders if someone on the outside would now be just as intrigued, watching all the people in the corridors.

Someone on the outside.

She knows that if they are inside then there must be an outside, but she cannot see anything that even vaguely resembles an *outside*. She has a very blurred memory of being somewhere else, doing other things – she assumes that it must have been on the *outside* – and then, for some reason completely unknown to her, she was suddenly here in these corridors with all these people obeying inane regulations. She has lost all concept of time: she does not know what day it is; she does not even know what time of the day it is. Her watch stopped some time back, and there do not seem to be any clocks in the corridors. She needs to know what is going on, but she is quite sure that no one around her would have any answers. When she very briefly catches the eye of an elderly man in a shabby grey over-coat, she is uneasily aware that she is not the only one thinking such thoughts.

She can already feel a film of sweat on the inside of her hands and the back of her neck. The sweat on her neck is cold, and, somewhere within her brown corduroy jacket, she knows that her heart is beating faster than normal. As she reaches the end of the corridor, she draws in her breath and lifts her head.

The man in the enormous Reception Hall had said while

handing her a long, thin key on a plaited leather ring: "Walk to the end of the corridor in front of you, then turn left. After twenty metres, you will see another corridor running off to your right; follow it to the end and then turn right again. The room you are looking for is the third door along that corridor. You can't miss it: there is a large number one painted on the door." He had then handed her a brown pill from a large jar on his desk, saying: "Breakfast, lunch and dinner." When she had looked at him, completely dumbfounded, he had added, "Everything you need and nothing you don't."

There had been so much that Tilda had wanted to ask the man, but she had not had the slightest idea where to start.

Now, thinking back to the Reception Hall and the Receptionist, she has the feeling that she is an intelligent woman, and she believes that, somewhere in her past, she has been used to dealing with people. Asking questions, delegating work and formulating procedures have most probably been an important part of her life. She is quite sure that she knows how to stand up for herself, so she is confused and perplexed that she should be meekly taking orders and keys and even pills from someone with a fixed smile sitting behind a large white desk.

Then, while she is still trying to conjure up some kind of picture of her past and who she actually is, she finds herself wondering why Door One should be the third door and what numbers might be painted on the first two doors. Nought and minus one? It does not make any sense that the third door should be Door One: everything must always begin at the beginning and then move forwards. There is a distinct feeling of unease rushing through her body.

Before, when she had still been standing in front of the Receptionist, she had wanted to ask him why the beginning was the third door down the corridor, but while she had been formulating the words in her head, the dapper young man with the carefully waved hair and the advertisement-like smile had moved on to the next client, and Tilda had realized that she had already been forgotten.

Average height with short, greying hair and blue eyes, she is still an attractive woman, in spite of her fifty-plus years. Her body is supple and well-trained and her face, more oval than round, is perfectly balanced – a balance that often instils a feeling of calmness in others, similar to the effect that can be derived from a beautifully crafted portrait hanging in an art gallery. She is wearing a pair of dark blue jeans, a soft white cotton shirt, with the top button undone, and her brown corduroy jacket. It is what she was wearing when it all began, though of the actual *beginning*, she has absolutely no memory.

As she turns left, she clenches the large key between her sweaty fingers. She can feel the ornate bow of the key that has been cleverly moulded to simulate two tightly inter-twined branches. Her fingers run down the shaft while she thinks of tree trunks. She tries to reassure herself: trees are friendly things – they indicate growth and life – the complete opposite of this maze of corridors going nowhere. Her mind is quickly filling with images of all kinds of trees, layer upon layer of green and brown and even yellow and orange. She thinks about autumn, and then she thinks of winter, and the images become stark and grey, and she can no longer see any leaves.

Left, right, right. Would she remember it all correctly?

She is nervous, and she knows how easy it is to forget things when one is nervous. Or to mix them up with other things. She knows that she must have often forgotten things before. Before what? She wonders about the word *before;* then she thinks about the word *after.* Would she experience an *after,* or would there just be a *before* and then nothing?

Without actually looking around, she is conscious that there are not as many people in this corridor, and she feels less intimidated – she has not been able to understand why she, of all people, should feel intimidated – and she is able to keep her gaze straight ahead of her instead of some-where near the floor. Her mind is still attempting to process images of trees and leaves and different seasons and the two words: *before* and *after.* She turns right, into a new corridor, the sound of her hard-soled shoes echoing on the compact timber floor.

There are no windows in any of the corridors, and there is only cold artificial light coming from what seem to be long, thin, white tubes running along the ceilings. She had not reflected on the lack of windows earlier, and this new awareness is beginning to push in on her, like some kind of tight blanket. Once again, she thinks of the Ghost Ride and the solid darkness broken suddenly and erratically by exag-gerated figures of death and dying. She remembers the high-pitched screams of people who knew that no one had died, or would die, and who were quite sure that the ride would soon burst out into the sunshine – people revelling in the controlled sensation of fear.

But now the sensation is not controlled, and everything within her seems to momentarily stop working as her mind gingerly fingers the idea that there may not be any way out. She gasps for air, like someone breaking the surface of the water after having been submerged too long, and then she turns to her right.

The man in Reception, with his well-cut, grey suit and his blonde, wavy hair, had smelt strongly of some kind of spicy aftershave. Tilda had not been able to put a name to the aftershave, even though the olfactory sensation insisted on lingering; she is still unsure as to whether the sensation had been unpleasant or not. She remembers the man's smile. It had been a Reception smile, white and sterile like something pasted across a poster, without any real feeling. The man in Reception with his hair and his aftershave and his smile was obviously used to dealing with clients: handing over keys and giving directions.

Tilda can already see the door with the large numeral one painted boldly in black, just like the man had said. It is an ordinary door, and, like all the other doors in that particular corridor, it is oak, completely flush and without panelling; on its right-hand side, there is a large round doorknob, most probably brass. A couple of people walk quickly past the door without looking at it. Tilda wonders if she might be brave enough to walk past it. Perhaps she could then continue on down the corridor, past all the doors; perhaps, somewhere, she might find an exit. Perhaps she might even find some trees.

She sighs, but then, as though she is trying to convince herself that what she is about to do is her only option, she shakes her head. Somehow, she knows that she cannot just walk past the door, even though, more than anything, that is what she wants to do. She finds herself actually envying the people who are now much further along the corridor, but, while she watches them, she knows that there are many other doors. She stops in front of Door One and fits the key into the lock. She takes a couple of deep breaths, looks furtively behind her, and then, turning the key, she opens the door.

Fragment Two

Tilda felt the door shudder ever so slightly as the lock freed itself. She disengaged the key and, for a moment, stood statue-like, gripping the doorknob, too terrified to turn it, completely aware that there was an unknown space behind the door and that it was waiting to engulf her.

She did not have to turn her head to know that the maze of artificially lit, grey corridors had not disappeared. She stood there, for a moment completely paralysed, clinging to what she believed was the present, yet knowing that she had to step into a future which gave absolutely no indication of anything, either positive or negative. She knew that there was no way back – the man in Reception would never allow it – the only way forward was through that door. Attempting to regulate her breathing, she argued with herself that opening the door could hardly be any worse than anything she had already experienced since being caught up in the nightmare of rooms and corridors.

Once again, she found herself trying to remember something, anything, from her past, while, at the same time, she struggled to work out why she should have been uprooted from a life that was most probably safe and secure, only to be deposited in an interminable maze of corridors. She did not know: she had no memory of how it had happened or why it had happened. She was no longer sure who she actually was or where she fitted in; perhaps that which she believed was her past, and which she could no longer remember, was not her past at all.

She closed her eyes, turned the doorknob and passed quickly through the door. Behind her, the door closed with a dull heaviness, and she heard a faint click as the lock fell back into place. When she quickly turned her head, Tilda noted that the inside of the door had neither a doorknob nor a keyhole.

There was obviously no way back.

Tilda did not want to think of there being no way back. If the Ghost Ride had an exit, then there had to be an exit here as well; it was just that she had not yet found it. Everything had to have both a beginning and an end – an entrance and an exit – but everything had been so peculiar of late, and, if she were honest with herself, she could no longer be completely certain about beginnings and ends. In fact, she could no longer be certain about anything. As she pulled her fingers through her hair, she was aware that her hands were shaking.

She looked around her, and all she could see was blue, not blue walls, a blue floor and blue furniture but, instead, an infinite expanse of blueness, completely unbroken by anything whatsoever. It was like stepping into a summer sky, and, for a brief moment, she forgot all about exits.

When Tilda was a small child, she would sometimes lie on the uneven patch of prickly, dry, green and yellow grass behind the house where she lived, and she would look up into the sky. Pretending for a moment that the dreary brick buildings and the weathered, grey paling fences did not exist, she would see only an upside-down world of blue. Sometimes the blue was broken by weightless white and grey clouds skidding across its surface or congregating in strange shapes, blocking out some of the blue. As she lay there, the grass sticking into her bare arms and legs, the street sounds fighting their way into her consciousness, she knew that if only she could step into this blue and white world then everything would suddenly be wonderful.

This time she did step into it.

She expected to sink downwards, but her feet were still connected firmly to some kind of hard surface. She spread out her arms to prevent herself from falling and took a second hesitant step. The blueness was now all around her, while, at different levels, long thin streamers of cold, almost transparent, cloud moved slowly, like strands of seaweed in deep green-blue water. She could no longer see any walls, just an infinite stretch of blue.

This was not what she had expected: there was nothing around her that even remotely resembled a room. While she was wondering why she had been sent to such a place, she remembered that the man in Reception had been quite certain about Room One. "That's where *you* have to start," he had said, turning to smile at the next customer.

Start? She trembled involuntarily as she took a few more uncertain steps into the cerulean sky. She sneaked a quick look behind her and saw that the blue had packed itself closely into a solid wall; she could no longer see the door.

She continued in a direction that she believed was straight ahead. She had no idea where she was supposed to be going. There were no signposts, not even a path; all she had was the understanding that she was moving further and further away from where she supposed that the door had once stood and probably still stood. Her entire being was focused on the need to find some kind of exit.

Then the thought suddenly occurred to her that she could be moving in the wrong direction.

Tilda stopped walking, wondering about the words *right* and *wrong* and what it was that made one direction more right or more wrong than any other direction. She stood perfectly still, trying to work out what it was that made *anything* more right than wrong. Was it right for her to be here in this place, or was it wrong? She was quite sure that she had not had a choice. But, was it right for her to be going in the direction she had chosen? She did not know, but she was quite certain that she could not simply stand in the middle of all the blue, she had to keep moving. Perhaps the direction itself was really not so important.

As she moved slowly in the direction she had chosen, fragments of opposing ideas were rapidly replacing each other in a bid to answer her question: what was it that made something more right than wrong or wrong than right? She had always found the question difficult to answer as she was fully aware that wrong decisions sometimes resulted in positive outcomes, while some positive actions could have devastating consequences. If her choice of direction proved to be wrong, and she failed to find the exit, then she was not sure if her choice could be considered wrong or right. Perhaps she was not supposed to find an exit. Perhaps she was supposed to spend the rest of her life in this endless blue firmament, in which case she would have made the right choice from one perspective but, most definitely, the wrong choice from her own.

Tilda was not prepared to believe that there was no exit and no way out, and her thoughts refused to seriously contemplate what such a thing might imply, but, even assuming that there was a way out, there was still nothing saying that her choice of 'straight ahead' had been the right one.

Once again, she stopped walking, assorted feelings of panic clutching at her body. Her stomach was swirling into a maelstrom, and there was a thin river-like line of cold edging itself up her spine. She gulped after air, telling herself that she had to remain calm: there would be no one rushing to her assistance if she were to start screaming – no one who would hold her hand and comfort her and tell her that everything was going to be all right. She was completely and utterly on her own.

Or was she?

Perhaps, hidden somewhere within all that blue, there was something or someone – something that was very carefully watching her every step; someone who, heaven forbid, might even know what she was thinking and what she was likely to do next. It struck her that there were many things that were much worse than being all alone.

Tilda took a few more hesitant steps forward and shuddered instinctively as delicate ribbons of cloud brushed across her face. She was still concerned about direction and whether or not she was moving in the *wrong* direction, but her anxiety now had an added layer: there was also the worry that someone might be watching her. She tried to concentrate on her breathing: she knew that, above all, she must not panic.

She focused her thoughts on images of tired yellow grass and miserable buildings and paling fences. It was somewhere in the middle of those, and similar, images, that she had been born more than fifty years ago. She remembered how her mother had once pointed out the narrow terrace house with its wrought-iron balconies and the large fading sign *Community Hospital* affixed to the front wall. The actual place of her birth had not really interested her: it was not much different from everything else around her – brick buildings with façades shifting in tones of grey, boarded-up windows, balconies sighing with things that were no longer wanted, cars that had stopped running... Although aware of the sign, she had tried to concentrate only on the image of the blue sky.

But, back in all the blueness, Tilda was becoming un-mistakably apprehensive that something was wrong: she was not anywhere near fifty. The realization had begun as the merest sliver of a feeling, squashed between all her other feelings and anxieties, and it had first appeared just after she had entered the room and the door had locked behind her. Now, as she thought about run-down buildings and grey streets, the awareness had pushed its way to the forefront of her mind.

Lost in thought, she ran long, thin fingers through shoulder-length, thick brown hair that she knew, in the sun-shine, would show scattered streaks of red, and, when she looked at her hands, she saw that they were completely unblemished. Although she had no way of actually being able to look at herself, she guessed that she was probably no more than twenty-five. The more she thought about it, she decided that, in spite of all the stress and confusion, she definitely did feel younger. Had she simply imagined those extra three decades? She thought of all the things which had happened or which she imagined had happened – was it possible to imagine life in such detail? Perhaps she had even imagined her birth date? She closed her eyes tightly, thinking of people and places, of things that had been said and thought and experienced, wondering if any of it had in fact been real.

Was it possible that her past existed only in her imagination? All the people she had met; all the places where she had been; all the things she had done – were none of them actually real? She frowned, still with her eyes closed, as she slowly understood that all of the many things and happenings rushing past her mind could only be part of her past if she w*ere* actually in her fifties, otherwise they had to be part of her future. A future that she had possibly already experienced.

As Tilda stood there, wrapped in a kind of blue blindness, struggling to find something in her past or her future that would confirm a connection with reality, no matter how tenuous, an indistinct image of her mother flickered across the darkness behind her eyes. At first, she tried to ignore the image as she was more concerned with trying to find an answer to what was actually *past*, *present* or *future*, but the image was persistent, and, finally, she gave up and let it come into focus.

It was an image of a small angular woman with dark hair pulled back into a loose bun on the back of her head. Tilda recognized it immediately as it was the image that had followed her through her childhood, sometimes entwined with other images, like those of the small grey-brown sparrows foraging for food up and down the dusty street. As the years passed by, one after one, the image Tilda had of her mother melded into the sparrow-image, the sparrows became more mother-like, and thoughts of the one always brought to mind thoughts of the other.

In that one very important image, her mother had always worn a dark blue dress. Tilda knew that there must have been other dresses – there was a heavy, brown wardrobe, with clumsy claw-like feet, standing in the room she shared with Tilda's father – but, for some reason, that was the only dress Tilda could remember.

Her father, a tall, well-built man with heavy features and thick, black hair, wore a grey hat on the back of his head and glasses with horn-rimmed frames. He was not overly large, just large, and yet, no matter where he was, he always seemed to fill the space around him, pushing everything and everyone to the edge and even beyond. As a child, Tilda could sense his coldness, but she did not understand his calculated cruelty. When he became angry, which was frequently, she would slip out of the house and curl up on the grass near the woodpile, hoping that he would not find her. Often she would look up at the sky and imagine herself in a world that was completely blue.

By the time she turned six, the space had become far too small for the three of them. Tilda even felt that the blue sky may have shrunk, and then, without fully understanding how spaces could become smaller, she was sent to live with her maternal grandparents. She travelled from Sydney with a man she had never met before, but who she was told was her grandfather. Later, when she looked back, there was not much that she remembered about the train trip, though she did recall her mother on the platform, hugging her. Then there was a gap and next she saw herself boarding the train, holding the hand of the strange man with the grey hair and the beard, and she remembered looking out of the train window and seeing her mother still standing on the plat-form. As she stood, watching her mother wave, the train slowly pulled away from the station, and clouds of grey-white smoke spread out across the platform – the grey pushing aside the blue.

Tilda no longer had any idea of where she was in relation to the door with the numeral one painted boldly in black on its surface. She did not know how far she had come, and she certainly did not know how far she had to go. At times she feared that she was just moving around in circles. She had read that lost people will often move in a circular formation when there is no landmark or reference point, and she definitely had nothing to guide her. This terrifying thought was just one of many heaping themselves on the panic side of her equilibrium scales. Very soon that side of the scales would be touching the ground, though, in a room that is not really a room but a space completely filled with blue, it was no longer possible to say what was the ground and what was the sky.

The blue was a definite cornflower blue colour, very soft and gentle, but strangely oppressive. If only it were possible to see something beyond the blue. If only she knew the extent of the room. Was there an exit, or was this how everything would end, with her wandering in the blueness for ever? Was this moment not only her present but also her past and her future?

She stretched out her arms again. For a moment, she had some wild idea that she might connect with something other than blue, but then she thought of all those things that could be hiding within the blueness, and she quickly drew in her arms, wrapping them tightly around her body. At the same time, she wondered if it might be possible to become part of the blue, somewhat like a bird disappearing into the sky. She had always envied birds the apparent ease with which they separated from the security of the branch or the tiled roof, launching themselves into an element without any footholds. She made a small jump but landed almost immediately back on the hard surface beneath her feet.

Tilda thought again of her mother standing at the train station, and the grey-white pushing away all the blue. At the time, she had most probably believed that they would soon be reunited, but, years later, she understood that a reunion had never been part of the plan, and the last time she ever saw her mother was at Central Railway Station in Sydney. The remembered image of her mother standing on the train platform, with clouds of smoke swirling around her, merged together with the images of a blue dress and brown sparrows, and became labelled *mother,* assuring her that she was no different to anyone else. "My mother," she remembered telling her friends at school, when she was about seven, "was quite small, and her favourite colour was blue."

Not being able to see beyond the blueness, she felt as though her eyes were closed and that she was actually looking inwards instead of outwards. Perhaps she had stepped into her own head and, too late, had discovered that there was actually no way out.

She closed her eyes, and the blue disappeared. Small, minute, multi-coloured particles and hazy, ever-changing shapes flickered behind her eyelids. She had not really expected to be able to see herself, and, for one surreal moment, she wondered if were even possible to step into one's own head.

Tilda's grandparents lived far to the west of Sydney, where saltbush and red dust plains competed with vast blue skies. After many hours, the train had finally stopped alongside the almost deserted railway station, and her grandfather had jumped off the train before lifting her down on to the platform. The guard, in his dark blue uniform, handed Tilda's bag to her grandfather, and the train had then moved off into another present, extricating itself from that which, until then, had been a combined past. Tilda remembered watching the disappearing train and feeling very alone, a feeling that did not diminish, not even when she looked up at the unbelievably blue sky.

Her grandfather had placed his large rough hand on her shoulder and cleared his throat.

"Come on, love," he said, and Tilda had thought, '*Love*? Why *love*?'

They had walked out of the small brown weatherboard station house and across an expanse of red dirt to where an old green utility truck was parked. Between the blue and the red, white sunlight was dancing along the horizon, obliterating the line between tangible and intangible, painting realities where there were none. Tilda's life in the country had begun.

Pushing her way through the blue, Tilda thought how she had always wanted to be part of that blueness, but now that she was, she was not sure if the reality was exactly what she had imagined. She had always expected to experience a sense of limitless freedom and lightness, but she could feel neither.

She remembered that she still had the key in her hand as she suddenly became aware of her fingers moving backwards and forwards over the pattern of branches, sliding up and down the shaft, slipping around the circle of leather. She dropped it into her jacket pocket, while she wondered briefly whether she would ever be able to return it to the Receptionist. She had begun to have doubts: she was no longer sure that she would get out of Room One. This is where everything would end, in the blueness that was part of, and yet so contradictory to, her childhood.

The panic-weighted end of the scales finally touched some kind of firm ground, settling with a soft, barely audible, thud, and Tilda screamed.

It was a scream that exploded outwards from some hidden place inside her. It may have been prompted by anxiety, frustration and fear, but it had been lying dormant for a long time, long before the corridors and the doors with numbers. It had been waiting for this particular moment, and now it surged upwards and outwards, filling the space around her, forcing sharp erratic lines through the blue.

She found herself on the ground, pushed down by the scream that, like some genie escaping from a bottle, had grown to enormous proportions and had now taken on a life of its own. She was only vaguely aware of the blueness above her and around her; she was no longer wondering why she was where she was – all her fear and anxiety had collected together into that one enormous high-pitched cry for help.

As the sound very slowly dissipated into the oppressive blue void, leaving only sound-shadows poised like icicles on the edges of white clouds. Tilda, still tightly curled up in a foetal position, saw it: a thin line of light, far off in the distance, level with the ground. She rolled over on to her hands and knees. The light had not disappeared, it was still there. She closed her eyes and then re-opened them – the light had not moved. She did not have to walk in circles any longer; at last, she knew where she was going.

First on her hands and knees and then in a crouched position, she began to move towards the light. If she stood up, it disappeared, but, when she once again crouched down, the perspective changed, and the light was there where she expected it to be. The blueness was already beginning to break up: fast-moving clouds were obliterating the blue, changing everything to white. The light was becoming stronger and stronger, and it was dominating everything around her. She could feel herself breathing faster; perhaps she would actually find the exit. Perhaps she would get out of Room One.

Fragment Three

Tilda takes several minutes to orient herself before grasping the fact that she is back in the Reception Hall. There had been an explosion of bright white light; she remembers the blue being eaten up by the white, and everything after that happening at excessive speed, too fast for her to comprehend. Somewhere, there must have been an exit, or otherwise she would not now be back in the Hall. She tries to remember, but her head is still full of erupting white light. She tries to focus on things around her, and she can see that there is a Receptionist sitting at the desk in the centre of the very large open space, but it is a different person. He is short and rather plump, with black hair and a pair of rimless glasses. If she had been expecting anyone, she had been expecting to see the other Receptionist, but then she thinks about it for a moment and understands that he cannot be there all the time. She notices that there is a long queue in front of the desk.

She looks around her, noting the enormous domed ceiling, at least twenty metres above her head, the white marble walls, the huge timber and glass reception desk on a low podium in the middle of the Hall and the ten corridors branching out like carefully spaced spokes in a wheel.

The queue circles around the Hall, and there are people everywhere, both in the queue, and, like herself, standing on the edge, looking rather bewildered and lost. There are large, beautifully printed signs stating that under no circumstance is anyone permitted to leave the queue, and anyone who does so will be severely reprimanded. There is also a sign saying that conversations are to be kept to a minimum and another sign urging people to join the queue as soon as possible after returning to the reception area.

She brushes her hand over her forehead before straightening her jacket. As far as she can tell, she is still twenty-five. She scarcely dares wonder if it will be a permanent change, or whether she will suddenly revert to her normal age. She has nothing against being twenty-five again, but, while she is thinking about losing three decades so quickly, she wonders if it actually is a case of *again* or if it is something totally different. She has given up trying to work out if she is in her own past or future. She attempts to catch the eye of the Receptionist, but the man seems to be busy with a customer.

Or is it a client? Tilda is not quite sure; labels change so quickly nowadays.

She is still wondering about the significance of the two words and whether one is actually more appropriate than the other, when she starts walking towards the end of the queue.

She finds herself behind a man in a large green duffel coat. He has long, fair hair pulled back into a ponytail that cuts the green of the coat into two halves, and Tilda resists an impulse to run her hand down the length of hair. Without touching the hair, she imagines its softness caressing her fingertips, but the man in front of her does not seem to be aware of her: he is looking straight ahead. Perhaps, like her, he is looking at the back of the person in front of him, wondering about impulses and tactile sensations.

Tilda asks herself whether or not she should speak to him. She is not normally shy, but she knows that there must be some kind of social etiquette to be followed even in a situation as bizarre as the one in which she has found herself. She is not sure of the etiquette – she is not sure of anything any longer. As a rule, she does not stand in such a queue, waiting to be handed a key to a room which, in fact, is not a room. While she is wondering what she should do, she tries not to think about corridors and keys and rooms with numbers.

She leans forward and taps the man gently on his shoulder. "Excuse me," she almost whispers. "Have you been waiting very long?"

The man turns suddenly, obviously surprised that anyone would be addressing him in such a place. As he turns, the ponytail swings ever so slightly across his back. Tilda notices that he is only a few years older than herself – thirty, at the most. She wonders if that is his correct age, or if he is actually much older, or younger.

"Not that long; what about yourself?" He looks at her for a moment, and, without waiting for her answer, he says, "But, then again, everything, and I really mean *everything* – time, things around us, places, you, I, even what we think – is all so very relative, don't you agree?" He is still looking at her when he adds, "I really don't believe that anything can exist entirely on its own, so the length of time we have been waiting is really quite irrelevant."

Although Tilda finds the answer quite astonishing, she is aware that some people believe that things can only exist in relation to other things, though she is not sure if she agrees. She looks at him, weighing up whether or not she should answer him, and then she says, "You may be right – yes, you probably *are* right – but, at the moment, I'm not sure what is relating to what. Actually, I'm terrified of getting bogged down with all the things on the periphery and losing track of the central point, and then…"

"You'll start walking in circles… "

She is more than slightly taken aback, thinking about Room One.

There is a suggestion of a smile around the man's mouth and eyes. He says, "Oh, yes, it does happen, but we must never let go of the relationship between things, not even between ideas. This is what forms the web that holds everything firmly together. It lets us move between things, not necessarily always in a physical sense. It puts us in control." For a moment he looks down at his hands; then he looks back at Tilda and continues, "To tell you the honest truth, just now I have no idea who is in control; we are certainly not –"

Tilda interrupts him, touching him lightly on his arm. "I'm sorry, but you must tell me: how did you get here? I mean, *here,*" she asks, indicating the room with a gesture of her hand.

While she has been mentally adding the man in front of her to an ever-lengthening list of peculiar and unexplainable happenings, she knows that she wants to ask him how it is possible to move between things if not in a physical manner, but she also knows that she has not got much time, and there are still many other things she desperately needs to ask him.

He says, "I'm not sure, like everyone else, I guess. I really wish I could remember. I have tried to remember, but my mind seems to be completely blank on that topic. It's possible that it was not particularly pleasant, but, as I said,

I really have no idea."

Once again, the enigmatic half-smile.

Tilda nods her head slowly. Perhaps he was not that strange after all. Perhaps he was no different to herself, trying to make the best of an insane situation.

She says, "You're right; it's all very hazy. There may have been a lot of people involved, but I really don't know, not any longer." An almost imperceptible wave of anxiety crosses her face, and she is quiet for a moment, trying to remember that which now seems to be forgotten.

In front of them the queue has begun to move again after a short period of inactivity, and they concentrate on keeping up with the people ahead of them. When, after a couple of minutes, they suddenly come to another stand-still, Tilda again taps the man on his shoulder. As he turns around, she asks, "Do you think... do you think we will ever get out?" She looks around her as she says the last three words, terrified of something, but of what she is not quite sure.

He looks at her, an expression of disbelief on his face. "Of course we'll get out," he says. "That is the one and only certainty; it has to be the central point."

The queue is moving quickly, and they have to hurry to keep up. There is now only one person ahead of them. Tilda has an instinctive feeling that she must not lose contact with the man in front of her. Still processing his answer to her question, she asks him, "Your name? What's your name?" She is aware of the desperation in her voice, but she has too many other things to worry about, and she knows that in less than a minute he will be gone.

He half-turns to face her again as the Receptionist impatiently beckons him to come forward. "Oswald," he says. Then he adds. "Something to do with German woods."

Images of trees.

Tilda is still thinking about Oswald after he has disappeared down one of the corridors, and she is standing, once again, in front of the Receptionist. For a moment she stands there, saying nothing while she wonders if she will ever see him again. If it is at all possible, she feels even more alone and isolated than she has done since she ended up in the maze of corridors and rooms, though she cannot remember when that was, so she decides that *lonely* and *isolated* must somehow belong to some kind of default situation. In spite of his rather strange ideas, Oswald was a real human being, someone who obviously understood her fear and anxiety, someone who probably felt much the same as she did. At least this is what she wants to believe. She thinks that nothing is even vaguely reliable any longer.

"Can I help you?" The Receptionist smiles directly at Tilda. "There are many people behind you in the queue, and, as you must understand, it is important to keep things moving as smoothly and as quickly as possible." The smile remains, poised between them.

Tilda thinks how strange it is that an expression can become concrete and, at the same time, be completely disassociated from the source of the expression.

Her eyes move away from the smile, which continues to fill the space in front of her, and she concentrates on the man's face. In spite of the situation, or perhaps because of it, Tilda is strangely fascinated by the small round glasses and the way they reflect the man's eyes. She wants to ask why it is so necessary to keep things moving; in fact, she wants to ask him why they are all standing in the queue in the first place, but, instead, she says, "I was thinking that nothing is reliable any longer. Not even my age."

The smile recedes, and the Receptionist picks up some papers from the desk in front of him, bundling them together and then spreading them out in front of him. He says, "Do you really think so?" The smile is different now, more restrained, and his eyes behind the small rounds of glass are wandering past Tilda along the line of people waiting in the queue. He fixes his gaze on Tilda and says, "Reliable or not, we can't stand here all day."

Tilda remembers the key and pushes it across the desk to the Receptionist. "I'm not sure if it was the right room," she ventures, "It ended so strangely… nothing was…"

"Nothing was?" There is an impatient nuance to the Receptionist's voice. He quietly slides open a drawer in the massive desk and drops the key into its own special box. Before closing it, he picks up a new key and hands it to Tilda. From a jar on his desk he also takes one of the brown pills and pushes it across the desk towards her.

"Of course it was the right room," he says as Tilda picks up the tablet and places it hesitantly in her mouth. "Every room is always the right room." He has regained both his composure and most of his smile. "Room Twenty-Seven," he says, pointing along a corridor running off to his right.

"It is a very long corridor, so don't despair. Eventually you will reach the end and then you must turn left. At the end of the new corridor, turn left again. Door Twenty-Seven is the tenth door along on the left-hand side."

Tilda still wants to ask him lots of questions about Room One and why she is only twenty-five and why she must eat small brown pills instead of proper food, and, most of all, why she is where she is, but the Receptionist is already smiling past her, and the man behind Tilda moves up to the desk. Tilda sighs and walks slowly in the direction of the corridor. It is not the same corridor down which Oswald disappeared, and she is feeling strangely depressed, even lost. She wonders briefly if there is actually any point looking for Room Twenty-Seven, but she has a distinct feeling that she has no other option.

Fragment Four

When Tilda was eighteen, she married Milford. He was three years older, and neither of them should have married, at least not each other. They married at the registry office with two of the office workers as witnesses. Over the years, the office workers had witnessed many marriages; it was part of their job description, and they both managed to convey an air of slightly bored superiority.

It was March, and there was a slight hint of autumn in the air. Tilda had a new pink dress, and Milford wore a suit that was, already then, at least ten years out of date. Holding each other's hand and only vaguely aware of the sombre timber panelling, the leather-covered furniture and the small window looking down on to a traffic-infested street, they said "I do", both of them desperately wanting to believe that they were on the threshold of something wonderful.

But the *wonderful* eluded them.

Her steps echoed softly along the corridor, each echo adding itself to the one before, filling out and creating new echoes and new sounds. The sounds were filling her head, interacting sharply with memories of Milford, memories she had desperately tried to erase. She found it annoying that she should be thinking about him now, when she had so many other things to worry about. Tilda had relegated Milford to her past, but perhaps there was no such thing; perhaps everything was part of an enormous *now,* and there was no past. Not even a future.

There had to be a future; she had to get out of this place; there had to be something after all the corridors and rooms and… But what if this *were* the future? What if this is how everything was going to end? She shook her head, trying to rid herself of such thoughts. This is definitely not how she had imagined the future: there were so many things she had not yet done, and, quite apart from what she had done or not done, she had absolutely not calculated ending her days in an intricate jumble of rooms and corridors.

Her erratic inner monologue came to an abrupt stop; she had reached the end of the first corridor, and she could see two new corridors stretching out to the left and the right, forming the top of a T. Unexpectedly, a string of T words ran through her head as she turned to the left.

Taffeta, truculent, tansy, tip… The words made no sense, but they did help to push Milford to the edge of her mind, and, as the deluge of half-formed images and sentences faded, she forced herself to focus on the small weather-board house where she had lived with her grandparents.

It was a box-like house with narrow verandas at the front and on both sides. Even in the short-lived winter months it was constantly dusty, and, when the summer storms came, the dust turned to rivulets of red that sketched fleeting patterns across the iron roof and over the walls and windows. It stood a little to one side of the town, two streets back from the main street. From the front veranda, Tilda could see the town's two churches: the Catholic and the Anglican where she had been told God resided, moving haphazardly from one to the other.

Next to the house, there was a shed with a corrugated iron roof and, behind the shed, a small hen run with buckled wire fencing. When she first came to stay with her grandparents, there had been a vegetable garden behind the house, but, as the years passed, weeds had invaded the garden until, eventually, there was no clear differentiation between the rest of the backyard and the garden.

When she had arrived at the house with her grandfather all those years ago, her grandmother, a small unassuming woman with salt-and-pepper hair plaited and twisted around her head, was already standing at the gate, waiting for them. After they had extricated themselves from the car – it was a long step down to the ground – Grandfather took Tilda's bag up to the house, while Grandmother bent down and gathered the little girl into an uncomfortable and awkward hug before leading her into the house, the wire door slamming behind them.

Inside the house, Tilda was met by a mixture of smells that only helped to emphasize the fact that she was now somewhere else and no longer at home. The smells came from strange furniture and furnishings, from unfamiliar people and different foods, even from the bushes growing close against the veranda posts and from the paint on the very walls of the house. And they were all linked together by the heavy, earthy smell of red dust. While her nose was busy isolating different smells, her eyes were carefully noting the layout of the house where a long narrow hall stretched from the front door to the back of the house. There were doors leading off the hall – the first one, closest to the front door, was open, and Tilda was able to see a wine-coloured sofa and some armchairs around a polished table. On the table, she could see some lace doilies, a glass vase and several books. The three remaining doors were all closed.

The hall opened into a large kitchen which occupied most of the back part of the house, its floor covered with worn brown and green linoleum, and from the kitchen, there was a wire door leading to the backyard. Moving her eyes quickly around the room, Tilda noted that there was a door to a small room to the left of the kitchen, and that the door was open.

"Used to be your mother's room…" her grandfather said, his words hanging heavily in the air somewhere between the kitchen and the room.

Tilda looked at him then, wanting to hear more, but her grandfather, having dropped her bag inside the door, disappeared up the hall towards the front of the house. Her grandmother placed a hand tentatively on Tilda's shoulder. "You know, he loved her… he loves her, very much."

In the room at the back of the house, Tilda told herself that she also loved her very much and that she missed her dreadfully. She also tried to tell herself that she missed her father, but the emotion was not there, and she was not sure why. She would lie in bed at night, listening to the crickets and the shrill night birds, or, when it was raining, to the rain beating against the roof above her room, and she would conjure up the already-fading images of her parents and wonder about love and what it was, if anything, that she actually missed. She was not particularly worried about the separation: her parents were still living in the grimy little house in Sydney, and eventually she would be put on the train and she would be sent back to them.

Quite certain that nothing had changed, she was often confounded by her grandparents' silence those few times when she mentioned her mother, and, as time wore on, she mentioned her less and less.

Grandfather, with his short grey beard and glasses and blue-grey overalls, worked at the produce store in the main street, ticking off sacks and bales, and tins with clamped-on lids. On those frequent occasions when Tilda accompanied him, she loved standing in that space, surrounded by the smells of feed and wheat and kerosene and sawdust and petrol, the cages full of chickens, the tools, the old green tractor, the tyres.

At home, her grandmother made food every day on an enormous black fuel stove, which took up half the kitchen, washed the clothes in a large black copper – also in the kitchen – looked after the hens and the vegetable garden (until it silently disappeared into the confusion of the back-yard) and often baked cakes for functions run by the CWA.

Within only days of Tilda's arrival in the outback, she was enrolled in the local school, and, when the other children asked her why she lived with her grandparents, she told them, for some reason that she had never been able to understand – not then nor even later – that her parents were both dead and that she was an orphan. When pressed for more information, she would sometimes add that her mother's favourite colour had been blue.

In the beginning, there was the occasional letter from her mother, but when Tilda was eight, the letters stopped altogether, and when she asked her grandmother if her mother had forgotten her, the elderly woman shook her head without saying anything. Two years later, Tilda asked her again, and her grandmother told her that her mother had died – she mentioned nothing about her father – and

Tilda then spent many sleepless nights tossing and turning in her little bed at the back of house, quite certain that her thoughtless chatter in the school playground had been the cause of her mother's demise.

Her thoughts had been so insistent and so colourful that she had not paid much attention to the corridor, and she had not noticed that it was completely empty, except for herself. As the thoughts slowly swirled back to where they had come from, Tilda became aware of the emptiness all around her and the extent of the corridor stretching off into the distance. It was like a long funnel joining an unfathomable present with an uncertain future. As she looked at the corridor, she thought how even her thoughts were being funnelled – they were being pushed back towards Milford: thin and slightly freckled Milford with the blue eyes and the nondescript type of fair hair which would eventually recede from his temples. Tilda did not want to think about him, but, in spite of what she wanted, she remembered that he had been much taller than she was, and how easily he had claimed the space above the heads of everyone around him. This was a space that even Tilda felt she had some claim to as long as she held tightly on to his hand, and she remembered how, at least in the beginning, she held on to him as tightly as she could.

They had met in a pub not far from Central Station. Tilda had only just moved back to Sydney and was living at the YWCA. She had not expected to feel so lonely; she knew no one, and then she met Milford.

Milford was also from the country, and Tilda gathered that his family had a small property in the south-west of the state. "Wheat," he had said the first evening they met, "as far as you can see."

In spite of, or perhaps because of, the wheat, they had something in common; they both understood the wide, uninterrupted expanses of blue sky and red dust. She moved closer to him and smiled. Perhaps Sydney would not be so lonely after all.

Then the corridor abruptly came to an end.

Fragment Five

T ilda is so caught up in her thoughts that she is quite startled when she suddenly reaches the end of the corridor. She looks at the blank wall in front of her and is aware that she has no other option than to turn to the left: there is no corridor running off to her right. She closes her eyes. Somewhere inside her head, she can hear the Receptionist's words: "At the end of the new corridor, turn left again. Door Twenty-Seven is the tenth door along…"

She turns left and counts the doors along the corridor.

The key is a perfect fit, and Door Twenty-Seven opens without a sound.

The cemetery is small with a low iron railing cutting through squat cement supports, dividing the dead from the living. Beyond the railing there is a wide red-brown dirt road, and beyond the road there is only the blue, cloudless sky. Tilda is aware that the line between the road and the sky is almost straight with a handful of scattered buildings and trees breaking into the blue. She knows this without even having to look: the buildings and the trees are already imprinted on her memory: they have been there for years.

In spite of the summer warmth around her, she suddenly

feels cold without any kind of warning, and she shudders slightly as if waking from some disagreeable dream. She looks across the grey-white headstones to where a small group of people are gathered around a newly-dug grave. Most of the people are dressed in black. She walks closer and stands next to her grandmother, slipping her hand into that of the older woman. When she looks down at herself, she sees that she is only fourteen years old.

There is no room; there are no walls. Tilda wonders about the corridor; perhaps there was an exit after all.

She is holding her grandmother's hand; she can feel a certain tenderness in spite of the dry, papery skin. She knows that it is her grandfather inside the coffin being lowered into the hole. She knows that he is dead and that *dead* is the end of everything. She looks at her grandmother who is focusing on something beyond the coffin and the hole and the graveyard, trying not to let her tears fall.

The postmistress, a fat woman with short, tinder-dry, grey hair puts her large hand on the older woman's arm, believing, perhaps, that the gesture will somehow dilute the sorrow. Tilda's grandmother almost reluctantly moves her gaze from beyond the graveyard and looks at the postmistress briefly, but whether it is with thanks or not, Tilda is unable to say.

Tilda lets go of her grandmother's hand; the coffin is now in place. The minister says a last farewell, and the little group breaks up slowly and haphazardly. Later, the gravediggers will return to fill in the hole.

As people are moving away, Tilda stands at the edge of the hole and looks down. She thinks of her grandfather and the box and the darkness and that she had actually known him longer than she had known her own mother. Then her grandmother calls to her, and she whispers goodbye as she hurriedly turns away from the grave and joins the others further down the path.

Tilda is still looking for some sign of her previous imprisonment. Surely, beyond the dust and grey-green trees and the small group of black-clad people, there must be a wall, and, beyond the wall, another corridor. She wants to feel free, but she dares not assume that she is free. She slips her hand back into that of her grandmother, trying to find some kind of reassurance in the immediate physical contact.

It was his heart that finally killed him. He had been at work, helping the store boy move sacks of fertilizer, and, as the boy would later tell the police, he had suddenly dropped the sack he was holding, and, looking at the boy as though he wanted to say something, he had fallen to the floor.

"He was already dead, sir," the boy had said later, overwhelmed by the uniformed man standing in front of him. "I'm sure of that; there was really nothing I could have done."

The policeman had nodded, returning his pen and notebook to his pocket. There was nothing he could do either: it was quite obvious that the man was dead.

At first, her grandmother had refused to believe that death could happen so quickly, without any warning. When her daughter died, she had anticipated it for years: her mind weaving together all the different possibilities, tying them together with a 'do not open' sign. Although she never wanted to admit it to herself, she had known that her daughter would die, but she had not expected that her husband would die.

Grandmother fills the kettle from the tap connected to

the large water tank on the outside of the house and puts some kindling into the stove. While the water is boiling, several ladies from the CWA move around the kitchen, arranging cakes and carefully-cut sandwiches on porcelain plates with floral borders. Tilda stands near the door, feeling superfluous, then she walks back up to the hall to the lounge room at the front of the house.

A couple of the men are smoking; the store boy is standing with his back to the room, looking out the window. He has never been to a funeral before.

"It must have been awful…" begins Tilda. "I mean, it did happen right in front of you."

The boy nods and turns slightly to look at Tilda. He is a couple of years older, but he has known Tilda for a long while: they went to school together.

When he does not say anything, Tilda says, "I've never seen anyone die." Then, after an extended silence, she adds, "You know, my mother died."

The boy nods again. He has turned around completely and is facing the room. "You must understand, I couldn't have done anything, nothing at all." he says. "The policeman agreed with me: there was nothing I could have done."

Now it is Tilda's turn to nod. "I know that," she says. "It really has nothing to do with anyone else – death. I mean – it just happens." Then, for some reason that she does not fully understand, she adds, "Perhaps it has something to do with the relation between things?"

The boy looks at her, more or less as she would have looked at herself had she been able, with a puzzled expression on his face.

"I'm sorry," she says. "I really don't know exactly what I meant by that." She pauses for a moment, and then she continues, "But there is always some kind of relation or connection between things – the way they happen or don't happen – I mean, we're alive and then we are dead. Both things are connected; it is impossible to have one without the other, and the one is the way it is, or isn't, simply because of the other." She looks at him, and, when he does not say anything, she asks, "Do you agree or…?"

The ladies from the kitchen have arrived, setting down their plates of food among the cups and saucers already arranged on the best lace tablecloth covering the table in the middle of the room. Grandmother follows with the teapot.

The boy is thankful he does not have to answer.

Tilda has already moved on to thinking about confined spaces. She feels as though she desperately needs to be hanging on to someone; she does not want to slip back into the corridor. She thinks about Oswald.

Fragment Six

Oswald cannot get the image of the woman in the queue out of his head; he must have seen her somewhere before. Before what? He is not sure. Everything is so uncertain at the moment; there is no longer any reliable reference point. At the Reception Desk the Receptionist handed him the meal-replacement pill and a small key to a room on the fourth floor. Oswald was not even aware that there was a fourth floor. He had assumed that there was only one floor, but now his nightmare has expanded exponentially. He tries to visualize all the layers of corridors, bringing them together into one compact image, but it does not work. He feels trapped in a drawing by Escher, and, try as he may, there is no way out.

But there is a way out; he knows that for certain. He is a mathematician, and, for him, everything is based on logic: if there is an entrance to this maze of corridors (and there has to be, otherwise they would not be where they are now), then there also has to be an exit, a way out. Everything in the universe is determined by a collection of mathematical formulae. He remembers telling the woman that getting out is the only certainty. He has to hold on to that certainty; if he lets go then he will have nothing to hold on to, not even mathematics.

He is still not sure how it all began, but he knows that it must have begun somewhere. Everything has to have some kind of beginning, in the same way that everything has to have an end.

He turns out of a long corridor and begins to climb a flight of stairs. Like the corridors, the stairs have been made from some kind of timber, but, in spite of the large number of people who must have used them, there are no marks of excessive use; in fact, there are no marks at all. He thinks of other stairs he has used with a slightly worn indentation on each step, more or less in the middle where people normally walk. These stairs appear new, yet he is almost certain that they are not.

Again he thinks of the young woman. He realizes that he does not know her name: all he has is an image of a slightly-built girl with shoulder-length dark blonde hair and blue-green eyes. He is not completely sure about the colour of the eyes: they only talked for a few moments, and there was so much going on around them. He knows that she was concerned, probably extremely worried. His mind moves around all the images he has of her, and he wonders where she is now.

He has reached the top of the first flight of stairs and is faced with yet another corridor. There are not as many people on this floor, and he does not feel that he needs to hurry. He tries to remember something, anything, from the time before all the corridors, but his mind is like a brick wall with no openings.

A great deal of his thinking is based on the idea that everything is related to everything else; he sees life through the lens of some enormous mathematical formula that links everyone and everything. He has actually been trying to find a connection between all the room numbers he has been given to date. Initially, they were all prime numbers: thirteen, sixty-seven, eighty-three, seven, and he believed that he was on the verge of some kind of breakthrough, but then he was given number forty. He is still looking for connections; he is almost sure that the problem can be solved mathematically.

He reaches the second flight of stairs and sits down on the bottom step. He has a feeling that he should not sit down anywhere, and he wonders if he is being watched. Several people walk past him and continue along the corridor. A woman looks at him, an expression of concern on her face, before carefully stepping past him and walking up the stairs.

He suddenly remembers that he was sitting when they came. Everything is very hazy: a bit like being half awake and trying to piece together some disjointed dream. He remembers the feeling more than any actual images. It is a feeling of anxiety, even terror. He had a glass in his hand; yes, he can actually remember that. It was a squat glass with a heavy bottom. He can even remember how it felt in his hand – smooth and yet substantial – and the memory gives him a brief burst of self-confidence: if he can remember the glass, he should be able to remember everything else.

An elderly man, in a coffee-coloured sports jacket, stops momentarily in front of him and mouths to him that he must move on. The man looks worried, and Oswald is not the type of person who would want to worry anyone unnecessarily. He smiles a vague kind of *thank you* at the man and stands up. The man continues resolutely along the corridor, his head bowed; Oswald begins to climb the second flight of stairs.

Now he remembers that it was a whisky glass, and there were other people nearby, but he cannot remember any of their faces; he cannot even remember the room. It had to be a room within the confines of walls and a ceiling and a floor – all spaces have to be limited, he argues with himself, irritated by the fact that he cannot remember what he really needs to remember. Thinking of the whisky glass, he decides that he would be very grateful for a glass of anything at the moment.

The second flight of stairs opens out into a new corridor, which stretches into the distance. Standing at the top of the stairs, Oswald is unable to see the end of the corridor, and he feels that it parallels his present predicament. He does not like to be so much in the dark: he wants to be able to see all the facts laid out in front of him, and he wants to be in control of his life again. But then he wonders if he ever had been in control; perhaps he just thought he was and that was why he felt relatively happy and secure. Perhaps things happened the way they did because everything had been programmed to happen in certain ways. Perhaps the corridors are all part of this programming.

He meets a man and then a woman coming from the opposite direction; he does not talk to either of them, but he can imagine that they could very well be thinking many of the same thoughts as he is thinking. He reflects on what might happen if everyone refused to walk along corridors and open random doors. He even wonders why everyone is actually doing it without objecting. As his mind hurtles over and around centuries of war and political dispute, he feels that perhaps there are many reasons not to wonder, but then he thinks of himself and he continues to wonder.

By the time Oswald climbs the third flight of stairs, he is quite tired. The corridors have a claustrophobic feel about them, and the artificial lighting is beginning to make him depressed. He knows that he needs the sun and, if possible, something strong to drink.

He is still thinking about what he would like to drink when he reaches the door and slips the key into the lock.

Fragment Seven

Room Thirty-Four was a room about three metres cubed. The floor, the walls and the ceiling were all covered with sheets of dark timber laminate, which gave anyone inside the room the feeling of being completely enclosed inside a large box. The only light came from a naked light bulb hanging from the ceiling, positioned exactly in the middle of the cube.

Tilda was sitting on the floor. She felt that the room could easily have been a coffin, except it was the wrong shape. She was a little amazed that she should be thinking about coffins, and then her mind swung back to her grandfather's funeral. Her memory stopped at the wake when she was being offered a sandwich from a plate with a thin border of pink roses. Her grandmother was pouring tea; the store boy was... She could not remember what he was doing, because, just at the point where she was reaching for a sandwich and her grandmother was pouring tea into a pink and white cup, everything went black.

Back in Reception, she had sat on a low bench near the wall, watching people haphazardly attaching themselves to the queue. She was acutely aware that she was no longer twenty-five, not even fourteen, but was once again her correct age. Without really wanting to admit it to herself, she was extremely disappointed: losing almost three decades from her age had been the only positive thing about her present situation. She spent a few minutes thinking about the word *correct* and what it was that made one reality more correct than another. What was it that could possibly make fifty-five more correct than twenty-five? With the past and the future so curiously intertwined, she could no longer be sure which of the two was her actual reality.

A stout woman in a tightly fitting white uniform, with a white cap almost obliterating what was most likely a head of tired, yellow hair, came slowly into view. She was pushing a stainless steel trolley, and, as she stopped in front of Tilda, she offered her a drink, Tilda's clumsily formed thoughts about things being correct or otherwise collapsed like a house of cards is wont to do when someone inadvertently knocks the table. The woman stood, leaning on her trolley, waiting for an answer, and Tilda, having no time to gather together the fallen cards, nodded her thanks. She knew that there was no point asking the woman what the drink was – she could tell that it was neither coffee nor tea – but it was hot, and she accepted it thankfully. She had seen the woman many times before, pushing her trolley back and forth in the huge hall, the large silver-coloured urn sitting firmly in place on the trolley, the neat columns of paper cups swaying ever so slightly as the woman moved around the room.

She continued to watch the people in the queue while she drank, feeling the warmth spread throughout her body. The woman with the trolley had now moved on and was working her way around the enormous space, obviously in search of other people sitting on other benches. Tilda was really not interested; she was only happy for the warmth that had been encapsulated in the drink, whatever the drink might have been. She speculated fleetingly about how the woman had come by such a position: whether she had applied for it through some Employment Office or whether she had simply answered an advertisement in the newspaper: Wanted, woman to operate a mobile canteen serving hot drinks. Safe, enclosed working environment.

The man in Reception – tall and thin with receding grey hair – looked across at her. His gaze was direct and unfaltering; she looked away, but, when she looked back, his eyes were still fixed on her. She sighed and stood up, considering for a moment where she should discard the empty cup. Beyond the end of the bench, she saw that there was a slit-like opening in the wall under which there was a neat plaque, with the word *Rubbish* carefully engraved in a neat cursive script.

Tilda pushed the paper cup through the opening, rummaged in her coat pocket for a tissue, wiped her hands and then walked slowly towards the end of the queue.

When she finally reached the Receptionist, he gave her the key for Room Thirty-Four.

Now, sitting on the hard floor, she stretched out her legs. There was really not much else she could do; she had already walked around the room several times, searching in vain for some kind of exit other than the door through which she had entered. Perhaps the entrance and the exit were the same?

She could not understand why she should have to sit inside a timber box, and she wondered how long she would have to be there. As she had done on several occasions before, she began to worry that she might never get out. Her thoughts wandered past all the images of coffins and back to her grandfather's funeral.

Not long after Tilda's grandfather died, her grandmother became completely obsessed with everything and anything that had to do with death and dying. Grandfather's death had forced Tilda's grandmother to accept that death was inevitable and unavoidable and that it could happen at any time, anywhere. She would wake up of a morning, amazed to find that she was still alive, and she would spend the first hours of any day trying to equate herself with that fact. Death was the only definite, and everything she had ever done or thought was leading towards that one ultimate climax: death.

She was not a religious woman, so she could not find consolation in either of the churches visible from her front veranda; instead, she contented herself with doing all the things she had always done, thinking, as she dusted or washed or pushed the pieces of dark red meat through the mincer, that this might be the very last time she would be doing what she was doing. The idea fascinated her at the same as it disturbed her. As she took the cutlery from the drawer to set the table, she would think: perhaps I will never do this again; perhaps this is the last time I shall have to decide whether to match this fork with that knife or that spoon with that fork. She looked out of the window, watching the movement of light and dark beyond the white lace curtains and the glass. It did not much matter what she thought about the curtains or the glass or what was on the outside, because all those things would soon be someone else's responsibility, and her observations and thoughts would be no more.

It was the clean, razor-sharp cut between life and death that frightened her the most: we are and then we are no longer. She would have liked to have been able to talk to someone about it, someone who already knew what it was like, but she knew that that was impossible.

She was still trying to relate the reality of life with the inevitability of death; she had not been able to reconcile the two, and she felt that she was being propelled towards the second before she had had time to completely under-stand its irreversibility. There were no second chances and no way of avoiding that which someone had already pre-ordained. Was it God or had she herself, in that millisecond of conception, decided when and where she would die? She did not know. She would have liked to have been able to think of other things, but her thoughts nearly always came back to the question: what was it like to die? Would everything suddenly become dark? Would the birds simply cease to sing, like the switch on the radio being turned to 'off'? Would the smell from the red dust swirling down the street reach her nostrils and then disappear into nothing-ness? Would she be aware of that instant as she crossed over from something to nothing?

Tilda stood up and walked around the room once more. Perhaps she had missed a possible exit; perhaps there was a panel that needed to be slid up or down to reveal an open-ing or a door. She ran her hands over the walls as far as she could reach, but she found nothing out of the ordinary, nothing that moved in the slightest when she touched it.

She was bitterly disappointed, but that was life. She sank back down on to the floor, thinking about the day her grandmother had talked to her about her mother.

They were sitting at the table, the meal finished, and Tilda asked her grandmother to tell her about her mother.

"Your mother…" Grandmother had said, looking past Tilda towards a wall covered with family photos and a small oil painting of an English landscape, with unfamiliar trees, collected neatly within a heavy gold-coloured frame. "There's not much to tell. Not much that you would really want to know…"

"But I need to know. There must be something you can tell me?" begged Tilda. It was already six months since her grandfather's funeral and more than eight years since she had come to live with her grandparents.

"Just something, anything at all. What did she look like? What was she really like? Why did she move to Sydney?" All Tilda had was the one image and the blue dress; no one had ever wanted to tell her anything.

Grandmother moved her cup and saucer to one side. Without looking directly at Tilda, she said, "Your mother left here when she was seventeen – she'd heard so much about the city; *opportunity* was the word she used. 'Lots more opportunity in the city', she used to say. She worked for a while in a bar, and then she wrote that she'd found work in a big department store. She wrote a lot about opportunity in that letter."

Tilda's grandmother moved her cup on the saucer, the sound of china against china breaking into the snippet of silence. It was almost as though she needed the time to collect her thoughts.

"Then she met your father. He, your father, was at least eight or nine years older than she was – an accountant with some kind of import company."

Tilda had never known what her father had done for a living, though, if she really tried, she could remember the important-looking, brown briefcase standing in the hall, and her mother's repeated warning not to touch it because it was her father's.

"After she'd mentioned the accountant, there were no more letters, not for several months, not until she wrote and told us that she and the accountant were getting married. Later, when we looked back, we understood that she was already expecting you…"

Tilda said nothing.

"We said we'd travel to Sydney for the wedding, but she insisted that it wasn't necessary. She said that they'd come and visit us as soon as things had settled down." Grandmother ran her forefinger around the lip of the cup several times.

"After you were born, she was not at all well. She didn't write as much, but we knew that something was wrong. So your grandfather took time off from work, and we took the train to Sydney."

Perhaps there was an opening in the floor. The thought had not occurred to her before, and a small surge of excited anticipation ran through her body, a bit like a wave confidently riding above other, slower waves. For some minutes, Tilda remained sitting where she was, moving her eyes across the floor, section by section. Finally, she got up on to her knees and crawled around the floor, moving her hands over every square centimetre of the timber flooring, checking the edge of each timber plank along the entirety of the join.

Nothing.

Tilda had been so certain that everything was going to end in the blueness of Room One, but now she wondered if, perhaps, it was here where it would all end, in a room that somehow resembled a coffin. As she contemplated the line between reality and whatever it was that existed beyond reality, she was thinking much the same thoughts as her grandmother, and, like her grandmother, she was dubious of anything existing beyond that line: to her way of thinking, it made no sense. There was a beginning and there was an end, a past and a finite future. Once the end of that line was reached then *now* automatically became *then*. She wondered how long it would take before *now* became *then*. She tried to absorb as much of the *now* as she could, knowing that once *now* became *then*, she would no longer be aware of anything.

Her hands and knees were sore from crawling around on the floor, and her body was rapidly filling with a feeling of cold emptiness as she began to accept the fact that there was absolutely nothing she could do. The inevitable would happen no matter what she did or did not do. She sat for a while, considering her fate, and then she curled up on the floor and, eventually, went to sleep.

Fragment Eight

Oswald was back in the Reception Hall. At first, when he became aware of his whereabouts, he decided that the room on the fourth floor must have been somewhat of a disappointment, because he had no memory of what had happened there. Though, as he dwelt on his inability to remember anything from the room, he decided that not being able to remember did not necessarily equate with the experience being unimportant: he could not remember what it was that had caused him to be in the situation he now was, and, as far as he was concerned, it was an extremely important situation that was demanding all of his attention. He felt much the same as he would have felt waking up in the recovery room after an operation, still remembering the anaesthetist talking calmly to him before he was wheeled through the swing doors into the operating room but unable to remember anything that happened afterwards.

After being in the room – at least, he assumed that he had been in the room – he had found himself sitting on the second floor near the stairs leading down to the ground floor, completely filled with a heavy, formless depression, the key still in his hand. He had not needed a mirror in front of him to know that he was older; he had run his hand over his chin, feeling the roughness of his beard. The pony-tail was gone, and he was wearing glasses. He removed them and studied the heavy black frames. While he looked at the glasses, he tried to unlock any memories about what had happened in the room, but all he could remember was that he had opened the door and gone in. Beyond that, there was nothing.

However, as he sat there, the glasses resting in his hand, he did remember the significance of the whisky glass. As the image of the glass itself became clearer, he recalled that he had been at a party. The picture in his mind was still not very clear, but he assumed that the party had been at someone else's flat, and he could vaguely remember a harbour view and a myriad of lights marking out a very wide expanse of water. He could see himself standing on the balcony, and he had a feeling that he had been fascinated by all the lights: the actual colours and the way they all clustered together, forming ever-changing light patterns and new, exciting colour combinations.

After standing on the balcony for some time, he had moved back into the flat. The memory was becoming much clearer – the fuzzy bits at the edge were beginning to fade – and he remembered that there was soft jazz playing on the sound system and that the room was filled with people. In the centre of the room, a man and two women were moving in time to the music: there was really not a lot of space for dancing. Oswald had watched them for a while, wondering if moving one's limbs in time to music could still be called dancing.

He sat down on a modern, white leather lounge which was facing the balcony and the view beyond. His host – Oswald assumed that it must have been his host – offered him a choice of drinks, and Oswald took a whisky before nodding his thanks. A largish woman with a thick mane of black hair and a low-cut, tight-fitting, red dress sat down next to him. She was holding a glass of white wine, probably not her first, and Oswald remembered watching, with a vague kind of fascination, the erratic path of the glass as the woman moved the hand holding the glass first in one direction and then in another. At the same time, he felt himself being engulfed by a cloud of distinctly floral perfume. As he attempted to force his attention away from the glass, he was only vaguely aware that the woman was in the middle of some convoluted story involving her neighbour, her husband, a large four-wheel drive and the police. By now her perfume was suffocating, and Oswald felt that he really needed some fresh air, but he was not completely sure how to extricate himself from the situation. He drank his whisky quickly and was about to stand up, an excuse already on his lips, when there was a loud knock on the door.

The large lady suddenly stopped talking, and she looked around hesitantly for somewhere to place her glass. The knock sounded insistent; Oswald remembered speculating as to whether anyone else was expected.

The owner of the flat opened the door. From where he was sitting, Oswald could see both the door and the man who was opening it. From the look on the man's face, Oswald calculated that no one else had been expected. The knock had intruded like a stone flung into water, and the ripples were still making their way across the surface.

As the image of the door being opened became clearer in his mind, Oswald knew for sure that this is when it all began. Small fragments of memory bobbed along the surface as the ripples pushed further and further towards the shore. On the shore, the fragments slowly began to join together.

Six men entered the room. They were all dressed the same: black combat trousers, black shirts, black boots, black leather gloves and dark sunglasses. They were also wearing ear-pieces, so they were obviously all in contact with someone who was not in the room.

They pushed past the man who had opened the door for them, without saying anything. One of them turned off the music, and the sudden silence pressed forcefully against the walls, screaming to be let out. Another pulled the curtains across the windows, negating both the water and the constantly changing lights.

Some of the people in the room looked at each other; others, placing their half-empty glasses on tables, looked around for another way out of the flat. A couple took out mobile phones, unsure of whether to use them or not. No one dared say anything.

Then one of the men in black indicated that everyone should stand up and move towards the door. One woman attempted to fetch something from one of the other rooms but was forcibly brought back to the main room. Everyone was being ushered out of the room, yet not a single word had been spoken.

Oswald pressed his fingers against his head: yes, now he could remember, this was how it had all begun.

Fragment Nine

He was a tall, gangly man with ginger hair, touched with grey, that was already receding from his temples. He wore glasses in thin brown frames, a pair of shapeless, black-grey trousers that had most probably once been completely black, and a short-sleeved shirt with blue, white and green checks. The shirt was not tucked in and covered the fact that the top button of his trousers had gone missing. The thumb and first two fingers of his right hand were stained yellow-brown from years of smoking, and, even now, as he sat on one of the long benches in the Reception area, there was a cigarette between his lips.

A middle-aged woman, wearing a voluminous orange and purple blouse over a pair of beige-coloured stretch trousers, was in the nearby queue; as she came level with the man sitting on the bench, she looked in his direction, frowned, and then waved her hand in a symbolic attempt to disperse the smoke.

He ignored her and continued smoking. He had not seen anything saying that smoking was not allowed: it amazed him a little, but he was not about to question such an absence of regulation. There were plenty of small signs telling him not to leave the queue once he had joined it, and now he noticed a larger sign further down the hall, to the right of the bench. He stood up and ashed his cigarette in one of the large green pot plants standing at various intervals along the wall – he guessed that they were probably some kind of jade – then he walked over to the sign and looked at it with a tired disinterest.

It was a carefully printed sign, black on white with a very narrow red border. He read it through quickly at first and then he read it more deliberately a second time. The sign said:

> *Our goal is to provide you with a*
> *pleasant environment, but it is important*
> *that you co-operate and follow the*
> *regulations below.*
>
> *Keys are to be returned to the*
> *Receptionist on duty with as little delay*
> *as possible; benches have been*
> *provided in the Reception Hall where*
> *you are welcome to rest for no longer*
> *than fifteen minutes at any one time.*
>
> *A mobile canteen, serving hot drinks, is*
> *available twenty-four hours a day. As*
> *well, you will be given a sustenance pill*
> *each time you collect a key; these pills*
> *contain all the nutrition you need while*
> *eliminating the hassle of a normal meal.*
> *No actual food will be served.*
>
> *Rest rooms with facilities for showering*

are available, with access from the
Reception Hall: please register with the
attendants supervising these areas.

Conversation is to be kept to a minimum
in the Reception area, and there is to be
no talking in the corridors. As you will
have already noted, there is no mobile
phone coverage.

Finally, once you have joined the queue,
*you are **not**, in any circumstances,*
permitted to leave it. Penalties are in
place for those who leave the queue, fail
to return keys and/or who carry on
conversations in the corridors.

He shook his head, wondering *why,* not only about the sign, but about everything. He could still not understand why he was where he was: nothing made even the slightest bit of sense. At least there was nothing about not smoking, and he decided that that was the only positive thing about the whole situation. He stubbed out his cigarette in the same pot plant and began to walk towards the end of the queue, when his attention was caught by the sight of a woman already there. He guessed that she was about the same age as himself. She had short grey hair and was wearing a white shirt and blue jeans; she was also carrying a brown corduroy jacket over her arm. When Milford noticed her, she was standing next to a man with a beard, and they seemed to be deep in conversation.

Milford stood for a moment, looking at the woman. There was something about her that reminded him of someone. He squinted a little while he tried to piece together bits of images caught up in layers and layers of memory. It took a while for the pieces to join together, but the final image was indisputable: it had to be Tilda. The long brown hair might have gone, and she was older, but, the more Milford looked at her, the more he knew that he was right. It could not possibly be anyone else.

Milford remained standing just beyond the queue, deep in thought. He wondered whether he dared go up to her, but he decided against it. Not only was it probably against the rules, there was a very good chance that she would not want to talk to him, not even after all these years. Not after all that had happened.

As Milford joined the end of the queue, he was still thinking about the woman who looked so like Tilda. He was also reflecting on everything that happened all those years ago, things that he may have tried to relegate to his past but which had wound their tentacles around his present and would most probably still be with him in the future. Life was like that, he thought. Nothing really disappeared; everything just kept piling up, year after year. It was no wonder that life was so difficult.

He would have liked to have lit a new cigarette, but he decided against it: he would wait until he was in one of the corridors. If he were lucky, he might be sent somewhere where there were only a few people. He began to focus on the cigarette: in his mind, he could see himself taking it out of the packet and then tapping it softly on the side of the packet before he placed it between his lips. He could already feel the cold metal of the lighter between his fingers and the overwhelming sense of satisfaction as he inhaled, and the flame connected with the end of the cigarette.

The queue seemed to be moving a little faster than he had expected; perhaps he would not have to wait so long for that cigarette.

His mind refused to let go of Tilda, not now that it had finally found all the pieces and put them together. Even if the person in the queue was not Tilda, his entire consciousness was now completely filled with the person whom *he* had known as Tilda: her image from all those years ago, her smile, her perfume… He had not really thought of her for years, and now, as she laid claim over his mind and his complete being, he wondered if she ever thought of him; not that it was really something that he expected, but he wondered nevertheless.

He recalled the first time he had met her; it was at a pub somewhere in the city. She had told him that she was from the country and that she knew no one in Sydney. He believed that he had told her that he was from the south-west, adding something like: "Wheat as far as you can see." It was when he said that, looking at her face, that he knew that she assumed that his family owned all that wheat. He was on the point of correcting her misconception, but he decided to remain silent. He enjoyed having a pretty girl believe that he was someone with a secure, almost enviable, background; someone who had 'made it'. It had never happened before. His family did not own any kind of property, large or small; in fact, they owned practically nothing. They moved around a lot, his father picking up work wherever he could find it, usually on someone else's property. His mother was an alcoholic. His older brother eventually moved further west and did a bit of fencing and droving before getting himself killed in a brawl. Milford thought: that would have been at least twenty years ago.

His only sister, the youngest of the three siblings, married a man from the irrigation area further south, a big man with lots of curly black hair. He drove huge semi-trailers inter-state and was away for days at a time. Milford wondered if this were still the case: it was years since he had seen either him or his sister. He knew that they had two boys, but Milford guessed that they would both be grown up by now.

He really needed a cigarette. The queue had noticeably slowed down; obviously there was some kind of hold-up at the reception desk. He tried to see what was going on, but it was impossible to see anything without actually stepping out of the queue, and that was strictly forbidden.

Realizing that it would clearly be a while until he could have a cigarette, he forced himself to return to his previous train of thought, following a number of dubious secondary tracks until he was back on the main line. Once again, he could see himself in the pub, and he was watching Tilda's face as she carefully processed wrong assumptions into something that she probably labelled *information*. Information about Milford.

It probably would never have mattered, but they saw each other again. And then again, and again. Before they knew what had happened, all the *agains* had piled up to-gether, and they began to look at themselves as a couple. It was then that Tilda began to talk about visiting his parents, and, when he had finally run out of excuses, he told her the truth. At the time, Milford felt that she really did not mind about the land and the wheat stretching as far as one could see, but she did mind that he had been less than truthful. He promised her that it had never really been his intention to deceive her and that it would not happen again, to which she simply replied that, if it were to happen again, she would never ever have anything more to do with him.

The queue had begun to move again; Milford was not sure if the woman who looked like Tilda had already passed the Receptionist. He had no way of knowing, because, standing in the queue itself, it was almost impossible to see who else was there. He thought about it for a while and then decided that whether she had passed the Receptionist or not probably made very little difference. His hand was playing with the lighter in his pocket, and he was thinking that, as far as he was concerned, Tilda belonged in the past.

He remembered that they had got married at the end of the summer. He was not sure how it happened: it was a bit like riding a roller coaster – once it is in motion, it becomes almost impossible to jump off. His thoughts hesitated over the roller coaster image, wondering whether or not it would actually be possible to open the restraint and jump. He had not jumped, but, thinking about it, he wondered if it might have been better had he done so.

The queue had suddenly opened up in front of him, and he saw the Receptionist beckoning to him. His hand hard around the cigarette lighter, Milford walked up to the desk.

Fragment Ten

Ten minutes earlier, Oswald, who was already standing in the queue, turned around and thought he saw the woman he had spoken to earlier. She was several places behind him in the queue, and, at first, he was unsure if it actually was the same woman, but there was something familiar about her face. He waved at her with a restrained, yet nonchalant, hesitation that made the wave resemble someone trying to brush away an irritating fly. At first, she stared at him with a slight frown, but then time must have taken a jolt either backwards or forwards, and, possibly understanding that the man with the beard several places ahead of her was actually Oswald, the man from the German forest, she gave him a smile of recognition.

For a moment, Oswald considered dropping out of the queue and joining her further back, but he knew that it would not be permitted. He was annoyed and irritated that he should be so confined by a collection of regulations which made absolutely no sense, and he was also upset with himself for complying so readily.

He waved again – this time more confidently – but he was still feeling strangely ineffectual. He could sense that the man directly behind him was also irritated, but that was to be expected: everyone was irritated in one way or another.

The woman's face was completely devoid of expression. She nodded in Oswald's direction, and then, still looking at him, she stepped out of the queue. Oswald breathed deeply and held his breath, trying not to imagine what might happen next. His annoyance only increased as it became very clear that she had done what he had wanted to do but had been unable to do.

Nothing happened. No one came forward and dragged her forcibly back into the queue. Oswald slowly exhaled. Through the corner of his eye, he could see the woman watching him. He slid out of his place in the queue and moved backwards until he was standing next to her.

"You really gave me an awful fright," he whispered as they both joined the end of the queue. "It's just that we really don't know what could happen…"

It was not that Oswald was trying to process a sense of fright, it was more that he was trying to convince himself that he was not a complete failure. He just did not understand what was happening with him – he had always been a person with strong views on things, someone who did as he wanted. Until now, that is.

The woman looked at him, but Oswald could see that she was not really listening.

"You've changed. You're older. I didn't recognize you at first, but then I remembered…" she said. "By the way, I'm Tilda," she added, holding out her hand to him.

Oswald took her outstretched hand while thinking of his short hair and beard. Instinctively, he ran his hand across his face. He smiled, looking at her. "We're both older."

Tilda whispered, "I know, but it's all wrong somehow. It just doesn't make sense: are we experiencing the future or the past? Is this our past or our future? Are we really this old, or are we actually younger or even older, much older than we are now?"

He could detect a certain panic that she was doing her best to hold at bay. "What did you remember?" he asked.

"That I may have seen you some place before."

Oswald could not hide the fact that he was startled; he had, after all, been thinking the same thing. He knew exactly what she meant, but he said, "We saw each other only recently – at least, I think it was recently. It could have been ages ago, or it could even have been two or five years hence. If I remember correctly, I had a pony…"

She shook her head impatiently. "Yes, I *know* that. I mean *before*. Before all this." She spread out her arms, looking at him intently all the time. "I think we may have known each other, but I can't catch the pieces and there's no way I can see the whole picture."

Oswald nodded. "You could well be right; perhaps we did know each other…" He decided to be more honest. "Actually, I have been thinking the same thing: that we may have met before, but everything is a bit of a blur." He paused for a moment, and then he said, "Or perhaps we *will* know each other; we just haven't got there yet."

For a moment, neither of them spoke, and the queue moved forward a couple of metres.

Tilda's voice broke into the silence: she said, "I really must find out what's going on here. More than anything, I have to know how it will end. Because, it will end, won't it?"

Oswald nodded, and then, suddenly remembering something, he said, "I don't know if it helps at all, but I think that I now know how it all started."

Tilda turned and faced him. She repeated very slowly, "… How it all started?"

Oswald removed his glasses and then breathed on each round lens before wiping it on the sleeve of his coat. As he was putting the glasses back on his nose, he added, "At least, I think so."

The queue was moving slowly forwards, but there were still at least twenty people in front of them. Tilda touched Oswald on the arm. "You must tell me; perhaps if we know how it began then we might be able to work out when it will end. It might even give us some hint as to *how* it will end."

"It will end, of that I'm quite sure." Oswald was becoming neurotically aware both of the people in front of him and those who had joined the queue behind him. He was a very private person, and he did not like the feeling that anyone around him might be listening to what he had to say. While trying to keep some kind of invisible lid on his words, he did understand that, even if anyone was actually listening, it was most probably not intentional but simply because there was not much else to do while standing in a queue winding slowly towards a reception desk. It was to be expected that everyone was hoping that someone, anyone, might have stumbled on to an answer.

Having an understanding of people's listening habits did not remove any of Oswald's discomfort; all he really wanted was a quiet corner somewhere away from queues and people and corridors, but he knew that it was not going to happen. The more he thought about it, he had to admit to himself that what he *actually* wanted was something much more than a quiet corner.

He bent forward and, speaking very softly, told Tilda what he had remembered about the party and the men who had knocked on the door.

"But those people…" began Tilda. Then she said, "It is

making less and less sense; in fact, it makes absolutely no sense – no sense at all. I wonder if it might have something to do with time? In fact, perhaps there is actually no such thing as time – at least, not as we understand it."

The same thought had been gnawing at Oswald – no time or perhaps a kind of time dimension where everything happened at once. He was really not sure which it was.

He said, "You could very well be right; of course, you *must* be right: I really can't see any other explanation. I'm quite sure that everything that has been happening, and still is happening, must somehow be related to the way we experience time." His eyes lit up for a moment as he added, "Yes, actually it makes a lot of sense – there being no time – and perhaps you are correct when you say that there is no such thing. My theory is that time, or the concept of time, is simply something we have invented to make life easier, more accessible, more controllable –"

The queue was shuffling slowly forwards.

Tilda interrupted, "But knowing that time might simply be a figment of our imagination is hardly going to help us get out of this intolerable situation?" She paused, as if collecting her thoughts, and then she said, "Or, perhaps we are already back in the past or years ahead in the future, and we actually did get out. Or will get out, or…" She held her hands against the sides of her head. "Oh, honestly, I don't know anything any longer."

Oswald tried to smile sympathetically, but he suspected that the result was not quite as convincing as he had hoped. While he worried about expressions and how they could, or could not, be perceived, he continued to think about time. He knew that the idea that they could actually be back in the past or even somewhere in the future sounded absurd, but then everything was absurd at the moment. But, if there was no such thing as time then the idea was not at all absurd. It was completely logical.

He said, "There is, of course, a very slight chance that it could simply be a bad dream, and we will soon wake up." His smile began to tip over into subdued laughter as he thought of the hundreds of people all having exactly the same dream at the same time.

The queue had begun to move much faster.

"Have you seen any of the other people from the flat since…" She looked around herself and lowered her voice. "… since arriving here?"

Oswald shook his head.

The Receptionist, the one with the blonde, wavy hair and the aftershave, looked impatiently at Tilda, who was next in line.

She breathed in deeply and, before walking up to the large Reception Desk, whispered "Goodbye" to Oswald.

Most of the time she had been in the queue, listening to Oswald, she had also been thinking about her own state of mind. She was very aware of her extreme exhaustion and confusion, and she was beginning to worry that she might be on the verge of some kind of mental breakdown. She was quite certain that she was rapidly slipping head first into clinical depression; she could recognize all the warning signs: losing control was just one of them. Whatever else she did, she must not lose control.

Standing at the desk, Tilda waited while the Receptionist organized some papers, and, while she waited, she remembered how she had desperately wanted to ask Oswald if everything would be all right, if the end would be something that she could look forward to. She had wanted to ask him even though she knew that he would not have the answer. No one had any answers; everyone was simply being swept along in the same direction, but no one had any idea what the direction was, and no one knew where they would finally end up.

Her thoughts dissolved as the Receptionist, having finished with his papers, enunciated slowly and distinctly: "I noticed that you left the queue. You do know, of course, that it is not permitted?"

Tilda was taken aback: how did he know that she had stepped out of the queue? There were so many people in the Hall. She tried to imagine herself sitting where the Receptionist was sitting, and she wondered whether it was humanly possible to see all parts of the Hall and the queue at the same time. Then the thought occurred to her that the Receptionist might not even be human.

While she continued to reflect on the Receptionist's question, and whether or not he was human, she watched him nervously. It was almost as though she were searching for some kind of answer that he might be able to accept. Of course she knew that it was not permitted – there were signs everywhere telling her that. She replied: "But I only left it for a moment: I simply moved…"

The Receptionist tapped a gold-coated pen on a small pad of handmade paper positioned in front of him. "No one leaves the queue," he stated, emphasizing *no one.* "There is absolutely no acceptable reason for leaving it – not even for a moment. It simply messes with the order of things." He looked at her and sighed almost inaudibly.

Tilda was thinking about the word *messes*, and she was trying to work out how leaving a queue could mess with anything and whether it was not she who was going mad but, instead, everyone around her.

He spoke softly into a small microphone on his desk. An

invisible door in the wall closest to the Reception Desk silently opened, and a man, clothed entirely in black, stepped out and walked towards the Receptionist.

Tilda could feel her stomach constricting. She had not forgotten what Oswald had said about the flat and the black-clad men. She wondered if perhaps the nightmare was turning even darker.

"Room Fifty-Seven," said the Receptionist, still with his eyes on Tilda, while handing a key to the man in black.

The Receptionist had, however, not quite finished with Tilda. "Just keep in mind, *no one* leaves the queue," he added. He was about to call the next in line when he remembered something and beckoned to the man in black. "Her pill," he said.

As Tilda was being led away, she dared turn her head to look back at Oswald, but she doubted that he saw her. Oswald was already standing in front of the desk, and the Receptionist was commanding his complete attention.

Tilda and her guide were about to turn into one of the corridors when Tilda heard the Receptionist saying quite clearly, "I believe that you also left the queue…"

Tilda was not looking at Oswald, but she could almost imagine his expression, and she was quite sure that he was no longer smiling.

Fragment Eleven

Room Fifty-Seven was closer to the Reception Hall than Tilda had imagined, but it was still a matter of navigating two separate corridors and a flight of stairs. Although her guard did not say very much, he was not in any way aggressive. He walked next to her, telling her when to turn and when to keep straight ahead. Tilda was aware that people were looking at him, wondering who he was and why he was escorting her, but she did not have the answers that they were searching for, and she avoided their looks, her eyes straight ahead. She was trying to work out if Room Fifty-Seven was going to be some kind of punishment for her having left the queue – perhaps it was even some kind of elimination room – and she would have liked to have asked the man next to her why leaving the queue was such a problem, but she was quite sure that he had been told not to answer any questions.

She had been very relieved to see Oswald again, but Oswald had changed, and she had also changed. It was no longer sufficient that she traipsed along interminable corridors and opened doors to strange rooms, many of which were not even rooms, but now even time itself seemed to be against her.

When they reached room Fifty-Seven, the man placed the key in the lock and turned it. He opened the door half-way and motioned Tilda to enter. As she walked through the door, she thought she heard him wish her good luck. Later, she wondered if she had simply imagined it.

At first glance, the room on the other side of the door did not appear to be any larger than a normal broom cupboard, and, with the words *broom cupboard* filling and then pushing against the inside of Tilda's head, she heard the door lock behind her.

She found herself standing in a space that was not much larger than herself. The ceiling was not more than fifty centimetres above her head, and she could touch any of the four walls with her elbows. When she tried to sit down, she discovered that she could do so only if she hugged her knees very tightly. There was no artificial light source, only some kind of shadowy, diffused light that seeped in from one corner of the ceiling. Looking at the light, Tilda wondered what might be on the other side of the room, and, in spite of her anxiety, she found herself thinking about trees and sunshine.

The room may have resembled a broom cupboard, but there were no brooms, no mops, no cleaning things, no pots or tins of paint, not even piles of old newspapers. Instead, it was filled with almost-darkness, a suffocating sense of aloneness, cobwebs – real or imagined – and an acute feeling of helplessness.

She had not long turned six when, one evening while the two of them were alone at home, he had roughly pulled her from her chair at the kitchen table, knocking the chair to the floor, and pushed her into the cupboard under the stairs.

"Might teach you to behave!" he had said, slamming the

door shut and bolting it on the other side.

It had all happened so suddenly, and she had barely begun to wonder why before she heard the bolt shooting into place. As she stood there shivering in the darkness, she knew that it must have had something to do with the milk spreading white patterns across the dark red of the cheap oilcloth covering the table. She remembered the glass lying on its side as she had held her breath, willing time to stop or, at least, to return to the point when the glass was still upright with the milk safely inside it. She could not remember how the glass came to be lying on its side; perhaps she had knocked it. All she could remember was his face exploding into anger and his large hands gripping her arms.

She had banged on the door and screamed at him to let her out, but, even at six, she knew that there was no one to hear her and that he would definitely not be paying her any notice.

Her arms hurt where he had grabbed her, and her knee ached, probably from where she had hit it against the floor when he had pushed her into the room. Much worse was the darkness which had only the tiniest edge of light to it, sufficient for her to wonder about the shapes and things around her. She felt as though she were in the middle of a nightmare, but she knew that it would not be possible to open her eyes and simply watch it fade away. There was nowhere for it to fade to, because it was all around her.

She continued to bang on the door until her knuckles hurt and her arms ached. Slowly her screams turned to sobs, and, eventually, she sank to the floor among the brooms and the buckets, the strange smells and the flimsy cobwebs. The frightening creatures stirred up by her imagination continued to press in upon her, but there was nothing she could do beyond saying over and over to herself that her mother would soon come and that she would open the door and let her out.

Days later, or perhaps it was only hours, the door suddenly opened, and the bright, artificial light from the naked globe in the hallway swung in an arc, lighting up the cupboard, chasing away the monsters.

Her mother had wrapped her arms around her and told her how sorry she was. Tilda had held on to her tightly, knowing that it was not her mother who had locked her into the cupboard, and wondering why she should be saying that she was sorry.

A week later, Tilda went to live with her grandparents.

Sitting in almost the same room, Tilda relived the same feelings, as she had all those years ago, with the same overly cramped sensation of the walls and ceiling pressing down upon her. Once again, all she wanted to do was to scream, and, once again, she knew that no one would be taking any notice.

At least she was spared the brooms and the buckets.

The not-quite darkness was enveloping her exactly as it had all those years ago. The monsters of her childhood no longer had the same power over her, but now, as she looked into the darkness, she was filled with other fears and other anxieties.

For some reason, images of Oswald kept pushing their way to the forefront of her mind. He was the only person, other than the Receptionists, with whom she had had even the slightest amount of contact since she had arrived in the corridors – the only stable point in the nightmare swirling around her. If she was to retain her sanity, she must not lose contact with Oswald. But she knew that neither she nor Oswald had any say in the matter, and her thoughts veered off towards the flat on the harbour and the men dressed in black. She was wondering why Oswald had not seen any of the people from the party in the corridors; she would have assumed that the large lady in the red dress would have stood out in any crowd.

The fact that she could barely move in the space was exacerbating her anxiety, making it difficult for her to breathe, and as bands of panic tightened around her body, and the beads of sweat on her neck turned cold, her head filled with surrealistic images of dying and death. Sand-wiched between the images and her fear was the realization that were she to die in one of these rooms, no one would ever know.

She would simply cease to exist.

Her father had been a violent man. It was not until she was an adult and that part of her childhood had shrunk to a small, dark smudge somewhere near the beginning – her beginning – that she was finally able to pull together all the images and the feelings and the fear into one terrible word: *violence*. Her memory of her father was so diffuse and broken, she found it difficult to pin down an actual physical form, but the dark hair and the glasses were always there, completely imbued with a feeling that began somewhere in her stomach and which then moved outwards and filled her entire body, making normal thinking almost impossible.

It was her grandmother who told her about her father, the day she talked about her mother.

"He was a very violent man, you know," she said, reaching across the table and taking hold of Tilda's hand. "When we went to Sydney, just after you were born, it was then we found out what he was like."

"We wanted your mother to come back with us, but she

wouldn't. She was so sure that things would work out. She told us that he had promised her that things would change, that he was trying to be better… "

Tilda's grandmother sat for a moment, holding Tilda's hand, not saying anything; then she sighed and said, "Perhaps it was love, I don't know, but I really do think that she believed him. Perhaps she also believed that there was no one else in the world who could help him be a better person."

She squeezed Tilda's hand gently and then let it go. "But she wouldn't let him hurt you, that was where she had drawn the line… She wanted you to be safe, yet for some reason we will never know, she wouldn't leave him."

Tilda asked her grandmother if everything had worked out as her mother had hoped, if her father actually did become a better person.

The older woman looked at Tilda thoughtfully before slowly shaking her head. "No, he didn't," she said, getting up from the chair.

Tilda knew that that was the end of the conversation.

She was thinking about the conversation now as she sat hunched up on the floor, reliving the fears and the terror of her six-year-old self. Although she now knew what had happened to her mother, and although she knew part of her father's story, she did not know how it had ended. She assumed that it had ended; unless, of course, he was still caught up in some kind of past while she, his daughter, had moved years beyond him into a distant future. In the awful half-darkness, she found herself hoping that he was dead: anyone who could torment a young child as he had tormented her deserved to be dead. She banged her hands against the walls and the floor, tears streaming down her face. She did not want to finish her life like this, in a box that was not much bigger than a coffin. She had imagined the end completely differently. She wondered how long it would take before she lost consciousness and how long it would take before she finally died.

Fragment Twelve

It was when Tilda was being led away by the man in black and when the Receptionist, leaning over his desk, looking straight at Oswald, had said, "I believe that you also left the queue," that Oswald suddenly had a premonition that, if things had simply been spiralling out of control for the last days or weeks or months, this was definitely the point where all the bits were about to break apart and fling themselves, completely unordered, out into space. While the thought was still taking form within his consciousness, and he was wondering about the physical possibility of such a thing, he was also aware of himself thinking that a spiral was a controlled form, but a disintegrating spiral could be anything at all.

There was no point in denying that he had left the queue. He nodded slowly, and the Receptionist sat back on his chair, his elbows on the table, the fingers of his hands forming something that resembled a steeple.

Oswald felt as he had when, as a schoolboy, he had been sent to the Principal's office. He disliked the memory and he intensely disliked the feeling. He did not want to give the man in front of him the satisfaction of feeling at all superior. He began, "Some regulations need…"

The Receptionist raised his hand, stopping Oswald mid-sentence. For a moment the two men resembled two immobile statues facing each other, before the Receptionist clicked his fingers, and a second black-clad man appeared; from where, Oswald was not sure.

"You're to go with him," said the Receptionist, who was already looking past Oswald at the next person in the queue.

Although, more than anything, Oswald did not want to follow any black-clad man anywhere, he understood that there was very little he could do about it.

He followed the man down an extremely long, narrow corridor before making a right turn into a relatively large open area, in the centre of which was an elegant white marble fountain surrounded by a multitude of green leafy plants. Everything was lit with soft, almost warm, artificial light. Oswald stopped walking and stood for a moment dumbfounded, looking at the clean, sparkling water splashing on the green leaves. Apart from the few pot plants in the Hall, it had been days, perhaps even months, since he had seen anything even vaguely resembling natural life.

Whether the man had no interest in indoor fountains or whether he was actually in some kind of hurry was difficult to tell, but he motioned to Oswald to follow, and, taking a key from his pocket, he opened a door at the furthest end of the courtyard. Oswald was dubious as to whether or not it could actually be called a courtyard, but that was the only way he could interpret it – an open space surrounded by walls.

He was still processing all the unbelievable images of water and lush green plants as he followed the man through the door and into a pleasantly furnished hall. He noticed that the walls were a soft cream colour which helped accentuate the two fuchsia-coloured armchairs and the medium-sized pastel drawing in a simple gold frame. There were three doors leading into the hallway, and, without hesitating, the man chose the one straight ahead and opened it. Oswald followed him, still thinking about dark green leaves and falling water, wondering what might happen in the room beyond the door but being completely unable to prepare himself emotionally. His mind was rapidly processing all the things that might, or might not, happen, and he kept asking himself why they felt that leaving a queue was so serious.

His thoughts had moved on to the word *they* and the myriad of possibilities it contained and what it actually could mean in the present situation, when a soft voice said: "That will be all. Thank you, you may go now."

The man in black bowed ever so slightly and left the room, closing the door quietly behind him. Oswald remained where he was, near the door, absorbing every aspect of the room and its one inhabitant while thinking that perhaps *they* was actually singular.

It was a reasonably large room with the same cream-coloured walls as the hallway. The floor was covered with a thick, light-grey carpet, and the windows were completely obliterated by heavy, embossed curtains in a slightly darker cream colour. Oswald wondered if there were actually any windows behind the curtains or if the whole thing was simply a sham. A few paintings filled the spaces between the curtains, possibly the work of the same artist who had done the work hanging in the hall.

A few armchairs – the same kind and colour as those in the hall – were scattered around the room, and there was a very comfortable-looking three seater couch to one side, beautifully upholstered in the same fabric as the armchairs. In the centre of the room, there was a heavy round glass coffee table on which a number of books and a small crystal vase of pale pink roses had been carefully arranged.

Sitting in the armchair directly opposite the door was a man who seemed to be about fifty. He was quite thin, and there was a lot of grey in his hair which most probably had once been completely dark. He was wearing rimless glasses on a long, almost ascetically thin, nose, and Oswald noted that his ears seemed to be completely out of proportion with the rest of his very thin face; they seemed to be far too big, almost as though they had been stuck there as an after-thought and someone had grabbed the wrong size.

There was something about the man: his face, the way he carried himself, his voice. Oswald was certain that he had seen him somewhere before, but he could not recall where. While Oswald was attempting to search through infinite layers of memory, the man stood up, and Oswald could see that he was of average height, just a little shorter than himself.

"So, you're Oswald," said the man in the same soft voice. He motioned toward a chair. "Please sit down," he invited and then resumed his own seat, carefully smoothing his beautifully tailored grey trousers.

Oswald sat down on the very edge of the armchair that happened to be closest to him. He was completely at a loss as to what he should say. He was still trying to remember if he had seen the man before, and, if so, where he had seen him. He was battling with so many questions and frustration and even anger – the image of a soon-to-erupt volcano filling his mind – but, beyond the inner turmoil, there was something about the man that made him speechless. He was not sure if it was the contrast to what he had been expecting: the man, apart from being carefully dressed, appeared to be wearily kind. There was even the hint of a smile playing around his mouth, and Oswald could not help but notice the smile wrinkles near the corners of his eyes.

He said, "I believe you broke one of our rules…"

Oswald wondered if the man might have actually been going to smile, but the sensation was fleeting as the man's face locked into an expression that seemed completely bereft of any kind of emotion. *Neutral* was the word that ran through Oswald's head.

The voice. Yes, he recognized that voice.

Oswald was still trying to equate this well-dressed, grandfatherly man with the nightmare all around him.

The man did not move his gaze from Oswald as he slowly shook his head. "But rules are rules, you know; nothing can operate successfully without them."

Oswald's legs were shaking, and he clamped both his hands firmly on his knees in an effort to still them. He was thinking about the virtual volcano within him and how there were so many things he wanted to say and needed to say. He breathed deeply and said, "I'm sorry, I didn't catch your name…"

The man sat looking at him for a moment – once again, the slightest hint of a smile – then he said, "You can call me the Administrator."

"The Administrator?"

"Yes, the Administrator, the man in charge."

Oswald wanted to smile, but he frowned instead. The name was meaningless; it was not a name that he could connect with anyone in particular. He really doubted if he was supposed to associate the name with anyone, and yet, he was sure that he recognized the man. If only he could place him. Beneath his hands, he could feel his knees starting to shake again.

"But what are you actually administrating? What's the point of all of this: the rooms, the building, everything…?" He lifted his hands from his knees, futilely attempting to demonstrate the extent of *everything*. "How did I and all those other people out there get caught up in this… this nightmare? I mean to say, we have no idea where we are or what's going on; it makes absolutely no sense to walk up and down corridors for the sole purpose of opening doors to rooms that aren't really rooms…" He paused for a moment, glaring at the man in front of him. "Or, is everything simply some hideous figment of my imagination? Is it actually possible that all of this is in my mind, and I am going completely mad?"

The Administrator sighed and looked at Oswald for a few moments without speaking, then he said, "You may not believe me, but I do actually understand you. We all need answers, don't we? No, nothing of what you are experiencing is necessarily in the mind – not in your mind or in anyone else's for that matter – but, then again, I suppose anything of which we are conscious – and even that of which we are not conscious – can be said to be in the mind."

He paused again, smiled, and said, "Regardless of the state of the mind, we need to be able to establish our place on the line; we need to know what is happening in the *now* so that we can confidently move from the what-has-been into the what-is-to-be." Then he actually laughed, and Oswald noted that there was no malice in the laugh.

After a short silence where the laugh faded into the heavy drapes in front of windows that probably did not even exist, he continued, "But what if there is no line, Oswald? What if everything happens more or less at the same time, on different layers, so to speak? What if…"

Oswald leant forward and interrupted, "No line? No past, no future? No time? Is that what you mean? Do you mean that we don't begin at the beginning and work our way through to the end?"

The Administrator put his fingers together and said, "We established an order so that we could feel that we were in control, and we gave the order a name; we called it *time*. We now have a line stretching from birth to death, and we call the line *life*. We know that the beginning of every line is birth and that the end must be death. We fear death because it is the end of the line, and we do not know what comes afterwards." He laughed and then added, "We automatically fear that which we do not know, that which we cannot control, that which is beyond everything that is ordered. We cannot control death; it happens no matter what we do, no matter which god we call upon…" He paused for a moment. "But, just imagine for a moment that we may have got it all wrong."

Oswald's brain was on full speed, computing what the Administrator had told him, adding it to what he already knew and what he already suspected. "Got it all wrong? Got what wrong?"

"The line with its beginning and end, sitting uncomfortably in an infinity of space and time." The Administrator sat quietly for a moment and then he said, "But, as I was saying, rules must be obeyed."

Oswald moved even further forward in his seat, to the point where there was a danger that he might lose his balance and fall on to the floor. "Yes, yes, I do understand that, but the line… Are you saying that time is actually not linear, or are you saying that time, as we think we know it, just does not exist?"

The man in front of him waved his hand, with the

slightest hint of irritation showing in his face. "It's fairly obvious, isn't it? That's why you're here, and when you have made the connection, well… In the meantime, all you have to do is to obey the rules; it's quite simple really."

Oswald knew for certain that he had met the man before. The knowledge – that he knew – insisted on pressing against his brain, wanting more information, wanting to be able to tie together all the pieces and make itself complete, but, no matter how he tried, Oswald could not fit the pieces together. He hesitated and then he asked, "But leaving a queue: what's so wrong with that? I can understand rules, but they have to make some kind of sense."

The Administrator nodded. "Of course. Of course. You are perfectly correct, but, you must understand these rules *do* make sense. Even if it is highly likely that the line does not exist, it can actually be quite dangerous to leave the queue."

"Dangerous?"

"It will make sense eventually; it is just a matter of slotting together everything that you already know." The man smiled again and continued, "That shouldn't be too difficult for you, Oswald: after all, you are a mathematician. The past, present and future may not be exactly as we have organized them, and, as you suggested yourself, *linear* may be the wrong adjective to describe something so complex, but we cannot take it upon ourselves to re-establish an individual order in something that, for want of a better expression, could be called 'ordered chaos'.

"You have already worked out part of the answer, and you will soon work out the complete answer. As you so aptly put it, 'getting out has to be the central point'. I must congratulate you on your astuteness; you are almost half-way there. In the meantime, obey the rules."

There was something about the way the man said his name; something resonated far back in what he might, at one time, have called his past.

"But I have to know *why*. I need answers. I know that I am going to go completely mad if I have to stay here much longer. It's not just the place, it's being confined within something that makes no sense, and it's the not knowing…"

"No, you won't go mad. And everything will make sense, eventually." The smallest hint of a smile was back on the Administrator's lips.

Oswald did not know whether to be angry or not, but he felt that the meeting was drawing to a close and that his opportunity to find out more was simply slipping away from him. "So that's it? I just keep walking up and down corridors and in and out of rooms while you sit here watching and…"

The Administrator nodded. "I'm afraid so."

Oswald shook his head angrily. "Then it's all a frightful waste of time, and what I think or don't think makes absolutely no difference at all."

The dapper little man laughed. "There's no such thing as 'a waste of time', and I wouldn't say *no difference* at all. Keep in mind that the essence of the thought may not be exactly what you believe it to be." Then he clapped his hands softly, and yet another black-clad man appeared from behind one of the drapes, and Oswald knew that the meeting was over.

Or almost over.

The man who called himself Administrator was talking again: "And Tilda…"

"What about Tilda?" said Oswald, turning around, amazed to hear Tilda's name – a name with which he himself was barely acquainted – on the lips of this man.

The man was smiling again. "It's all got something to do with there being no past and no future, or, at least, not in the traditional understanding of past and future. I'm sure you'll work it out."

By now, Oswald was beginning to feel extremely frustrated, but he was already being ushered from the room by the man in black. As he was on the point of leaving the room, some of the pieces suddenly fell into place, and he remembered a name: Taylor, Turnbull...

He turned around again. The Administrator had not moved.

"Turnbull," Oswald called out as the man in black was about the close the door. "Eugene Turnbull."

The expression on the Administrator's face did not change, and Oswald left the room in a state of utter confusion.

Fragment Thirteen

She has lost track of time, just like when she was six years old, and, although she is not absolutely sure, she may even have slept for a short while. Her legs and arms are stiff from being cramped together in the confined space. She stands up, but she cannot straighten herself properly; she stretches as far as she can, bending her arms and pushing her hands firmly against the walls. Her eyes are now reasonably accustomed to the dark, and the shadows are no longer filling her with fear. Her fear is of another kind: she wonders if she will ever be let out; she wonders, yet again, if she is actually supposed to die in the tiny, confined space. Perhaps this is what happens to people who leave the queue: they are locked into tiny, confined spaces and then forgotten.

She sits down and pushes her feet hard against the wall. She cannot straighten her legs, but the pushing gives her a sense of relief. Then, as she is pushing for the fourth or fifth time, she is almost sure that she can feel something move beneath her left foot. She holds her breath, and, very cautiously, she pushes again.

Whatever it is moves again. She pulls herself around and studies the wall near her foot. She runs her hands over the place, and she discovers that the wall is not completely smooth at that point. As she investigates further, she finds a thin ridge that marks out an area about fifty centimetres square – more than half the width of the wall – and it becomes very apparent that she is looking at some kind of door.

Frantically, she works her fingers around the edge, trying to find some kind of opening device. Initially, she finds nothing, but then her fingers stumble on to a small indentation at one side, and, by slipping them into the indentation, she finds that she is able to move the square.

It is not an ordinary door: it does not swing outwards or inwards on hinges. She lifts it upwards and it slides out of its frame on the other side of the wall. She leans into the hole and stands the square piece of timber against the wall beyond the hole.

It is extremely dark in the hole, and she is not sure if the ground is flat or if there are stairs or if it simply falls away into some infinite pit. She wonders if she dare enter the hole. She is quite sure that this is not part of the plan; if she squeezes herself through the opening, there is a possibility that no one will ever, ever find her…

She hesitates for a moment, her body filling with a sweat-filled anxiety and a strange sensation of excitement, then she decides that she has really nothing to lose, and if the hole should finally give her a way out – the only way out – she would be crazy not to grab hold of this sliver of good fortune. God only knows if she will be given another such opportunity. She pushes herself through the opening and then slides the cover back in place.

It is pitch-dark.

Tilda's heart is beating and her knees are shaking, but she is uncertain if the shaking is because of nerves or simply because her legs have been so cramped. Kneeling on the ground, she stretches out her hands in front of her and feels her way, ever so slowly, forwards. There is no floor, only a rough surface made up of hard-packed small stones and sand. There is a moist, enclosed smell that makes her think of rats, and she tries not to think of the things which might be hidden in the darkness. She runs her hand along the wall closest to her, and she feels that it is cold, almost moist, and quite rough; she understands that she is most probably in some kind of tunnel. Tunnels have to go from somewhere to somewhere; perhaps there will be a way out after all.

The darkness pushes around her; she forces herself to keep thinking of the word *exit*, in an attempt to quell the panic which is threatening to overcome her. Hand over hand, she moves slowly along the tunnel and away from the room. She remembers playing blind man's buff as a child and the feeling of dark disorientation behind the blindfold, the fear of knocking into things or moving in the wrong direction. While she is feeling pressed in on all sides by the darkness, she is also wondering what might happen if someone should come to release her and find that she is not there. The more she thinks about it, the more certain she is that no one will come; from what she has experienced so far, that does not seem to be the way it works.

The tunnel turns slowly to the left, and then it begins to move downwards. The descent is gradual, and it does not cause Tilda any undue concern. Although she could probably stand up, she is still on her hands and knees as she is frightened of stumbling and falling in the dark.

It is very quiet in the tunnel. Quiet and completely dark. She opens her eyes as wide as she can, but it is almost impossible to see anything. Tilda speculates as to whether this may be what it is like when one is dead. Then the thought occurs to her that perhaps she is already dead, and she has already stepped beyond her own future. She wonders about the concept of a future after one is dead and whether death is not only the line negating the future but also the line that puts an end to what we call time. Once she is dead, time can no longer have any meaning for her: there can be no present and no future and the past can no longer be of any consequence, because, once she is dead, her past belongs to other people. She decides that time has to be subjective, and, while she wonders about the possibility of a subjective collectivity or a collective subjectivity, her mind wraps itself around the idea of time coming to a sudden end – the death of time.

She makes a concerted effort and pushes away such thoughts, replacing them with the single word *exit*. The thought spurs her on. She imagines herself bursting out of the tunnel into bright sunshine. She believes that she can already smell the vegetation and even feel the warmth of the sun against her skin. The image and all the associated sensations are overpowering, and for a few moments her imagination runs away with her. She can see herself surrounded by green grass and leaves dappled with white sunlight, and further away she can see people doing ordinary things: mowing lawns or walking dogs or talking to each other over fences. She makes her way towards the people, and, when she finally reaches them, they are amazed by what she tells them: things about corridors and rooms and a tunnel. They sit her down on a garden chair stacked with soft, colourful cushions, and they bring her a cup of tea – milk and two sugars – and tell her that she need not worry any more and that she is safe. The image is comforting: it assures her that she made the right decision when she entered the tunnel. She knows that the nightmare is coming to an end, and she will soon wake up and everything will be normal again.

She feels sorry that Oswald is not with her. She would have liked to have saved him as well. There is something about Oswald that reminds her of someone; perhaps she had met him once, long ago, in another life.

She has now moved about fifty metres from the room. In front of her and behind her, everything is dark. The darkness is oppressive, and, in spite of her trying to hang on to only positive thoughts, there is one terrifying thought sidling along next to all the others: the tunnel might simply be going further and further inwards. There might not be an exit after all.

She would like to rest, but she does not dare; she knows that she must keep moving; if there is an exit – and she keeps telling herself that there *is* one – she must reach it as soon as possible.

The possibility of reaching an exit has filled her head with thoughts of light and sun and even blue skies, things which she has always taken for granted. She also thinks of streets and houses and gardens and normality. Normality has not been part of her life for... She stops and wonders just how long it has been, but she does not know. Perhaps it is days, perhaps weeks. Time is no longer something on which she can rely; she tries not to think about *when* and *how long*.

She finds that she is moving faster now, even though the ground is quite rough against her hands and knees. She prays that there really is an exit, and she prays that she will be able to find it. The thought of ending up in some cul-de-sac deep beneath the ground is too horrifying to contemplate.

And then, without warning, the tunnel comes to a stop. She feels around in the darkness, at first cautiously and then frantically. Her whole mind is filled with that cul-de-sac she was trying to avoid contemplating, but, from the loose rocks strewn around, she guesses that there could have been a rockfall. She has no way of knowing how long ago it happened: it could have been yesterday; it could have been years ago. Desperately, she pulls at the stones and dirt in front of her, but, in the darkness, she cannot say if she is making the situation better or worse. She has no way of knowing whether the blockage is centimetres or metres thick. She crouches down, her head in her arms, as the dreadful truth slowly dawns upon her: there is no exit, and she will have to return to the room.

Fragment Fourteen

By the time Oswald was back in the Reception Hall, he had had plenty of time to think about his meeting with the Administrator or Eugene Turnbull: it did not explain anything; instead, it probably just made everything more complicated.

He was sure that the Administrator and Eugene Turnbull were the same person, but if the Administrator really were Eugene Turnbull then nothing made any sense at all. Eugene Turnbull had been his high-school teacher in mathematics. That was years ago, and yet, the man still looked exactly the same as he did then: he had not aged at all. Oswald remembered how he and the other boys in his class would laugh about 'doddery old Turnbull' behind his back. By all rights, Turnbull should have been dead and buried years ago.

Oswald rested his forehead in his hand and closed his eyes. His memory of Turnbull was that he had been an exceptionally good mathematics teacher; in fact, it was probably because of Turnbull that Oswald had continued with mathematics after leaving school.

But what was he doing here? And how could he possibly still be alive?

There were more and more questions piling up, and Oswald could not see any way of getting any of them answered. He decided that he should have been more confident, more outraged, even more aggressive. It made no sense that an ageing man with disproportionate ears, who should have been dead these last twenty years, should have been telling him to obey inane rules and regulations. He felt like turning around and running back to the courtyard, with its fountain and green plants and soft lights, to bang on the Administrator's door, but he was quite sure that, even if he managed to get that far, it would be completely useless.

Beneath all his confusion and frustration, he could still hear the Administrator telling him that he was almost half-way there. *Almost halfway there.* He had even agreed with him that *getting out* was indeed at the centre of everything. Oswald was not sure if he should be experiencing some kind of pride at having solved so much of the puzzle or whether he should be desperately worrying about the fact that the Administrator actually knew what he had said to Tilda when he had said that getting out was at the centre of everything. His head was filling up with equations, none of them with answers.

He looked around him at the crowds of people in the Hall, and he could not get past the thought: were all these other people really important? Were they part of some equation or were they completely superfluous? Was it possible that all the variables stacked on either side would finally equate, even if he were the only person left in the building? He wondered at the part played by Eugene Turnbull – he was so sure that it was Eugene Turnbull that he was already substituting the name for the uncomfortable-sounding name of *Administrator* – and whether it was

Turnbull, and not just *getting out*, that was the central point. As his thoughts hesitantly played with the idea of Turnbull's being at the centre of everything that had been happening, it also occurred to Oswald that perhaps it was not Turnbull at all and that perhaps he, Oswald, was at the centre. The thought was extremely disquieting; he shook his head and attached himself to the end of the queue. He knew that there had to be answers to all his questions, possibly just below the surface of what could be considered normal. Once he had those answers, then everything else would fall into place.

But, of course, that was obvious.

He looked around hurriedly just in case he might have been able to see Tilda, but she was nowhere to be seen. He wondered if she had also ended up in Eugene Turnbull's office, or if she had been taken somewhere else. He wondered why Turnbull had mentioned her by name.

The Receptionist with the round glasses said: "Room Six." He studied Oswald for a moment as though there may have been something else that he wanted to say, but, possibly thinking better of it or, perhaps, deciding that it was irrelevant, he simply handed Oswald the key.

Oswald took the small brass key and asked, "Why Room Six?"

The Receptionist looked surprised: people usually did not ask questions about the Rooms. They did not ask questions about anything. His surprise had obviously cut across one of the barriers. He began to say, "Because…"

Oswald was hoping that he might be about to tell him something of importance, but the man let the word, with its promise of more words, disappear into the air-conditioned space around them and, instead, said: "Follow the corridor on the left, then the second to the right. At the end of that corridor, take the stairs to the second floor and follow the corridor. Halfway along, you will see door Number Six. It's on the right-hand side."

Oswald said nothing: he had been hoping for something else, but he was not completely sure what that might have been. He put the key into his pocket and walked in the direction of the first corridor.

Room Six was, as the Receptionist had very carefully explained, roughly halfway down one of the corridors on the second floor, and it was on the right-hand side. The entire door had been painted blue, an attractive medium blue colour, and it was the only blue door in that corridor. When he first saw it, Oswald was reminded of something he had read about doors being painted blue to ward off evil, and, while he looked at the door, he was trying to decide if the blue was a good omen or a bad one. He came to the conclusion that it all depended on one's own moral perspective and on which side of the door one was standing.

He turned the key in the lock and went in.

When Oswald was thirteen, at the end of the 1950s, he was taken to the beach. It was not something that happened very often as Oswald and his family lived a long way from the coast, and Oswald's father did not own a car. The family – Oswald, his parents and his two younger brothers – took a train and a tram and finally reached one of the beaches on the edge of the city.

It was a beautiful late-spring day: the sky was powder blue; it was warm, and there was a feeling of joyful, relaxed expectancy in the air. It was most probably a Sunday, because the people on the tram and in the streets were obviously not hurrying to work, though this was not necessarily reflected in their clothing, which, in most cases, was completely respectable. Oswald's father wore a brown jacket and the hat without which he never ventured outside the house. His mother wore a red cotton dress with a full skirt, and although she had dispensed with wearing a hat for this occasion, she was carrying a white handbag and her hands were correctly hidden by white gloves. Oswald wore plain beige shorts and an emerald-green shirt.

From the tram stop, it was only a short walk to the beach, and, on reaching the wide steps leading down to the sand, the two younger boys rushed ahead, taking the steps two at a time, before running across the sand to the edge of the water. Oswald remained standing on the promenade. It was not that he had never seen the sea before – he had, several times – but there was something about the waves rushing towards the beach and then mysteriously sliding back out to sea that both mystified and fascinated him. As his parents followed their two younger sons down the stairs and on to the beach, Oswald stood statue-like, following the never-ending rows of waves with his eyes, watching each of them finally touch the wet sand before disappearing backwards under the oncoming waves.

He tried to follow a single wave, but he had to give up as waves were seamlessly absorbed into each other or, at times, moved sideways into other waves further along the beach. When it became obvious to him that he could not simply concentrate on one single wave, he watched the heaving pattern of blue-green water, following it as it rose and curled and fell until it finally swept up on to the sand, leaving long lines of quickly disappearing white foam.

Oswald had no idea why he was so fascinated by the moving water in front of him; he was too young to have some kind of philosophical interpretation that would cause him to think of birth, death and resurrection – all he could do was to look, drinking in the image with all its related sounds and smells.

Oswald's father turned, waving to him impatiently, and Oswald pulled his eyes away from the waves while he walked slowly down the steps. The sand crept into his sandals, and he kicked them off, carrying them in his hand the last few metres across the beach.

He sat down on the sand next to his parents; his father had removed his jacket, and his mother had placed her gloves in her handbag. Oswald's brothers, however, were already on the very edge of the surf, daring each other to be the first to dive under the next wave, or the next, or...

Oswald watched them for a few moments as small interruptions sketched across the more important image of the waves, then he pulled off his shirt and shorts, and, dressed only in a pair of black swimming trunks, he ran down to the water. His brothers were still hesitating on the edge when he ran past them and dived into the cold, restless, churning water. No longer on the outside of something looking in, he was now part of the movement and the noise. He moved upwards through the water, feeling its strength – finally part of the birth, the death and the rebirth.

Once again, he was standing on the exact same beach, looking at waves pounding the sand. There was no one else on the beach, no flags indicating where or where not he should swim and no stray dogs chasing imaginary sticks.

Nothing.

He was completely alone.

He remembered how he had felt that day when he was only thirteen years old; in fact, it was as though he was thirteen all over again, and he was standing, looking at the beach, and his brothers were rushing towards the water while his parents were wondering where he was. He quickly looked around, but there was no one else anywhere.

Anyway, his parents were long since dead, and his brothers no longer lived in Sydney: one of them had moved to England years ago, and the other one, the one closest in age to himself, was now living in Perth. As he hesitated on the edge of the water, concerned about the cold, he thought about his brothers, wondering if they still went to the beach.

Looking at the waves, in much the same way as he had done when he was thirteen, he was almost certain that time itself was insignificant. The beginning, the middle, the end and even the new beginning, were all rolled together: there was no beginning and there was no end. Oswald remembered what he had said to Tilda: "I'm sure that it has something to do with time", adding that time might just be something that we have invented to make things easier.

He dropped down on to the sand, lying back and propping himself up on his elbows. As he felt the satisfying, almost sensual, warmth of the sand against his body, his mind played with the thought that he could easily change the time on his watch, and life would continue without any problem, except, perhaps, that he would be either too late or too early for appointments, that he would miss trains and buses, and that he would arrive for a dinner date at the wrong time. As he was thinking about missing appointments, he looked at his watch: the time on the dial – half past eight – told him absolutely nothing that made any sense. Half past eight was completely unrelated to his present situation. It could have been three in the morning or twelve noon; it really made no difference.

Since arriving in this complex of corridors and rooms,

Oswald had been completely disassociated from time. Lying on the sand, watching the waves curl on to the sand, he tried to get his mind around what was actually meant by time, and, in the middle of all of his contradictory thoughts, he remembered someone suggesting that perhaps *we* are time. When he first heard it, the idea had a certain appeal, but he had not given it very much serious thought; now, he shrugged mentally, thinking that anything was possible, and, if time can only exist in its relation to something else, it probably made sense that the 'something else' should be him and everyone around him.

It was difficult to get a grasp on something that had no limitations and no physical features. As far as he could see, time even defied mortality. Oswald frowned, thinking of what it was that separated his life into all the different compartments, each with its own label: weeks, years, past, present... He picked up a handful of the warm, dry sand and let it run slowly through his fingers. He picked up a second handful and let it follow the first; he enjoyed the feeling of the coarse, sun-warmed grains slipping past his fingers. After the days or weeks – he was no longer sure of the length of time – spent in the sun-deprived corridors, it was such a relief to be *outside*.

He did not believe that he actually was *outside*, but as long as there was sun and sand and water, he could at least pretend that such was the case.

His eyes moved along the length of the beach, from left to right, and then he stood up, brushing the sand from his trousers. As long as he was *outside*, he would make the best of it; he had no idea when he would get such another opportunity. He began to walk along the beach, but after a few steps, he sat down on the sand again and removed his shoes and socks, carefully stuffing his black socks into his shoes; then he rolled up the bottoms of his trousers, and, with his shoes in his hand, he continued walking along the sand, at an angle which would eventually bring him to the water's edge.

He thought: if there really is no time, then there is no past, no future and no present. He was trying to give the concept of *no time* some kind of visual form, and was thinking that it was bordering on the impossible, when he realized that he had reached the edge of the water.

The water was refreshingly cold, and he stood for a moment, savouring the sensation of it swirling around his ankles, rushing backwards towards the oncoming waves, making place for new waves and new sensations. He was watching waves further out from the shore move to one side or completely disappear beneath newer, faster waves, then he looked down at the water flowing over his feet. There was no special order in which the water reached his feet; he knew that it was his logical mind, needing to impose some kind of order on everything around him, that told him that the waves were reaching his feet in a strict chronological order. But what if that was not the case?

Oswald moved a few steps back from the water-line but continued to look at the waves. He was thinking about what the Administrator had said about *getting out* being the central point, and about the need to concentrate on the fact that *the essence of the thought may not be what we believe it to be*. In his mind, Oswald was putting an equals sign between the two statements, and, when that did not work, he tried a plus sign, and then he wondered what the result might be. But, no matter how he arranged all the facts, there did not seem to be an answer.

Then he thought again about time having no visible boundaries and no limitations, and he thought of the few times he had been at the beach before he turned thirteen, and the many times he had been there since, including the present moment, and he knew, without knowing why, that all those times were part of the one and same experience. When, as a thirteen year old, he had visited the beach with his family, he had also been there as his six-year-old self, and even as he was now, and even as he might be in ten years' time. He was excited at the realization, and he felt that, finally, he may have found a very small splinter of light.

As he moved his gaze from the water to further down the beach, he saw a figure standing on the sand a little way back from the water's edge, and he was almost certain that it was Eugene Turnbull.

Fragment Fifteen

E very optimistic, hopeful feeling that had pushed Tilda onwards through the tunnel suddenly ran out of her like water out of some hole-ridden plastic container. She sat in the darkness, her back leaning against the rockfall, her head resting in her hands. She had been so sure that she would get out, and now everything seemed ever so much worse than before she left the room. She had no idea what she should do. If she were to return to the room, someone may have already noted that she was no longer there, and as there would be no reason for anyone to check the room a second time, and, as it was completely impossible to unlock doors from the inside, she would obviously die in the room. No one would know, and she doubted that anyone would even care.

The fact that she was in an extremely unenviable situation was uncomfortably evident, no matter how many times she altered the details or attempted to analyse her perspective.

The moist, earthy smell of the sand and rock became more noticeable, and the claustrophobia that she had so valiantly been fighting against began to wrap clingy, cold arms around her. She began to actually wonder if there might be some advantage in dying and getting it all over and done with, but, as the thought took hold, she became very certain that she did not want to die and that the idea of sitting anywhere simply waiting to be overcome by unconsciousness did not particularly appeal to her.

The year Tilda turned seventeen, her grandmother died, which meant that Tilda was suddenly left on her own. The kindly, somewhat portly, accountant, with the thinning reddish blonde hair and the tiny pencil moustache, had been named as the executor of Grandmother's estate. He invited Tilda to stay with him and his wife, at least until things were sorted. She stayed for two weeks, feeling out of place and very aware of some kind of debt she would probably not be able to repay.

Both the accountant and his wife were extremely kind and understanding: they had no children of their own, and all that care and affection, which they had never been able to splurge on their own offspring, they now generously gave to Tilda. She appreciated their kindness, but she knew that she needed to reclaim her own space, wherever that might be, and, after those two weeks, she decided that she could not possibly stay any longer. When the estate was finalized, she told the accountant to sell the house for her and deposit the money in her account; then she packed together her few belongings and took the train to Sydney.

It had been more than ten years since she had left Sydney as a small child, her face pressed against the window of a train, and she had very little idea as to what she was going to do there. While something inside her was propelling her back to what she knew had to be some kind of beginning, there was another something nagging at her about the impossibility of retracing steps, and, torn between these two conflicting paths, she finally chose the first, telling herself that it was not a case of retracing steps but a matter of finding out what had actually happened.

She had been working in the office of the produce store for the last couple of years, and she was reasonably competent with both shorthand and typing. She had no concerns about not being able to find work in the city; her only concern – a concern that at times completely engulfed her – was to discover what had happened to her parents.

Among her grandmother's things, Tilda had found a small dog-eared notebook, and, turning the pages, her eye had caught her mother's name followed by an address in Sydney. The address did not say anything to her, but, as she looked at it, she understood that this is where she must have lived with her parents, all those years ago, before she was sent away. The address was to a house in an inner suburb of Sydney, and Tilda had closed her eyes, trying to make the words in the notebook collate with her very vague memories of grey houses and paling fences, but the two things remained distinctly separate. The address meant nothing to her; it did not conjure up a street or a building: it was just a collection of words in a notebook.

In Sydney, she found temporary accommodation at the YWCA close to Central Station, and the following day, she caught a train the few stations to her destination. It took her about twenty minutes to find the street, but, the moment she stepped on to it, she knew where she was. It had been eleven years, but as she looked down the street, memories began to swarm back, converging on the address, drawing connections where previously there had been none.

As the memories became clearer, Tilda realized that nothing much had changed: the few scrawny street trees, positioned at uneven distances along both sides of the street, had actually survived and were now taller than the power lines, and their branches had been pruned back to accommodate the lines. There were more cars parked along the street, and the upstairs veranda of one of the terraces had been built in, giving it a strange blind appearance; both things – the cars and the veranda – were uncomfortably out of place among all the vague, disjointed memories that were rapidly slotting together, making her believe that they had always been there and that she had always remembered.

Outside the house next to the one where Tilda had lived, there was a man working on an old car, and, behind him, down the side of the building, Tilda glimpsed discarded tyres and car parts that were either unwanted or still waiting to be used. As she walked past, the man wiped his hands on an oily rag he had hanging from the back of his jeans, and he whistled at her. She walked on, pretending not to have heard.

Later, lying on the hard, narrow bed at the YWCA, she thought back over the day, the narrow, grey terrace house where she had lived with her parents at the centre of her thoughts. It was not as tall as it had been when she was six, but it was still divided into separate flats, and, from what she could now remember, nothing much had changed. While the house retained the central position in her mind, disparate images – a dead plant in a pot on the downstairs veranda, a bike frame leaning against the iron latticework on the upstairs balcony, a gate hanging on only one hinge, a wooden box with the words *Pears Soap* lying at the side of the house, an obviously overweight woman in a mauve cotton housecoat, sitting on an old beige sofa on the downstairs front veranda – floated at the edges, occasionally threatening to assume the central position.

It was the overweight woman who finally filled Tilda's mind, pushing all the other images, including the house, beyond the edge. Her name was Joy and she and her husband, Alfie, had lived in the house for six or seven years – she could not remember exactly. She had never met Tilda's parents, but she felt that living in the same flat meant that she and Tilda must be connected in some indescribable way. Tilda sighed as she remembered Joy's undisguised enthusiasm.

Tilda had not intended to go into the house, she had just thought to look at it from the outside. Lying on the bed, gazing at the grey-white ceiling, she was, however, no longer sure what her intention had been. Perhaps there had been no other way of finding out what she had learnt; perhaps she had needed to re-embrace the house in order to make it divulge its secrets.

It was Joy, moving heavily on the sofa as she made room for Tilda to sit next to her, who had invited Tilda into the house or, at least, on to the veranda. And when Joy had run out of answers, she had called up to Frances on the top floor – Frances, who had lived in the house for ever.

Tilda's thoughts switched to Frances, an elderly woman in a pink dressing gown, a cigarette in one hand and a lighter and packet of cigarettes in the dressing gown pocket. There was not enough room on the sofa for the three of them, so Tilda had fetched the Pears Soap box and up-ended it. No one had protested. Frances straightened her dressing gown with her free hand and then looked closely at Tilda.

Tilda had not expected to recognize Frances: it had been too long, and she herself had been too young. All she could hope was that Frances might be able to tell her about her parents: how her mother had died and what had happened to her father.

There was an irregular darkish spot on the ceiling; Tilda wondered if it was mildew or something else. She looked at it trying to imagine what it looked like: some kind of African animal or a large whale. While she was trying to relate the shape to some concrete form, Frances' words were pushing their way to the front of her mind, fighting for attention: "Oh yes, love, I remember you. You were just a little one then, real skinny. And that father of yours…"

Tilda closed her eyes and the whale on the ceiling disappeared. She remembered asking Frances what had happened after her mother had died.

"Do you know what happened?" she had asked, "I think my mother died, but my father… Do you know where he is now?"

Frances had looked at Tilda in amazement. "But he's in gaol, love; he's been there for years!"

"But why?" Tilda was not sure that she wanted to hear the answer, because she already knew what it would be.

"He killed your mother, that's what he did!"

Sitting in the darkness with a very real sense of moist earth wrapped all around her, Tilda remembered what it had felt like, hearing that her mother was dead because her father had killed her. Somewhere, at the back of her mind, the idea had been lurking, ever since her grandmother had talked to her about her mother, but she had never wanted to take hold it and consider it seriously. Each time the idea had slunk out of the shadows, she had pushed it back again, refusing to accept what it was trying to suggest.

When, at the age of seventeen, she was forced to face the fact that her father had beaten her mother to death,

Tilda was completely overcome by an inexpressible feeling of isolation and loneliness; she felt as though she had been suddenly transported to some place totally disconnected from everything and everyone else, even from life itself. She was sad and angry and thoroughly depressed all at the one and the same time. She had listened, almost in disbelief, while Frances had talked about raised voices and screams and the sounds of furniture being moved, even thrown, and then the silence.

"It was the silence afterwards that was worse," she had said, shaking her head. "I knew then that something really bad had happened; I knew it in me bones."

"The police came and then the newspaper people; it was in all the papers, you know," said Frances, remembering how they had all asked her what she had heard, and how she had told them that it was her bones that had told her that something awful had happened.

"The front door was wide open. There were people everywhere – that was after the police came – and I looked in…" Frances sighed and shook her head again. "Blood everywhere and him sittin' there all dazed like."

Later, all those years afterwards, lying in a strange bed beneath a ceiling harbouring images of whales or rampant lions, Tilda wondered briefly if things might have turned out differently had she remained in Sydney, but, while her thoughts meandered around pieces of broken furniture, long since discarded, and blood stains, long since removed, she remembered the broom cupboard. As that awful memory of claustrophobic darkness descended upon her, she knew for certain that there was nothing that she could have done that would have changed the course of events which eventually led to her mother's death.

Still musing on what Frances had told her so many years

ago, Tilda recollected that she had refused Joy's offer of a cup of tea, and, turning her back on the house, she had walked back up the street. She never looked back, and she never returned. Without making a definite decision, Tilda knew, even then, that the past had to remain where it was, in the past; she needed to re-create some other kind of life for herself in the future.

Just as she knew, while standing on that street, that there was a future beyond the drab, violated terrace house, she knew now that there had to be a future somewhere beyond the tunnel; it was just a matter of finding it. Slowly she became aware that, although she had moved a long way into the tunnel, and, although the opening to the room was closed, the air in the tunnel did not feel at all close or tired; in fact, she believed that she could actually discern some kind of vague movement in the air around her. She licked her finger and held it up, and she could feel a small sensation of coolness on one side of it.

Tilda slowly moved back away from the rockfall, feeling her way carefully in the direction of the almost imperceptible movement of air. Her spirits began to rise: perhaps she would not have to die in the tunnel after all. Perhaps there actually *was* a way out.

Fragment Sixteen

Milford has been given a large key, and he sees that the wooden tag attached to the key by a metal ring has been decorated with the numeral One Hundred and Ten. The Receptionist has told him how to find the room, and he is now holding the key in his hand, walking along a lengthy corridor on what he concludes is the third floor. Milford finds it extremely irritating that there are no windows anywhere: he needs to be able to see the sky and to sense some kind of connection with the outside. He is beginning to feel rather confined, but he is not sure what he can do about the situation: if there are no windows, then there are no windows. He is fairly certain that the Receptionist would not be at all interested in hearing about his distress.

In an effort to focus on other things, he thinks about Tilda and wonders how he could possibly have believed that he had seen her. Their paths moved apart years ago, and Milford guesses that Tilda's life had gone in a very different direction to his own.

He turns from the long corridor into one that is slightly shorter and then into one that is shorter still. He is thinking about Tilda, but he is also thinking about the absurdity of his present situation. Nothing makes sense, and, try as he will, he cannot work out how it all began. He really needs to talk to someone, but it seems impossible, and he is feeling exceedingly frustrated.

He stops in front of Room One Hundred and Ten and slips the key into the lock.

Milford walks into an enormous library. As the heavy door swings closed behind him, he becomes aware of the smell of books: a very slight mustiness mixed up with ink and some spices, the names of which he cannot remember and probably never knew, and even the scent of summer grass. He cannot put his finger on the smell, but he knows that it radiates from the thousands of books on the shelves in front of him.

He looks quickly around the very large room, noting the rows and rows of bookshelves; the large brown-red polished reading tables in the centre with the simple, yet elegant, reading-lamps; the comfortable-looking leather armchairs; and, close to the door, the wardrobe area for bags and coats. He notes that there is nothing in any of the many purpose-built pigeon-holes and there are no coats hanging on the long stainless steel rods; the wardrobe assistant is nowhere to be seen.

Milford's eyes move past the wardrobe and he sees, at both sides of the room, open staircases leading to a gallery running around the room on three sides. When he raises his eyes to the upper gallery, he can see that even the gallery is filled with bookshelves and books.

Down on ground level, he expects to see a librarian sitting at the information desk, but there is no one there, and, when he scans the room a second time, he finally understands that he is the only person in the library.

Milford never goes to libraries, and he feels out of place and curiously ill at ease. He walks to one of the very large tables in the centre of the room, his rubber-soled shoes making small sucking sounds on the hard polished timber floor. He is at a loss as to what he should do: should he remove a book from one of the shelves? Should he sit down at one of the tables? Should he simply remain standing in the middle of the room?

It is many years since he actually read a book. He occasionally reads the daily tabloid, but not from cover to cover: he picks up the news from a scattering of commercial television broadcasts. His opinion on things is simply a reiteration of contemporary popular opinion sifted through talkback radio. When he reads the tabloids or watches television, it is mainly to follow whatever sport is being played at the moment; he has never really understood people who read books.

He lets his hand move over the smooth surface of one of the tables; it feels comforting, and his anxiety diminishes a little. He looks around hastily, and then, reassured that he is completely alone, he sits on one end of the first table, and, lowering himself on to his back and pushing against the surface with both hands, he slides backwards into the middle of the table.

Looking upwards, Milford is aware of all the books looking down on him, and, above him, at the top of the domed ceiling, he can see a square-shaped skylight, through which he can glimpse some blue sky. It tells him that there is an *outside*.

He lies on the table, enjoying the quietness, while he wonders about the word *outside*. Many years ago, he learnt not to take it for granted, but it is easy to forget things. Since entering this world of corridors and rooms, he has thought about the outside a lot, because he is no longer sure if he will ever get outside again.

Many times during his life, he had regretted losing Tilda. His relationship with Tilda had been very much like his acceptance of *outside;* he had always assumed that she would be there, and, in the very same way as his belief in the constancy of *outside* was eventually shattered, his assumption about Tilda turned out to be completely wrong.

One of the biggest differences between Tilda and Milford was Tilda's reaction when, having peeled back the thin onion-like layers of her present, she was confronted with her past. Faced with the horror that revealed itself behind those layers, she made up her mind that her future was going to be very different. Milford, on the other hand, had no need to search for his past – it was so much part of that which he called his present – and he had decided, long before he met Tilda, that, as long as he had a roof over his head and a meal in his belly, there was really not much point in changing anything: his expectations of life were not particularly high, and he was, therefore, not easily disappointed. He may have left the country and moved to the city, but he was still firmly connected to his past in the same way that long tendrils of some insidious creeper can stretch themselves far beyond the trunk, appearing both self-sufficient and autonomous while still displaying all the characteristics of the parent plant.

By the time Milford and Tilda met at the pub not far from Central Station, Tilda was working in the office of a small legal and insurance company in the city, and Milford, already into his third position since moving to Sydney, was working at a factory that turned out cardboard boxes in many different sizes. As he told Tilda on their second meeting at the pub, the factory building was long, low and uninteresting, close to the railway line and coloured a dingy mottled black from the constant onslaught of smoke. The work areas may well have been huge, but the windows were small and grimy, which caused Milford to often wonder what had happened to open spaces and blue skies.

By the time they married as summer was turning into autumn, Milford had changed jobs again, finally breaking through one of those small, soot-smeared windows in an effort to reconnect with everything, or at least something, on the outside.

Tilda was sympathetic: she understood the expanses of brick-red and blue where one straight line divided the heavens from the earth, and she felt sorry for Milford. But, twelve months and one miscarriage later, Tilda's sympathy began to wane as Milford walked out of yet another job, putting the blame on a vaguely expressed kind of incompatibility and, above all, a need for change.

Milford slowly rose up into a sitting position and rubbed his neck carefully. He slid off the table and sauntered to one of the two staircases leading to the gallery that skirted the walls above him. Each polished timber step raised him just that much further above the floor below, and he enjoyed the sensation of the slowly changing perspective. When he reached the gallery, he followed it casually along its entire length, occasionally leaning over the balustrade to look down on the library below. Behind him, along the walls of the gallery, there were books crammed into every shelf of the many bookcases, and, at reasonable distances, there were sliding ladders, allowing access to the top shelves.

Arriving at the other side of the gallery and the identical

staircase leading to the floor below, Milford sat down on a grey upholstered chair. Stress and anxiety had always been part of his persona, but of late he was more fraught than usual. He took out his packet of cigarettes and counted the cigarettes he had left; there were not as many as he had hoped, and he sighed audibly. He emptied one of the cigarettes into his hand and returned the packet to his pocket. Placing the cigarette in his mouth, he flicked open his lighter and, holding the flame near the end of the cigarette, he inhaled a couple of times. He leant back in the chair and closed his eyes, enjoying the deep feeling of relaxation and satisfaction that was filling his body, wanting it to last for ever.

Milford was extremely frustrated not knowing what was happening to him or why it was happening. Nothing seemed to be making any sense. He did not want to have to return to the Hall, and he would have liked to have remained where he was, with an endless supply of cigarettes, but he knew that that was not likely to happen.

He opened his eyes and took a cursory look at the titles on the shelf closest to him. He leant over and pulled out *Being and Nothingness* by Jean-Paul Sartre, flipping open the first few pages, attempting to read a word here and a sentence there; then he returned the book to the shelf and, still smoking his cigarette, he walked back down the stairs.

Fragment Seventeen

Oswald has returned to the Reception Hall and is now sitting on one of the benches against the wall. His mind has drifted, and he is imagining what it would be like to be sitting at a table with a hot meal in front of him. If he concentrates very hard, he can actually smell the food, and he knows that when he has eaten what is on his imaginary plate, there is more on the table. In his imagination, he almost reaches out and lifts a schooner of amber-coloured liquid to his lips. His stomach rumbles, and he forces himself back to reality: there is no table, no food, no drink…

If it were at all possible, he would take all the meal-replacement pills and tip them into one of the letter-box receptacles marked *Rubbish*, but he knows that it is not possible, and, if it were and if he did, then he would probably starve, which, on second thoughts, might not be such a bad idea. He desperately wants to be able to feel food in his mouth and in his stomach; he wants to return to a normal routine of breakfast, lunch and dinner with, per-haps, morning and afternoon tea; he wants definite times for things. As it is now, he never knows whether it is day or night, this week or last week or next week.

Although the pills seem to adequately satisfy his hunger on one level, he longs for the physical act of eating, and he spends a lot of time thinking about food. He rubs his temples with his fingertips and tries to make himself think of something else. More than anything, he needs to be able to implement his own routines over and above the inane routines that are running his life at the moment.

He looks along the wall, and sees that there are a few other people either sitting or lounging on some of the benches. The tea lady is further down the hall, working her way towards where Oswald is sitting. He decides to ask her for something to drink when she gets close enough. The drink – whatever it is – is definitely not tea and it is not coffee, but it is hot and Oswald has actually learnt to enjoy it.

A couple of people are chatting quietly; they seem serious and their voices are muted. Oswald reflects on the fact that it is seldom that he sees anyone looking the least bit happy; everyone seems so very anxious and subdued. Without any effort on his part, the word *funeral* pushes itself into Oswald's consciousness.

Further down the Hall, Oswald can see a couple of men in black standing near the wall, possibly checking to see that people join the queue correctly. They seem to be slightly bored, but Oswald is fully aware that looks can be deceiving.

He closes his eyes, thinking how wonderful it would be if, when he next opens opens them, he might be back wherever he was before all the madness began. His memory of his own past, before the party, is still very sketchy. He knows that he is a mathematician, but he is not sure where he was working or even if he was working. He cannot even remember where he was living or if he was married. The thought pulls him up with a start: perhaps he *is* married, and perhaps he has a wife and children, possibly even several grandchildren, somewhere. Perhaps they are all wondering where he is and what has happened to him, or perhaps they are also here in this infinite maze of corridors, but they all keep passing each other without actually meeting. Then he considers the possibility of having been propelled into his own future, in which case, he may not even have met the wife or the children and definitely not the grandchildren. The thought is disturbing and extremely sobering.

He feels that he needs to focus on other things, and he takes a small notebook and pen from his coat pocket. He jots down some numbers with an equals sign between them. He sits for a few moments and looks at what he has written, and then he scribbles over everything. He takes a new page and writes *past*, *present* and *future* in block letters. The words look up at him from the white page, challenging him to make the right connections and to understand.

While he is sitting, very much in thought, the lady with the drink trolley reaches his bench, and he gratefully takes the drink that she pours for him. He looks at her briefly: she is probably not much younger than he is. He wonders how she perceives the situation – whether she finds it strange like he does or whether she feels that it is quite normal to be walking around an enormous Reception Hall, handing out cups of something that is neither coffee nor tea to people who really do not want to be where they are but cannot do anything about the situation.

He sighs and, having taken a mouthful of the hot drink, looks again at what he has written. He knows that the answer lies somewhere there, but he is unsure where. There is obviously no such thing as past, present and future – he is quite sure of that now. If time is eternal then there can be no past, because that would indicate something before what was past – a beginning – and there cannot be a beginning to something that has always existed. And if there is no past, then there can be no future – there can only be a continual, eternal state called *time*. He does not want to even consider the present, as its existence is too short to warrant any form of consideration, but, then again, perhaps time is just one continual present and contains that which we call both the past and the future. This is why he is so sure that there is a way out: at some point, the way in and the way out *must* coincide.

He notes a couple more numbers, and then he writes: *almost halfway there, getting out* and *the essence of the thought.* He puts a large question mark after the last few words, before taking another mouthful of his drink. His mind continues to grapple with the figures and the words, moving them around, adding them, subtracting them, underlining them. His gaze falls again on the men in black further down the hall, and he wonders whether they really are disinterested or whether the look is simply part of the uniform. It occurs to him that they could be anticipating the end of their shift, assuming, of course, that they work in shifts, but how such things are regulated is something that Oswald feels he does not have the energy even to begin contemplating.

His mind returns again to the figures he has written in his notebook, and he decides, somewhat belatedly, that it could very well be forbidden to write things in notebooks or anywhere else for that matter. Instinctively, he feels that he cannot afford to lose either his notebook or his pen, so he slides both of them back into his pocket and finishes his drink, his thoughts still rummaging through numbers, words, different probabilities and the likelihood of what is or is not forbidden. Oswald reprimands himself for using the notebook, and he hopes that no one has seen it, then he chides himself for worrying about unnecessary things when there is so much else to worry about.

He screws up the empty paper cup that is still in his hand, savouring, for a moment, the physical contact between the smooth, even surface of the demolished cup and his fingers. Then he stands up and walks a couple of metres to the closest rubbish slot where he drops the redesigned cup. He listens, waiting to hear it connect with other rubbish further down, but there is no sound, and Oswald turns away, slightly confused, slightly disappointed – why he is really not sure – and heads for the end of the queue.

He is feeling very tired. Beyond occasionally being able to grab some sleep in the rooms, depending on the particular room experience, adequate sleep definitely does not seem to be part of the plan. He attaches himself to the end of the queue, hoping that the next room will allow him to stretch out and sleep, at least for a couple of hours.

As the queue moves slowly forwards, Oswald continues to contemplate the concept of time. If there is no time, no past, present or future, then everything is happening at the same time, and that which might appear to have belonged to the past might very well be part of the future. Or the other way around.

Or perhaps, he thinks, he has been thrown into some parallel universe, and somewhere, in what could be called the real world, there is another Oswald, who is the Oswald he has always known, who is doing all the ordinary things that he has always done. Perhaps he is with the wife he cannot remember and the children and the grandchildren who may not even exist. He remembers a girl called Irene with dark brown hair and brown eyes, whom he believes he may have liked many years ago; perhaps they married and settled down in a suburban brick house with a tiny backyard. Perhaps she is the mother of all those children and the grandmother of all those grandchildren he cannot even bring to mind. He had read something once about how life is all about choices, a bit like forks in the road, and how choosing one option did not necessarily negate all the others which continue to play out parallel to the chosen option, like shadow-plays that are out of sync with the actors. Perhaps there are lots of Oswalds out there, all doing different things, thinking different thoughts, having different experiences.

Oswald presses his fingers hard against his forehead, trying to get his mind around the possibility that there may be a myriad of parallel universes. He knows that he is too tired for such mind gymnastics, and he finds it difficult to cope with such thoughts when he no longer knows where he is or even who he is or whether what he is experiencing is in the past or the future, and whether or not this past or future is actually connected to him. The idea of having such confusion multiplied an infinite number of times makes his head spin. He really wants to add a few new thoughts to his notebook, but he dares not: he will simply have to try to remember them for later.

He wonders how difficult it is to pass sideways into another parallel universe; to be another Oswald doing other, happier things.

The queue is now moving reasonably fast. Oswald is attempting to focus on the concept of movement in relation to time when he suddenly realizes that he is almost level with the Reception desk. The Receptionist, a young man in his late twenties, dressed in black trousers, white shirt and pink paisley vest, gives an impression of ordered efficiency which Oswald feels is completely at odds with how he himself is feeling. The man slides a couple of papers into a drawer under the desk and then gestures to Oswald to step forward.

"Room Nineteen," he says, holding the key in his right hand halfway across the desk.

Oswald waits, feeling instinctively that there is more to come, feeling his stomach tighten and his breathing become worryingly irregular.

"You were using a notebook; no notebooks allowed here. If you have anything to say, you can always say it to me or one of the other Receptionists. Open and transparent, no secrets."

Oswald looks at the man with a face completely devoid of expression, or as devoid as he can possibly manage in such a situation.

If the man in front of him is at all taken aback by Oswald's lack of emotion, he does not show it. He simply jingles the key on its large ring and puts out his other hand. "The notebook," he says, "and I'll take the pen as well; after all, you won't be needing it any longer."

In any other situation, Oswald would most probably have objected, but he knows that this situation is different; it is disassociated from everything that can be considered normal. In the same way that he has begun to question the order of time and whether time even exists, he knows that he must also accept that the rules governing cause and effect no longer seem to function as expected. He slowly removes the notebook and the pen from his pocket and places them both on the desk in front of him. He is angry with the Receptionist, but he is more angry with himself for having been so stupid. He is already beginning to feel naked, having now lost his only means to note and record. He should have been more careful, but now it is too late.

While the very smug Receptionist is explaining the way to Room Nineteen, Oswald is frantically trying to remember everything he has written in the notebook, and whether or not it will incriminate him; of what, though, he has absolutely no idea.

Fragment Eighteen

With a burst of renewed energy, Tilda began to move back along the tunnel on the side where she felt that there may have been a very slight suggestion of air movement. Feverishly, she ran her hands over every square centimetre of the rough wall, starting at the top and working down towards the ground, hoping to be able to find something that would confirm that she was right – that there actually was another way out of the tunnel. It was difficult trying to find what she was looking for in the dark, and she tried not to think of all those things that her hands might stumble upon, things that her eyes were unable to see.

About three metres back along the tunnel, her hands finally encountered what she was groping for: a small break in the surface of the wall, about level with her waist. Frantically, she worked her hands around the break and discovered an opening not much bigger than the actual opening to the tunnel from the room. She began to wonder how she could possibly have missed it earlier and realized that she had then been on her hands and knees and that the opening was higher up.

She removed her jacket and pushed it through the hole,

then she pulled herself up into the opening, trying not to think too much of the sad state of her clothing. She had no idea what she would find on the other side of the hole, but she was certain that it could not be worse than her present situation. As she squeezed through the hole, she kept telling herself that this had to be the way out and that, very soon, she would be free.

Vulnerable was the only word she could think of as she forced herself through the narrow opening in the darkness, having not even the slightest idea as to what might be beyond. Although she did not want to dwell on the possibility, she knew that she could well be throwing herself into some bottomless void, though, realistically, she did not believe this to be the case. But, even if there was solid ground beneath the opening, she had no idea what else or, for that matter, who else, might be lurking in the darkness. She had to rid herself of such thoughts, otherwise she would become paralysed with fear, and then she would not be able to move in any direction whatsoever. With a slight surge of confidence, she noticed that the darkness in this new tunnel did not feel as compact as in the first, and she wondered whether it actually was lighter or whether her eyes had become used to the darkness.

From the opening, she slid about three metres down on to what felt like a flat surface. When she felt around with her hands, she guessed that this new tunnel was roughly the same size as the old one, and that the ground and the walls felt very much the same as those she had been crawling over and past for the last hour or more.

After some rummaging in the dark, she found her jacket, which she wriggled back into, and then, still on her hands and knees, she moved along the new tunnel. Having found the entrance to the new tunnel, she felt strangely positive and optimistic, and each time the tunnel swerved a little to one side or the other, she expected to see an exit beyond the next bend. She still did not dare stand up for fear of tripping should the ground become uneven, and, as a result, her progress was quite slow.

All her thoughts were focused only on the exit and everything beyond: the light; the diversity of greens captured in a mixture of vegetation and trees; the sky, its blueness and even its greyness; and, finally, the people. She dwelt on the possibility – the probability – that was almost within her grasp, of actually meeting ordinary, normal people doing ordinary, normal things. There would be no Reception Hall, no corridors, no rooms, no keys, no regulations. She crawled faster, spurred on by the hope, which was quickly becoming a conviction, that she would soon be out of the nightmare and safe once again.

Then, without any warning, the tunnel became much wider, almost like a small cave, and the darkness became grey and shadowy. She was able to make out the sides of the tunnel, and, when she looked down at the ground, she could actually see the sand and the small rocks over which she had been crawling for almost two hours.

She stood up, confident that she would now be able to continue on foot, and, as she rounded the next bend, she was met by sunlight streaming in through an opening curtained with some kind of silvery-coloured thorn bush.

Tilda ran the last few steps, bursting out into the sunshine through the thick, tangled barrier, completely oblivious as the thorn bush drew thin red scratch lines across her arms, and as it grabbed haphazardly at her clothing in one final, vain attempt to keep her in the tunnel.

For a moment, she stood perfectly still beyond the opening, barely comprehending that she was indeed free, that she had found the exit and that now all the corridors and rooms and madness were behind her.

As she became more aware of her surroundings, she saw that she was standing on the side of a small hill, and, below her, verdant grass ran in one long wide sweep all the way to a small creek. On the other side of the creek, the ground seemed to be relatively flat and had been divided up into small fields of irregular sizes. A dirt road ran through the fields, and, in the distance, Tilda could see the squat spire of an old stone church and the roofs of houses – there was something familiar about the spire that pricked her memory, but she could not recall what it might be.

She brushed herself off as best she could, knowing full well that there was not much she could do about most of the marks on her clothing. Then, while she was running her hands through her hair in an attempt to bring it into some kind of order, she began to think about the possibility of washing herself, at least her hands and face, in the creek. All the time she was also thinking that it would have been nice if she had reverted to being twenty-five again, but that was evidently not to be. She began to suspect that being twenty-five again had probably been something she had dreamt and that, in reality, it had never happened.

The walk to the little town – Tilda was not sure if it could actually be called a town – was not at all arduous; in fact, after hours of crawling over through a dark tunnel, it was extremely pleasant. The green grass felt wonderful beneath her feet, the air was fresh and the sun was shining. When she reached the creek, she discovered that it was not deep, and there were sufficient flat stones for her to cross without getting her shoes too wet. On the other side of the creek, there was a small pool, where she was able to wash away some of the dirt and grime from her hands and face;

she even managed to remove a few of the smudges from her trousers.

When she first sat down at the edge of the water, she removed her shoes, and, while she was rubbing at the marks on her trousers, she let her feet dangle in the clear, cold water. The initial shock, as her feet entered the water, was quickly replaced by a feeling of deep satisfaction. She was outside for the first time in what seemed like weeks, and, no matter what she looked like, she was free, and just that knowledge filled her with an indefinable happiness. She found it quite unbelievable that she could be sitting on soft green grass, her feet immersed in crystal-clear, running water, the warmth from the sun seeping into her body, and that everything to do with rooms and corridors had simply evaporated. She could hear birds singing and, further across the fields, she could see some cows. She looked at the sparkling sunlight shifting in small irregular shapes and bubbles across the surface of the water, and she thought: perhaps the building with its corridors and rooms had been part of some awful dream, and perhaps none of it had actually happened.

After about twenty minutes or so, she removed her feet from the water and let them dry in the warm air, then she pulled on her shoes and continued on her way towards the town. However, the closer she came to the few uneven streets of disparate houses, more and more images began to nudge at her memory. As she reached the nineteenth-century stone church, with its low wooden fence and its noticeboard advertising Sunday services, the long clean shadow of the church falling across the path in front of her, she became acutely aware that this is where she had been when it all started.

The memory was both startling and liberating. She had

been visiting a friend, Amy. Amy had phoned her one evening, completely out of the blue: "You must visit, Tilda; we haven't seen each other in ages; it would have to be at least six months. What about next weekend? You are free, aren't you? Do say that you are; we could have a couple of days together – just the two of us. I'm sure we've lots to catch up on. You will come, won't you?"

Tilda had arrived by bus on the Friday evening, and Amy had met her at the bus stop. Amy lived a kilometre further out of the town, but it was a balmy evening, and they had enjoyed the walk. Tilda remembered that Amy had prepared a lovely meal with baked fish and a Greek salad, which they had eaten on the veranda at the back of Amy's house overlooking the garden. Tilda had brought a bottle of Pinot Grigio, which she placed in the fridge while Amy was preparing the salad.

Tilda had met Amy some years after she and Milford had divorced. By then, Tilda was living in Balmain, and, after having received the one and only promotion she was ever likely to receive at her first place of employment, given the size of the business, she had moved to a reasonably large law office, on the top floor of a sandstone building on Kent Street in central Sydney. It was a pleasant office and Tilda got along well with the other employees. Also, the office was only a short bus ride from where she was living. Amy was working as a saleswoman in Farmer's department store, on the corner of George and Market Streets, and the two women met by chance one day when Tilda went into Farmers to buy some stockings.

They had a number of things in common: they were the same age, they were both divorced and they had both moved to Sydney from the country. After that first chance meeting, they saw a lot of each other, and then, a couple of years later, Amy remarried, left her position in the department store and moved to a semi-rural area on the edge of Sydney. For a number of years, they continued to keep in irregular contact, and only very occasionally caught up in Sydney. Then Amy's husband suddenly died, leaving Amy once again on her own, and, since then, Tilda and Amy had begun to see more of each other. When they got together, it was as though all the years in between had never existed.

Tilda was thinking about Amy as she tried to remember the way to her friend's house. It occurred to her that Amy must be wondering what on earth had happened and why she had just disappeared, and then she recalled that Amy was with her when it all began. Tilda stopped walking and pressed her hands against the sides of her head: nothing was making any sense. If Amy was with her when... She tried not to stop her thoughts from rushing headlong into what had actually happened – it was easier to edge around such thoughts carefully – but, if Amy was with her then, then where was she now? She had no memory of seeing her in the corridors or the Reception Hall – not anywhere.

As she reached the centre of the town, she could see the large bus with the windows painted black so that no one could look in or out. She saw the group of people near the bus, and she could feel the anxiety and the consternation that was pressing down on everyone like some kind of fog. Everywhere she looked, there were men in black trousers and shirts.

But she had seen all this before: this had already happened exactly as it was happening now. She wanted to go up to someone, anyone at all, and ask what was going on, but, at the same time, she knew that it was not necessary: she knew exactly what was happening.

Two men in black were ushering people on to the bus. Tilda looked around her and, although part of her knew what to expect, she could still feel the terror mounting within her when she saw that she was standing next to Amy.

Amy said absolutely nothing about Tilda having been absent for so long; it was as though Tilda had been standing next to her all the time.

Amy whispered: "What on earth is happening, Tilda? Who are these people, and where do you think they could be taking us?"

Tilda said that she had no idea, but, of course, she did know. Images of the corridors, the rooms, the men in black, the Hall and the Receptionists were filling her head, but she could think of no simple way of explaining all of this to Amy; she could not even explain it to herself.

Amy squeezed Tilda's hand. "It must be some awful mistake, and someone will realize it very soon. Perhaps it's simply a military exercise that has gone wrong – you know, wrong place, wrong time." With the slightest hint of a smile, she continued, "There must be some explanation; I'm sure that there's really nothing to worry about."

Tilda could hear that she was not at all sure. She nodded and returned Amy's squeeze. They were in the queue, and they were being directed on to the bus. Tilda knew that they would both be told to sit three seats down on the right-hand side of the bus. She also knew that the large lady with the red hat would begin to scream hysterically just as the bus was ready to pull away from the kerb, and that a young man from the back of the bus would come forward saying: "Perhaps I can help: I'm a doctor."

She covered her face with her hands and sobbed. There was obviously no exit, there was no way back to what had been before.

Then it all became frighteningly clear: she had never been outside the building; she had been in Room Fifty-Seven all the time.

Fragment Nineteen

Back on the ground floor of the library, Milford looked around for a few moments, wondering what he should do next. Apart from the skylight that gave him a connection with the outside, he found the atmosphere of the library extremely suffocating, and he was beginning to feel acutely ill at ease. He walked over to a shelf and pulled out a book. It was a medium-sized book with semi-glossy pages. Milford held the book up to his nose and smelt the paper, inhaling a strangely satisfying mixture of glue, ink and paper. He placed the book on one of the large polished tables, and, after looking around to make sure that he really was all on his own, he slowly ripped out one of the pages.

As the page parted, almost reluctantly, from the thin cotton backing of the book, the sound it made was barely audible, but, for Milford, it encased a special sensuality, which was curiously addictive. The action of tearing, together with all the other sensations, actually freed up some of the stress he was experiencing. He screwed up the page and threw it on the floor, quickly ripping out another page and then another and another... The floor was very soon littered with small paper sculptures, and Milford left the carcass of the book on the table and pulled out a new one.

When six dead books were spread out on the table and their contents were piled on the floor, Milford sank down and began blowing the small paper sculptures first one way and then another. As the bits of paper changed position, touching each other with barely the whisper of a sound, Milford was reminded of himself. If he could have verbalized something as vague as the feelings and emotions within him, he may have equated them with the small paper shapes moving erratically, pushed in different directions by some force beyond themselves. He certainly did not suffer any form of existential angst over any decisions he may have made. As far as Milford was concerned, he was simply a pawn in the enormous game of chess that the universe was playing.

He picked up a couple of the paper balls and threw them in the air; then he threw a whole handful. Life had not been kind to Milford, and he had still not worked out why.

He had never been able to remain in any job for longer than a few months. Once the job acquired a veneer of monotonous routine, Milford usually tired of it, and then he quickly became restless, imagining new possibilities and experiences further afield. Tilda told him that it was because he was lazy and unfocused; Milford knew that it was because he hated the feeling of being tied down – to anything. Sometimes, when he moved on, ignoring the questioning glances of his fellow employees, it was his employer who, having seen all the signs, had asked him to leave; other times, he had taken the initiative himself, and, always confident that there would be something else around the corner and longing for what he saw as certain freedom, he would hand in his resignation.

But there was one particular job where he did not cut all the ties. Even after he left, there was still one thin and slightly tenuous cord linking himself and the plump, blonde girl who worked in the office and who laughed a lot, and who, when she was not laughing, often smiled in Milford's direction. On those occasions when he used to drop into the office, she hung on to his every word, carefully placing everything he said between unabashed smiles meant only for him. He had enjoyed the laughing and the smiles and the fact that she listened. Even before he decided to resign, he had already followed her home on two occasions, telling himself that it had nothing to do with love and trust – things that were bundled together and filed under the name *Tilda*. This was different; it was simply part of his need to be free. Yet, even after he had left the job, he saw her once again, before finally letting go of his end of the cord, but, by then, it was too late.

He had no idea how Tilda had found out about the girl from the office, but she had. When she confronted Milford, she simply reminded him of what she had said she would do if he was ever to lie to her again, and then, without giving him a chance to explain, she left him. Milford could still see her wiping her eyes as she picked up her coat and handbag before walking out of the room, the flat and his life.

When Milford heard the front door close that terrible evening, he was filled with the knowledge that, from that moment onwards, nothing would ever be the same again. He stood there in the small kitchen while all that was good about his past was sucked out, beyond the walls of the room, into some invisible dimension. A sense of in-expressible loss had descended upon him at the same moment as she had confronted him, because he knew that he had no answer that she would be able to accept; instead, he allowed the guilt and the pain to fuse together into an anger that he had no way of controlling. He picked up the few glasses and plates on the table and hurled them against the wall, the sudden noise giving him a few seconds of relief, but, moments later, the scattered pieces of glass and porcelain littering the floor only emphasized the futility of his situation. After she had left, her eyes filled with fear and some other emotion he was unable to decipher, he sank to the floor and sobbed uncontrollably.

He had then sat hunched up on the kitchen floor, his back against the wall, wishing that there was a way of erasing the present and returning to the past. The word *idiot* kept pushing itself through his mind, but he was not sure whether he was an idiot because of what he had done or because he had been found out. After consideration, he decided that it really did not make a lot of difference: however one looked at it, he was still an idiot, and Tilda would not be coming back.

Fragment Twenty

Losing his notebook and pen made Oswald feel as if he had been subjected to some kind of virtual earthquake which measured quite high on the Richter scale and had disturbed the very core of his equilibrium. He had been trying to remain focused and positive, but without his concrete collection of ideas and the means to add more, he was at a loss as to how he would be able to hold himself together in at least some semblance of sanity. Just the fact of being able to physically relate to his ideas and calculations – black figures against white paper – gave him a connection, if somewhat dubious, with reality. A connection that he needed, if he was to survive in a situation where nothing any longer was ordered and nothing seemed associated with any kind of reality.

When he moved away from the Reception Desk, he was aware of the Receptionist standing and watching him for a few moments before abruptly turning to attend to the next person waiting in line.

The Receptionist had said that Room Nineteen was on the fifth floor, but Oswald had barely been listening to him. Not only was he angry about losing his notebook, he was also completely frustrated by the endless monotony and absurdity of everything to do with corridors and rooms; nothing seemed to be leading anywhere, and he was even beginning to doubt that he had been right when he said that they would definitely get out. His frustration was balancing on the edge of a deep depression, and, spreading beyond the edges of all the greyness, there was a shapeless anxiety over what he may have written in the notebook and how it could be interpreted.

Caught up in all these fairly negative thoughts, he followed the corridor to its very end where, instead of the expected flight of stairs, there was a heavy metal door, similar to those leading to a fire escape. He opened the door and found himself on a narrow landing leading on to a spiral staircase. The staircase itself completely filled the round stairwell that stretched both upwards and downwards as far as he could see. At repetitive equal points along the spiral, in both directions, Oswald could see landings, similar to the one on which he was standing, and which doubtlessly led to other corridors and other rooms.

Oswald closed the door behind him and stepped off the landing on to the first stair. The metal stairs had been constructed with an open grid pattern which meant that he was very aware of the drop beneath him and the spiralling staircase above him. He began to feel quite dizzy, and he gripped the railings running up both sides of the staircase, his hands damp with perspiration and his heart pounding. A wave of nausea came over him, and although, more than anything, he wanted to sit down, the idea of sitting in such a place, poised over an abyss, made him feel even worse. For a few moments, he hung between the two railings, unable to move.

The nausea passed, and he dared take a quick look downwards, fascinated and yet terrified by the sight. He wondered if life were not a bit like the void, but whether one began at the bottom and worked one's way up to the top, or whether one began at the top and simply fell to the bottom, he was not quite sure. In either case there was a complete absence of being in control. He took another look, and this time, with his hands securely clutching the railings, he was able to allow his gaze to linger, without closing his eyes. The fact that he was securely anchored to the railings, while he looked both up and down, helped him retain a slight sense of balance. The drop was alarming, but he was beginning to come to terms with it, and he focused on the landings, thinking that, behind each landing, there was most probably a door leading to a corridor which, in turn, led to other corridors. At this point, Oswald did close his eyes, not to block out the drop, but in an effort to try to fully comprehend the unbelievable image of an over-whelming maze of corridors stretching out, both below him and above him, on so many different levels. The concept was staggering.

For Oswald, this could well have been a concrete representation of time: a stairwell without beginning or end, a bottomless crater criss-crossed by corridors and rooms dipping into what most people would term the past or the future while attempting to cling to something called the present but which, in spite of its name, was constantly disappearing into the past.

He gritted his teeth, and, fixing his eyes on each individual step, while he endeavoured to block out the reality of the drop below, he continued slowly up the stairs without once removing his hands from the railings. His mind was still completely focused on the stairs and the terrifying space both beneath him and above him, and, although there was some very small part of his mind still grappling with the problem of what he had written and how it might be construed, such thoughts no longer seemed so very important.

When he was level with the fourth floor, he stopped again and rested; he was relieved that he had only one more flight ahead of him. His mind, removed for a moment from the staircase and the drop below, decided that perhaps there was some small advantage to be gained if Eugene Turnbull or the Administrator, or whoever was actually holding all the strings, knew what he thought. Perhaps, in the end, it might actually turn out to be positive. It was definitely time for someone to start protesting. Oswald was becoming more and more amazed that no one had protested and that everyone, including himself, was so easily controlled.

Sheep, he thought, turning on to the last flight of stairs. The images filling his mind were making him smile, but the idea that this might actually be the way that others were also looking at him very quickly removed the smile. He was not the type who followed the crowd: he believed that he had always been an extremely independent person. It did not make sense that he should now be accepting things that, normally, he would have shied away from completely. He wondered how a handful of people, or even just one person, could make so many people do things that they did not want to do. It was absolutely absurd.

By the time Oswald had reached the fifth floor and crossed the small landing to the door, he was slightly out of breath but relieved that he was finally able to leave the stairwell. Once he had closed the heavy metal door behind him, thankful that he no longer had to contend with the infinite chasm below and above him, he stood for a few minutes, catching both his breath and his composure before walking slowly to the end of the corridor in front of him. For months he had been telling himself that he should start exercising more – he had even picked up a brochure from the local gym – but that was before the corridors and the rooms. As he thought about the gym, he felt a slight surge of positive energy as it became clear that he had actually remembered something else from before.

At the end of the corridor, he turned to the right and then, almost immediately, to the left.

He found himself in a very small dead-end passage, and Room Nineteen was right in front of him, at the end of the passage. He studied the door carefully for a few moments: it was an average-sized door with narrow panels in either white oak or Nordic pine. There were eight vertical panels all standing completely flush with each other, and, as he stood in the passageway, looking at the door, his mind turned to paling fences. But before he had had time to definitely equate the images of paling fences with the panelling on the door, his thoughts had already moved on to Paddle Pop sticks and sticky, melting ice blocks, and he smiled in spite of everything.

The number of the room was painted boldly in white paint right in the middle of the door, across three of the panels, and on the right-hand side, halfway up – or was it down? – there was a large round brass doorknob. The keyhole had been placed exactly under the doorknob.

Oswald slipped the key into the lock, and put his hand on the doorknob. He was about to turn the key and unlock the door, just as he had done on so many previous occasions, but something was stopping him. Something without any kind of physical form was pressing down on his arm, telling him to return the key to his pocket, telling him that he did not have to enter Room Nineteen.

Very slowly, Oswald pulled the key back out of the lock and wrapped his fingers tightly around it. An amazing sensation of calm rushed through his entire body. He did *not* have to open the door; he did *not* have to enter the room. He was not a *sheep*; he would do exactly as he wanted, and, right now, he definitely did not want to enter Room Nineteen.

Fragment Twenty-One

Tilda is back in the Reception Hall. She is feeling quite shaken, having understood that absolutely nothing is the way she believes it to be. There is nothing any longer that she can cling to in the belief that it is normal. The tunnels, the green grass, the creek, the town, even the bus were all simply part of the Room. Although she feels that she is getting very close to banging her head against the wall – any wall at all – and screaming out her frustration, she is beginning to understand that, just like a hamster running on its wheel, there is absolutely nothing that she can do. She is going nowhere because, no matter what she might have hoped, there is nowhere to go. Perhaps she is already dead, and what she is experiencing is actually hell.

Her mind, having brought up the image of Amy, pushes her thoughts in the direction of her friend, and Tilda wonders where she might be. She is quite sure that she has not seen her since they stepped on to the bus – the first time – and, although she would have liked it to be otherwise, she does not completely believe that Amy was part of what she just experienced. The Amy that she met at the bus stop was probably not Amy at all, or else it was some reflection of

Amy. But then she thinks that it might have been some kind of rewinding of time, in which case it would have to have been Amy.

She is extremely confused and despondent, and she is dubious as to whether or not she has the energy to go through the merry-go-round of corridors and rooms again – and again and again. There does not seem to be any way out of the nightmare, and she can see herself disintegrating into an infinite number of very small pieces – a bit like a thousand-piece jigsaw being scattered all over the floor. When the thought occurs to her she wonders what it would be like if she were actually to split off into lots and lots of tiny, unfettered pieces, and she decides that perhaps, for that very first split second, it could be extremely liberating.

Nothing has changed; everything is exactly the same as the last time when she was part of the endless routine of corridors, rooms and Reception Hall: the same long queues with the same dazed, haunted people moving slowly forwards before disappearing down one of many corridors, the same men in black, the same efficient-looking Receptionists. She knows that she could rest for a while on one of the benches but decides against it. She is in too much of an inner turmoil to be able to sit somewhere quietly by herself, and, instead, she attaches herself to the end of the queue which is already winding halfway around the Hall.

She can feel the nervous, sharp-edged anxiety that flickers outwards from the queue as it creeps slowly forwards. Most of the people have probably been in the queue before, but, for some, Tilda guesses that this could be their first time. She looks around, hoping to catch sight of Amy, but it is as though she simply evaporated somewhere between the bus and the Reception Hall, When that actually happened, Tilda is no longer sure. She tries to remember exactly when she last saw her friend after they stepped on to the bus, but there are enormous gaps in her memory, and the bits that remain intact are becoming very diffuse on the edges. Images seem to fade in and out of each other, and she thinks about dreams and how difficult it can be to remember them.

She wonders if, at some stage, way back when it all began, Amy may have actually managed to escape by slipping out of the nightmare; perhaps she never actually boarded the bus, or perhaps she stepped off while the lady in the red hat was having hysterics. Although all such ideas are illogical, Tilda regains a small shred of enthusiasm as she thinks of Amy calling the police and all the emergency services, and then the shred fades as she is forced to admit that even if it there were the slightest possibility that Amy were still on the *outside*, she would have absolutely no idea where Tilda was. As the queue moves slowly forwards, Tilda still hopes that Amy did get away, and that she is safe.

She notices a man standing at the Reception Desk; he is probably about the same age as herself, and there is something about him that tells her that she knows him, or, at least, that she has seen him before, but she is unable to find him in any of the small boxes in her memory. He seems very agitated, and the Receptionist is talking with him. The man pushes something across the desk towards the Receptionist – a young man, probably still in his twenties – who then slips whatever it is into a drawer. He appears to say something to the man who is looking rather distraught. Tilda watches the man as he moves away from the desk and finally disappears down one of the corridors. She tries to remember where she may have seen him before.

The man behind her, a tall man in his thirties with a

slight stoop, taps her lightly on the shoulder, and she spins around just a little too quickly.

He says, slightly taken aback but still in a low voice: "I'm so sorry. I didn't mean to alarm you."

Tilda shakes her head slightly and forces herself to smile while thinking that there is really not much to smile about.

The man says, "Have you been waiting very long?"

The words play around between the boxes in Tilda's memory as she listens to herself saying, "No, not that long, but everything, and I mean everything, is so very relative, wouldn't you agree?"

The man is now looking at her very intensely. After a moment, he says, "I really don't think that anything can exist entirely on its own."

Tilda gasps as one of the boxes springs open, and she suddenly remembers the man called Oswald. She throws a quick look in the direction of the Reception Desk, uncertain as to whether there may be a connection there with the man called Oswald, a connection that she must have missed earlier, but the man has moved on, and the Receptionist is attending to someone else. Then she covers her face with her hands.

"I really don't think I can take much more of this." Her voice is verging on a sob. The man behind her looks quite concerned, and he leans over and puts his hand on her arm.

"I do hope I didn't say anything to upset you; it's just that…"

Tilda tries to pull herself together. "Honestly, it's not you; it's everything… everything else." She wanted to tell him about Oswald, but she really did not know where she would begin.

"Do you think we will ever get out?" he asks.

She looks at him, remembering what Oswald had said to her. "Of course we'll get out," she says. "I believe that that is the one certainty. I'm not sure why, but someone told me that it has to be the central point. He was very certain that we will, eventually, get out."

The man nods slowly. His hand is still on Tilda's arm, and he withdraws it apologetically. "It's all been a bit of blur," he says. "Really, I don't even remember how I got here…"

Tilda smiles sadly. "I doubt that there is anyone here who can actually remember how they…" She feels a sudden need to talk about something else. She asks, "Do you remember much about *before*? For example, do you remember if you have a family?"

The man shakes his head. "I don't think so. No, I'm almost sure that I was on my own. I think I may have been an engineer. It doesn't really make any sense: not to be able to remember anything about yourself. I mean, it was only yesterday – at least, I *think* it was yesterday – I should be able to remember what happened yesterday, don't you agree?"

Tilda is about to say something when the person in front of her steps up to the Reception Desk, and she realizes that she is the next in line. She turns around but not before she smiles a quick apology towards the man and says very softly, "Perhaps we'll meet again…"

The person in front of Tilda has already moved away from the desk, and the Receptionist is looking at her. "Next person," he says, tapping a pen on a neat block of paper. "I don't have all day."

Fragment Twenty-Two

Oswald has pocketed the key, and, although he is still feeling somewhat exhilarated, the fact that he did not open the door to Room Nineteen is beginning to take on other perspectives, and the initial feeling of elation is quickly becoming diluted with a gnawing anxiety over what he has done. He is still standing in front of the door, and he could very easily remove the key from his pocket and open the door, but something tells him that he will not be doing that. He has crossed a mental bridge, and, for him, there will be no turning back.

As he stands, looking at the door, he fears that there will be repercussions, but, having crossed the bridge, he has moved on, and the repercussions – if there are any – will be part of some other reality that he is hoping to be able to avoid.

It is extremely quiet, and there does not seem to be anyone else around. He pushes his thoughts and fears to one side, moves out of the dead-end passage and looks down the corridor. It is completely empty: there is not a soul to be seen anywhere. It is a strange feeling to be so utterly alone when he knows that there are actually many people moving around in all the layers of different corridors. He wonders how long it will take for the people in charge to realize that he did not enter the room, and that thought leads him to consider whether or not everything is electronically controlled, or whether there is some other kind of surveillance system. He is certain that they must have some kind of system, otherwise he does not believe that they would be able to keep track of so many people and so many rooms. He thinks about the word *they,* but he is not sure if it is *they* or if it is only *he*.

He does not have a plan, so he has no idea what his next step should be. All he knows is that he must get out of the building – it has to be a building, and an extremely large one – but he really does not know how to go about it or even where to start. For the moment, the only thing he can think of is that it is essential that no one sees him.

He looks around him, wondering if there is anywhere at all where he might be able to hide, but he is sure that whoever is in charge – *they* or *he* – would have made certain that there was nowhere to hide: nothing but corridors and rooms and every room securely locked, with everything linked back to a Reception Hall and men in black watching one's every move.

Oswald does not want to start panicking; he has made an important decision, and he trusts that he has already started moving in a new direction. He does not want to dwell on the very slight possibility that he may have made the wrong decision; he tells himself that it was the right decision and that soon he will be free. All decisions are right, he argues with himself. Each new decision simply marks a fork in the road; very soon there will probably be another fork, and even later, another one. Oswald knows that he has to believe in himself; now is definitely not the time for him to be having second thoughts.

He returns to the tiny passageway where Room Nineteen is situated. He feels that it is strange that there should be only one room in the passage, and he considers the possibility that he may have missed some other doors.

It only takes him a few moments to walk into the passageway, run his eye over the door to Room Nineteen at the end of the space, and then walk out again. He does not notice anything out of the ordinary, but, then, as he is about to walk back out into the corridor, he notices a door. It would have been very easy to miss it, which, of course, he has already done a couple of times. It is painted in the same grey colour as the walls and seems to be made of the same material. When Oswald looks at it more closely, he can see that it is a door with a very small handle and no lock of any kind.

The fact that there is no lock means that there is no key, and Oswald feels his heart beating faster. He quickly weighs up the advantages and disadvantages of opening the door, then he decides that he has nothing to lose by opening it and definitely nothing to gain by standing where he is, so he opens it.

The door opens inwards into a narrow, elongated room which seems to have been wedged in between two walls as some kind of afterthought. Apart from the fact that the shape seems all wrong for an ordinary room, it has two or three armchairs, a couple of ordinary timber chairs, a small table and even a long low bookcase with some books. There is a large rectangular mat on the floor – a sapphire blue colour with a complicated geometric pattern in reds and oranges – and, running along the opposite side of the room to the bookcase, there is a stainless steel bench with a hot-water urn, coffee, tea, disposable paper cups, disposable spoons, sugar in small paper packets and biscuits wrapped in plastic. At the furthest end of the room, there is a sofa bed, and Oswald wonders if this might be a room for staff when they are off duty.

The thought is somewhat troubling as it means that someone could very well walk into the room at any given moment. Oswald checks the door from the inside and sees that there is a handle, and, when he turns it, it opens. He feels a sense of relief surging through him: at least he now knows that he can leave the room whenever he wants to.

He walks around the room and picks up a few of the books: *The Stranger, Notes From the Underground, The Ethics of Ambiguity.* He places them back on the shelves and sits down on one of the armchairs. He would have liked to have remained sitting, but he is very tense, one ear listening to the door, adrenalin surging through him, his entire body in a state of constant readiness for either fight or flight. He does not want to have to consider either alternative, but he is not sure what he will do if someone does come in through the door.

He walks quickly around the entire room, checking for another door or another exit out of the room. When he finds nothing, he decides to leave as he is becoming far too anxious about the very likely possibility of someone suddenly entering. He opens the door very carefully – there is no one in the passageway – and he steps out, closing the door behind him.

It is becoming intensely apparent to Oswald that he must formulate some kind of plan: he cannot possibly remain where he is much longer, but he is still not sure where to go. Yet again, he looks out into the corridor which, as before, is completely empty, and he is about to turn away, when he sees a figure appear at the far end of the corridor. He is almost sure that the figure is female. He pulls back into the small passageway and waits.

After a few moments, he takes another look and sees that the woman – he was correct about its being a woman – is now much closer, and he notices that it is Tilda. When she is about ten metres from him, Oswald can see that she is about to turn into a corridor running off to the left. He walks out into the corridor, no longer worrying about not being seen, and waves his arms. He suspects that Tilda does not recognize him at first, for she stops and stands still for a moment, peering in his direction. He waves again, and she walks slowly up the corridor to where he is standing.

Oswald puts his finger on his lips, and then, opening the door to the hidden room, he indicates that she should follow him. He notices that she frowns at him and looks as though she could be on the point of hesitating, so he is more than relieved when she follows him into the room. Once they are inside, he pulls one of the chairs over to the door, and, tipping it slightly, catches the back of the chair under the handle.

Tilda seems both very nervous and very surprised. At first she refuses to move into the room, and she remains just inside the door, undoubtedly still weighing her options as to what she should do; then, as though she has thought through the situation and made an important decision, she moves away from the door and sits down in one of the armchairs.

"I *do* know you, don't I?" she asks. "I think I saw you in the Reception Hall, talking to the Receptionist, and I felt even then that I'd seen you somewhere before."

Oswald thinks that it is strange that she could have

forgotten him so quickly, but he also understands that, since arriving in the building that is not a proper building, *strange* has become extremely relative.

He says, "Oh yes, we have met a couple of times. Remember? I'm Oswald, the man from the woods." He almost smiles, and then he sits down opposite her.

An almost negligible film of recognition crosses Tilda's face, and she nods, mainly from a need to appear polite. She is still not completely certain who he is, but she is prepared to take his word that they have already met. The name Oswald rings a kind of a bell in her memory, and then she remembers talking to the man in the queue about getting out and how she remembered that someone – was it this Oswald? – had told her that *getting out* was central to everything.

"We have to get out of here," he says, looking at her directly, "but I'm not quite sure how we are going to do it." He pauses for a moment, absorbing her confusion, and then he continues, "I'm awfully sorry, I should never have presumed that you... I mean, if you would prefer to go back to the corridors... You must understand, there is possibly a fair amount of risk attached to all of this, and, to tell you the honest truth, I have absolutely no idea what might happen next. I really don't want to put you in any danger."

Tilda has been watching him attentively all the time he has been speaking, and now she sighs and shakes her head slowly.

Looking at her, Oswald feels that she may have finally fitted some of the pieces together and made a decision, and, while he is wondering what that decision might have been, she tells him that more than anything she wants to get out.

Then she tells him about her recent experience in the tunnel and what happened afterwards.

Oswald listens intently. Somehow it fits in with at least one of the many conclusions he has reached: that everything that has been happening has something to do with time. He has no idea how time can be controlled to the extent that it is evidently being controlled, nor does he know who is controlling it. In spite of all his thinking and all his calculations, there do not seem to be any answers.

"What do *you* think is happening?" he asks Tilda. "Why do you think everything seems to be going around in circles and there is no obvious way out? Why didn't you remember me? Why is the past and the future all mixed up with what is happening now?"

Tilda throws her hands in the air. "Honestly and truly, I have absolutely no idea; I only wish I did," she replies. There is a small hint of irritation in her voice. "I'm not a scientist." she continues. "But at least I now believe that I can actually remember you. It was you, wasn't it, saying that we would definitely get out?"

Oswald nods. "Because it all has to do with time, we have to return to the starting point…"

"But that is positively ridiculous! Time doesn't run backwards."

"No, I don't suppose it does – it just *is.* Don't you see? That has to be the point with all of this, otherwise we wouldn't be stepping in and out of experiences."

Tilda looks at Oswald for a moment as though she is considering whether or not she will take the discussion any further, then she breathes in, a bit like a diver before plunging into the water, and says: "This probably sounds completely insane, but do you think it might be remotely possible that while we are here in this dreadful place, walking along corridors and opening doors, we are also somewhere else? Perhaps we are in many places at the same time, doing different things. We might not be stepping in and out of experiences at all but stepping in and out of different versions of ourselves."

Oswald observes Tilda with a new kind of respect. The idea is not as insane as she would like to have him believe; he has gone down the same track himself, trying to link the whole thing to the possibility of what others might call parallel universes. The pieces of information are all there, but Oswald is having difficulty making everything join up together.

Although Tilda would like an answer, she does not really expect one; she is quite certain that no one can tell her what she wants to know. Her head is now so full of conflicting ideas and possibilities that, at times, she believes that she would like to be able to remove it and sink into a peaceful state of nothingness – no thoughts, no nightmare, nothing.

She has been closely contemplating the mat on the floor, following the lines in the pattern, musing as to whether or not the answer might be hidden somewhere in the pattern. When Oswald says nothing, she lifts her head and says, "Or perhaps everything is simply the result of our imaginations gone wild."

"Everyone's imagination at the same time? Exactly the same images and thoughts?" Oswald laughs softly. "No, I really don't think we are imagining anything; I don't think that we are dreaming either. Everything is, unfortunately, very real, and it is just as real for all the others stuck in this building or whatever it is."

"You may be right – perhaps we are not imagining all

this, but nothing is making any sense; just like nothing makes much sense in dreams," continues Tilda. "We have absolutely no idea about what is happening here: we don't know where the building is; we don't even know if it *is* a building. We don't know anything about the people behind it. And..." she pauses for a moment, "nothing is normal... things are simply not the way they should be; not even we are the way we should be."

Oswald regards her thoughtfully, absent-mindedly stroking his beard. Then he says, "It could be that we actually know more than we want to believe that we know."

Then, without any warning, they hear loud footsteps in the passageway outside the door. Someone stops outside the door and turns the handle. The chair holds. Whoever it is tries the handle again and, this time, gives the door a slight push. Still the chair holds.

Both Oswald and Tilda hold their breath; neither of them have any idea what they will do if the door is suddenly flung open and the someone on the other side enters the room.

The *someone* tries a third time and then gives up. They listen to the footsteps disappearing down the passageway.

Oswald and Tilda look at each other and Oswald whispers, "I'm only guessing here, but I would say that he has gone to get some kind of reinforcement. I'm not sure what we are going to do: we can't stay here, but, on the other hand, we can't go out into the corridor. I hate to be harping on about it, and, at the moment, it honestly doesn't matter whether it is past, future or present, but, whatever it is, we really don't have much time to make a decision."

Fragment Twenty-Three

After Tilda left him, Milford moved away from Sydney and hitchhiked south. While he focused on trying to find that piece of wide, uninterrupted expanse of blue sky he had been hankering after, he suspected that he was simply trying to run away from himself. Not for a moment did he have to wonder why Tilda had left him: as the final straw heaped upon his continual restless movement from one place of employment to the next, his thoughtless foray into infidelity had caused everything to reach breaking point. It had been just one more thing that had confirmed what Tilda already knew or thought she knew about Milford: he was not to be trusted.

The intense irritation and, to a lesser extent, the shame that he felt, when he was found out, very gradually developed into a dull, angry ache which occasionally dipped down into feelings of dejection and depression. When it all became too much for him, the ache expanded within him before exploding outwards. Sometimes on these occasions, he tried to tell himself that he was angry with Tilda; after all, had she been more understanding he would not be in the state he now was, but he knew that the anger was always directed towards himself, and, when he was unable to contain it, he would often find himself in pub brawls with people he did not know and about whom he did not care. He moved from one casual job to the next, his path across the country coloured by more frequent altercations as he tried to extricate himself from the realization that he was the only one to blame.

Because his present was so entwined with his past and because Tilda was his past, he thought of her often, and he wondered whether, if he had remained in Sydney, she might have eventually forgiven him. He would have written to her, but he had no idea where she was, and, instead, he drank too much, smoked too much, and, on those occasions when it became completely clear that it was impossible to return to the past, he vented some of his anger and frustration on strangers.

About a year after he had left, he briefly considered returning to Sydney just in case Tilda had relented, but then he remembered that he had no address for her, so he continued south. It was late summer, and the countryside was yellow-brown. The sky, more often than not, was blue, and if he occasionally experienced the brief sense of peace that an uninterrupted sweep of sky gave him, it was almost always book-ended by the resentment and the irritation that he could not escape.

Not far from the border between New South Wales and Victoria, he worked for some months on a sheep farm and then he moved further west, almost into South Australia. In a town with one main street and one pub, he got into yet another fight. The man almost died – "a tragic case", the judge had said – and Milford, who had already received a couple of warnings, was sent to gaol.

In gaol, he attempted to work out why it had happened, and

if there had been some way he could have prevented it from happening had he been able to catch hold of his past. There was no straightforward answer, and all he had to look forward to were years of locked doors and barred windows. The line between the past and the future was for ever drawn in indelible ink as the present pushed him into a future he did not want. Milford would have done anything at all to have been able to clamber back over that line and disappear into the past, but he was beginning to understand just how difficult it was to step back over a line that had already been crossed.

Sitting in his cell, he would sometimes try to alter the picture of the past that had entrenched itself in his mind, by first erasing the image of the police car and the policemen who collected him from the bar. He also tried to erase the image of the man lying on the floor of the pub and the people standing around him, but the picture in his mind insisted on reclaiming all the erased details, and Milford watched helplessly as the two policemen walked towards him. He remembered feeling much the same as when Tilda had confronted him about the rumours she had heard, and how, both times, the past and the present had run off him like fast-running water, and how all he had wanted to do was to be able to return to a point in the past before anything negative had happened. Even though this was what he wanted, he knew that it was impossible and that there was absolutely nothing that could be done to change what had happened.

When one is falling, and the ground is rushing up from below, and everything above is pushing downwards, there is a split second when it is possible to believe that one is completely separate from all the movement up and down, and that one will remain cocooned and safe in some dimension that is neither falling nor rising. Milford, attempting to assess just how dead or alive the man on the floor in front of him actually was and how long it would take before he opened his eyes and stood up, felt the split second brush past him; then, as he slowly understood that the man was probably not going to stand up for quite some time, he tried to stop his fall by clinging on to branches and rocks on his way down. The branches did not hold, and the stones simply slipped away, and it was not long before Milford and the ground collided. When he finally picked himself up, his life had changed, and he found himself in gaol.

Fragment Twenty-Four

Tilda said: "Perhaps there isn't another way out; perhaps it's just that we want there to be another way out, but there isn't one. After all, when you think about it…"

She had been looking very closely at the mat for some time, letting her eyes follow the brightly-coloured, complicated patterns; now she sank to her knees and began to roll back one corner.

As she was rolling back the mat, she said, with the slightest hint of excitement in her voice, "Perhaps there's a reason for the mat's being here." She looked up at Oswald and attempted a weak smile. "Perhaps it's more than just a mat."

Oswald looked at her quite blankly. His mind was already working like a computer, processing a multitude of possibilities in an attempt to find a solution to the problem, but there did not seem to be one, and he knew that the man would be back at any moment. As far as he could see, the immediate future – that is if it was the future – definitely contained no surprises.

Tilda had turned back part of the mat, and Oswald, suddenly torn away from his own problem-solving and his anxiety about the impending future, could see that the mat was affixed to something that looked like the door to a manhole.

He knelt down on the floor next to her, and, as they lifted the mat together, the small square door automatically opened, attached as it was to the underside of the mat. Oswald peered down into a dark passageway.

He glanced quickly at Tilda, who was already on her way through the opening. Oswald removed the chair from the door; then, after a last quick look around the room to check that nothing was out of place, he too lowered himself into the hole, pulling the door closed above him. As the door locked in place with a metallic clank, Oswald assumed that, on the other side, the mat would have hopefully returned to its original position on the floor.

"Ingenious!" he said, smiling at Tilda.

Standing directly below the manhole, Tilda was not sure whether Oswald was referring to the fact that she had been smart enough to stumble on the exit or whether he actually meant the exit itself. She decided, however, not to ask him for a clarification. Although it was not as dark as in the tunnel she had recently crawled through, she could barely see his smile. She could, however, sense his relief, and she knew that it paralleled her own. The main thing was that they were out of the room, and the future, that seemed so definite and so dark only minutes ago, had begun to move along a completely different tangent.

For a few moments they remained standing under the opening, listening carefully. They heard the door to the room open and then they heard the footsteps of what sounded like two men. One of the men was laughing.

Oswald could imagine the incredulous look on the face of the man who had first tried the door handle; the second man had probably decided that he was a bit of a fool.

At first it sounded as though the two men would stay in the room, but, after a few minutes and a short exchange of words, the gist of which neither Oswald nor Tilda could follow, they left again, closing the door behind them. Oswald and Tilda glanced at each other without saying anything and then began to move away from the opening above them.

A couple of naked light bulbs provided sufficient light for them to see that they were in a rather small cave-like room which was particularly low to the ceiling – between the top of Oswald's head and the ceiling there would have been no more than ten centimetres. At the furthest end of this room, a robust steel ladder took them down a long drop of about six metres into a passageway that appeared to slope gradually downwards. Oswald believed that the tunnel had probably been cut through a mountain or a hill, but, as he had absolutely no idea how things looked on the outside, there was no way he could be completely certain.

Tilda could not stop thinking about the other tunnel and how it all had ended; she was hoping that this time there would be a very different ending.

Fragment Twenty-Five

Although Tilda was irritated that Milford had walked away from yet another job, it was not until she found out about the girl at the office that what she had considered to be a reasonably normal life began to unravel. But, when she confronted him, the first few thin strands already pulling free, he lost his temper. She knew that he could get angry, but she had never before seen him lose his temper so completely, and, as the locked broom cupboard with its darkness and frightening images began to expand within her mind, fear pushed away any possibility of picking up the strands and twisting them into some kind of reconciliation. She decided then and there, fixated on the anger that was so obvious on Milford's face and in his actions, that she could not join her present to her mother's past. Although she still believed that she liked Milford, she was aware of the very narrow exit door that would become narrower and narrower until, finally, she would be unable to leave.

She tried to tell herself that he had never been violent towards her, but her head was filled with what might happen, and, at night, she dreamt about her mother.

After the first months had blurred some of the memories,

she occasionally wondered if she may have been too harsh, and if, perhaps, it might have been possible to retie the two ends of the cord that she had always imagined kept them together. But, as fear of what might happen took over all the unfilled spaces, the two ends continued to blow in different directions, and she finally understood that it was no longer possible to grab them. Milford would have to remain in her past.

Almost two years after she had left Milford, she met Gary. By this time she was living in Balmain, a waterside suburb slightly to the west of Sydney's centre. Still very much defined by its working-class image with docks and a plethora of small industries, it was very slowly showing the first signs of a richer population more interested in water views and closeness to the city. Tilda was not particularly interested in either the aesthetics or the logistics; the furnished room she found in one of the terraces was not overly expensive, and she was simply pleased to have somewhere to live.

She had started at the law office as one of many typists, but it did not take long before she had risen a few rungs up the ladder and, within a couple of years, she had been promoted to office manager. It was a large office with several lawyers, and Gary was one of the three partners. He was almost ten years older than she was: average height, reasonably good-looking, and a fastidious dresser. By the time she became involved with Gary, Tilda had forgotten all about narrow doors and broom cupboards; she was completely intent on pushing aside the past and taking the leap into a future that looked as though it might offer her everything she had ever wanted.

They circled a date for their engagement, and then Gary

ruined everything by getting himself killed. Tilda's leap, already begun, was pulled up in mid-air, and she found herself prostrate on the ground very definitely tied to a present that she was no longer able to understand.

It had been a wet, rainy night, and Gary and a friend, another lawyer, were returning from a late meeting with a client when a car travelling in the opposite direction slid across two lanes of traffic and collided head-on with Gary's car. Gary and his friend were killed on impact: the friend was thrown from the car; Gary went straight through the windscreen. The driver of the other car died in hospital. The accident was on the news and in the newspapers. Tilda listened to the news and read the paper and wondered, like her grandmother had years before, about the line between life and death – the present and the questionable future. A heavy iron door had slammed shut between herself and Gary; she wondered whether he still thought of her; she wondered whether someone who had crossed that line was even capable of thought.

She sat at the back of the flower-filled chapel during the funeral service. No one knew of the engagement that had now been wrenched from her future and remained somewhere with Gary beyond that line she could not cross. She was simply a colleague sitting at the back of the chapel. While the minister talked of resurrection and eternal life, Tilda thought how easily and how quickly the present can annihilate a future and force everything back into the past. She was caught somewhere between the past and future, but she no longer believed that she had a future; she wished that she too were dead.

Fragment Twenty-Six

Milford is no longer in the library, he is now back in the Reception Hall, standing next to one of the many benches. He has no recollection of actually leaving the library and then walking back along the maze of corridors, and he sits down on the bench for a few moments, trying to work out how he could have been in the library and then not there. He knows that he was tearing up books; his fingers still remember the satisfying sensation of the pages being ripped from the spine. He wonders vaguely if someone will come in and clean away the paper from the floor. He did not particularly like the library: he felt threatened by all the books, but he liked being able to see the sky. Here in the Reception Hall there is no sky, no outside, and he is no longer on his own.

He decides that there is no answer as to why he is back in the Reception Hall, so he sighs deeply, gets up and joins the queue. The queue is moving very slowly, and, several times, Milford regrets having left the bench – there he could at least imagine that everything was still reasonably sane and that he was not part of some interminable bad dream.

When he finally reaches the desk in the centre of the Hall, the Receptionist gives him yet another brown tablet and the key to Room Eight. Milford has not been able to accustom himself to the sight of all the keys and keyholes: they remind him too vividly of things he wants to forget.

He does not immediately leave the desk, but continues to stand where he is, undecided, the key in his hand. He is thinking of all the things he actually wants to forget, but he is also thinking of something else.

The Receptionist looks at him and asks, "Was that all?"

Milford focuses his thoughts on the sign he has seen that says something about creating a 'pleasant environment' for everyone. He leans closer to the desk and runs his tongue over his lips. "I… I was just wondering…" The words he needs are refusing to line themselves up correctly.

There is a momentary silence and a sense of suspended animation, somewhat like a film being paused; then the moment passes, the pause button is released and the Receptionist suddenly finds the recalcitrant words. "You'd like some cigarettes?" he asks, his eyes fixed on Milford.

Although Milford is taken aback, he tries not to show it. He says, "Well, yes… yes. Cigarettes – if it's at all possible." He is still mentally clinging to what he had decided the sign was promising him.

The Receptionist smiles, rummages for a moment in one of his many drawers and then pushes a packet of cigarettes across the desk.

Milford, trying to work out how the Receptionist knew what he wanted, nods his thanks, slips the packet into his pocket and moves away from the desk.

Room Eight is in the cellar, several floors down, but, in a building without any windows, a cellar is no different from any of the other floors, and Milford does not find the prospect of descending to the cellar particularly confronting.

He walks down the four flights of wide stone steps, buoyed by the knowledge that he is now twenty-five cigarettes better off, and he then follows a long stone-flagged corridor, his footsteps echoing emptily after him. There are no corridors running off the main corridor, and, as there are very few doors, Milford correctly assumes that there are very few rooms.

There is no one else in the corridor, and the positive edge on his mood begins to wear off as he is affected not only by a feeling of eeriness, but also by a growing sense of unease. Several times he thinks that perhaps he should turn back, but he is not at all sure what might happen to him if he does. As he has already done on a number of occasions, he wonders why everyone should be following inane instructions so explicitly. He has never liked others telling him what to do, and he cannot understand why he should now be accepting all these instructions so readily.

At the end of the corridor, there is a blank wall and a T-intersection and Milford can remember the Receptionist explaining that, after the corridor, he must then turn to the right. After about five minutes, he takes another right turn and enters a much shorter corridor with several doors, all of them with numbers clearly painted on them.

Room Eight turns out to be the third room on Milford's right-hand side. He hesitates for a moment, still wondering where the line goes between blind obedience and independent thought, but, failing to find the answer, he finally sighs, takes the key out of his pocket and carefully fits it into the lock.

The room is bursting with a blinding white light; in fact, it *is* blinding light. Milford feels that it is like stepping into a lamp, and, for a moment or two, he cannot see anything.

He closes his eyes tightly, and when he opens them again, the light is less bright, and he is able to make out an area covered with what appears to be concrete. The entire area is bounded on all sides by high concrete walls, and, on top of the walls, Milford can make out the long rolls of razor wire.

The exercise yard.

Instinctively, he takes a step backwards, wanting to escape, but the door has already locked itself behind him, and there is no way out. He is the only person in the yard, and, when he runs his eyes past the towers on the top of the walls, he cannot see any guards. He wonders what he is supposed to do, and, for some reason, not wanting to remain next to the door now that it refuses to open, he takes a few steps further into the yard. He recognizes the rough feel of the concrete beneath the thin soles of his shoes, the uninviting grey-white walls, the wooden benches, the basketball court at the far end of the yard, the watch towers, the lines painted on the concrete where the prisoners would have to stand more or less at attention – in fact, he recognizes everything except the emptiness.

It was the emptiness he had dreamt of and hoped for during those years. So many times, he had closed his eyes and hoped, when he next opened them, that the other inmates, the guards – in fact, everyone – would have totally disappeared, leaving him completely on his own.

Now he *was* completely on his own.

He opened the new cigarette packet and took out a cigarette. After lighting it, he walked slowly around the yard trying not to remember what it had been like. The sun was burning down on him, and, although he was feeling hot, he enjoyed the sensation – real or otherwise – of being partially outside. He kicked a stone across the concrete

space, the sound echoing emptily around the entire en-
closure. He waited for someone to appear, but no one
came, so he walked across to the stone and kicked it even
harder a second time.

Fragment Twenty-Seven

Oswald and Tilda were making good time along the tunnel-like corridor. It was very different from the first tunnel where Tilda had spent most of her time crawling on her hands and knees; here they were able to walk upright, and at times they could actually walk next to each other. It was dimly lit, although fairly irregularly, and there was a palpable sensation of late afternoon just before the sun disappears over the horizon. There was also an intangible *something* about the tunnel that made Tilda feel that it was probably used quite frequently, and she tried to force herself to think of other things without very much success.

More than ten minutes had passed since they had cautiously climbed down the steel ladder when Tilda said: "I probably shouldn't be saying this; I mean, I know that we have to keep being positive, but I just can't stop thinking that we could very easily meet someone down here… Someone whom we'd probably prefer not to meet."

Oswald nodded. His mind was already attempting to sort through variations of the same thought. If they were to meet someone, there was absolutely nowhere to hide. Since leaving the ladder, he had been vainly searching along the surface of the relatively smooth walls, hoping to find a cavity or even a door, but there was nothing.

"I agree completely about trying to remain positive. Best not to think about such a possibility; after all, it may never happen," he said, knowing that he had to think about it, just in case it did happen. He attempted a constrained laugh, which merely accentuated what he was actually thinking. "Perhaps it's best we hurry up," he added.

"But it could very well be our hurrying that causes us to bump into someone," said Tilda. "I mean, as you have said yourself, it all has to do with time. Or timing," she added. "A few minutes back or forwards in time can transform everything: things that, by all rights, should already have happened may not have…"

Oswald interrupted her. "Yes, of course, you're perfectly right, which makes it all so much more complicated; we really have no idea as to whether we should be rushing along or merely dawdling. A few seconds one way or the other could make a lot of difference to the outcome." He frowned slightly. "But let's take it all one step further: what if the outcome is not completely reliant on time as *time*? What if it's not so much our dawdling or our hurrying that impacts on our present – or is it our future? – and everything is actually tied up with what you mentioned earlier?"

He stopped in the middle of the tunnel and looked at Tilda with an eager expression on his face. "I'm thinking of what you said about parallel realities or parallel universes or simply parallel existences. I agree with you completely: what seems real, what *is* real, for you and me at this particular moment in time need not be anyone else's reality. We know that for a fact: there is no one else around, so there is no one who could possibly be experiencing *exactly* what we are experiencing right now." He looked around him quickly before continuing, "But, even if there were people here in this very tunnel, even people walking alongside us, there's absolutely nothing to say that their reality and our reality need be the same. Perhaps even you and I are actually in different realities that, just now, are running at a tangent to each other."

The thought was utterly disconcerting. Tilda wondered how much longer they would be sharing the same reality, and she sincerely hoped that it would last until they were out of the tunnel.

She nodded; she could hardly disagree; the idea about separate realities was something she had puzzled over for some time. Although she had initially felt that the idea might go a little way to explain part of what was going on, Oswald's interpretation seemed to add infinite layers to something that was already fairly incomprehensible. She had no intention of delving into the intricacies suggested by what Oswald was proposing, though the idea of their being in the same space as someone else, while being completely invisible because of the difference in the realities, was at least something she could hang on to, even if there were elements of the idea that were very difficult to accept. With every cell in her body, she wanted to be able to trust Oswald's theory; she wanted it to be true, but, at the same time, she decided that *hurrying* was probably still the more sensible option. At least she would be actively doing something. Once again, she set off down the corridor.

The tunnel continued downwards at a moderate angle with only the occasional bend or sharp turn. When, after twenty minutes of walking, they had still not seen another person,

Tilda allowed herself to relax a little. She began to believe that it might be possible to get through the tunnel without meeting anyone, but, while she was cautiously positive, the fact that there could be other people in the tunnel – invisible or otherwise – remained very much in the back of her mind. Thinking about all the different realities that might be piled on top of, or next to, each other, she wondered if it were actually possible to see from one reality into another, or if everything was vacuum-tight and completely detached.

"At least we're on our way down and not up," Oswald attempted another short laugh, placing his hand momentarily on Tilda's arm. "I guess one should always be thankful for such small mercies. Whether or not separate realities actually do exist, I wouldn't worry too much about our meeting anyone here; there wouldn't be many people who would want to climb up this tunnel..."

Tilda suspected that he was simply trying to calm her, which, in turn, succeeded in dragging forward even more anxiety-ridden thoughts from the back of her mind. Her positive feelings were fading very quickly, and she could sense that she was definitely becoming more worried, even though, on some level, she did appreciate his kindness. Focusing again on the reason for her anxiety, she had to admit that if they were to be discovered, she would at least have someone with her: she would not be on her own. She touched his hand, acknowledging his kindness.

Oswald was not quite as confident as he was attempting to appear. Like Tilda, he was concerned about being caught in the tunnel where there was absolutely nowhere to hide, and he did not have to wonder what would happen to them if they were found. He really did not want to end up back in the building, but it was pointless to focus on the negatives:

there was a chance that what he most dreaded would not even happen. He knew that the idea of countless different realities all running parallel to each other was not much more than a theory, but the more he thought about it, the more he liked it and the more he decided that the idea might somehow contain the answer for which he was searching. Apart from this dubious theory, he really had nothing, but, he had taken a decisive, independent step, and, if he remained focused and positive, then perhaps everything would keep moving the 'right' direction.

They had been walking for some time, one behind the other, the tunnel having narrowed considerably, and neither of them was talking. Both of them were concentrating on pushing their thoughts forward to a point where they could see themselves bursting out of the tunnel, knowing that they were finally free.

It was relatively quiet. Occasionally, they became aware of their footsteps on the comparatively hard ground, or of the soft, almost inaudible, sounds of their breathing. A few times, small stones slid across the path – probably dislodged by one of their shoes – and they both started slightly at the sound before grasping what the sound was and that there was actually nothing to worry about.

Then, suddenly, without any warning of any kind, they heard another sound.

There was someone behind them.

Tilda covered her mouth with her hand and looked as though she was about to either scream or faint. Oswald was not sure which would be worse; he held on to her arm and motioned to her to remain perfectly quiet. The sounds, both footsteps and voices, were coming closer, and, from the difference in the voices, Oswald guessed that there were two people. They were talking to each other quite loudly, and the words, many of them difficult to understand, were reverberating through the tunnel.

Tilda, thankful for Oswald's hand on her arm, was still standing, even though her body felt limp and strangely disassociated from her mind. She felt as though the important, essential part of herself was somewhere else, looking at her own body as it stood in a tunnel, waiting to be discovered. She managed a furtive glance at Oswald. Without saying anything, both of them were fully aware that there was nothing that they could do.

Oswald's mind was filled with the idea of different realities and the multitude of different spaces within time. If his theory was correct, then it would mean that the people in the tunnel might pass by without seeing them. It was a very, very thin and fragile straw on to which he was holding, but he was holding on to it as if it had been a heavy steel rod.

He dared not speak, but he indicated to Tilda that they should stand with their backs pressed against the tunnel wall, leaving as much space in the centre of the tunnel as possible.

Tilda had moved beyond being a composite being made up of a body and a mind: she was cocooned within her mind – a mind that was now elsewhere, completely safe. She looked down on her body pushed up against the hard wall and felt a strange sense of sorrow and even compassion.

As they stood next to each other, their backs against the wall, Oswald continued to hold on to Tilda's hand very tightly.

Then, for no obvious reason, Tilda's mind reconnected

with her body, and she whispered, "I really don't think I can do this, Oswald." There were tears filling her eyes, and her body was shaking. The fact that two men were loudly and forcefully making their way along the tunnel, along the exact same part of the tunnel that she and Oswald had passed through only minutes ago and who, in only a handful of seconds, would be confronting them, was like a concrete wall that her mind could neither break through nor climb over. If it had been possible, she would have willed herself into a state of blissful unconsciousness, but, given her unnatural state of high alertness, even that was not possible.

Oswald understood that she was terrified, because he felt much the same. All he could do was to squeeze her hand in some kind of dubious hope that it might help when there was no other kind of help available.

The voices, relaxed and boisterous, were moving closer, layered over the heavy sounds of boots against the hard ground. Oswald guessed that the men were running; they obviously knew the tunnel very well.

The sweat on Oswald's back and neck was cold, and, although he doubted that he would faint, he knew that the strain was affecting him just as much as it was Tilda. He clenched Tilda's hand even harder, and she returned the pressure but did not look at him.

He could hear snippets of what the men were saying: something about a band playing in the town and what they intended to do that evening. Oswald thought it quite strange that the men could be talking about such everyday things when everything around them was so utterly bizarre.

He looked back along the tunnel as the two figures came into view. He wanted to be able to mentally will himself into a state of invisibility, but he knew that that was not how it was done; either there were parallel realities or there were not.

The men came closer.

Oswald could feel Tilda shaking; perhaps she would actually scream. He could not stop her if she did; he could only hope that she would not.

The two men were level with them; they were both dressed in black. Oswald felt the breeze as they passed by, and one of the men's arms brushed within millimetres of Oswald's chest.

All the time, Oswald was aware that Tilda was trembling; he could even hear her heartbeat.

Then, suddenly, she was not shaking any more.

The men were much further down the tunnel.

Tilda was nowhere to be seen.

Fragment Twenty-Eight

Back in Room Eight, Milford is sitting on the ground near one of the walls. He is not really quite sure what to make of his present situation – the greatest part of the horror was always the other inmates. And the guards. With such a large part missing, Milford feels that the walls and the concrete, and even the razor wire, are not much worse than the corridors and doors. No matter how he looks at it, he is still locked in.

He thinks of the words *locked in*, and wonders what it is that he is locked into. There do not seem to be any answers, and no one to ask. He does not like being locked in any-where – he likes to be able to see the sky and to be able to move around as he pleases, not as someone else pleases. Yet, over the years, *locked in* has probably said much more about him than he would be happy to admit.

He lights another cigarette, confident that, when this packet is finished, he will be able to ask for a new packet. He thinks again of the person who looked like Tilda, and then spends a few minutes deciding whether or not he will get up and walk around the compound again. Because it is so empty and non-threatening, the place feels weird and uncomfortable, and Milford is somewhat at a loss as to what he should do next. When he finally decides to take another walk around the empty yard, simply for want of something to do, he finds it extremely difficult to get up; his legs do not respond properly and he has a definite pain in his back that was not there before he entered the room.

Eventually, he manages to pull himself to his feet, and he attempts to attain some kind of balance while supporting himself against the concrete wall. As he does so, he notices the wrinkled skin on his forearms and the raised veins on his hands. He looks down at skinny ankles protruding beneath the cuffs of his trousers, and then he runs a hand over unfamiliar stubble on his chin. There is no way that he can actually see what he looks like, but he knows that he is old. Very old. The idea frightens him. In fact, he finds it more frightening than a yard full of inmates and guards. He remains leaning against the wall, trying to compose himself. He wishes that he were back in the library – at least there *he* had not changed. He is not at all comfortable with this new old version of himself, and he feels as though he is locked into the space with a stranger. He knows for sure that it would have been easier to confront other inmates and guards than to have to confront himself tottering so close to death's door.

Milford is not philosophical, and he normally does not analyse situations: life happens, there is not much that he can do about it. However, standing in the exercise yard, looking down at his decrepit body, he begins to wonder if this is how the end is going to be, alone in a gaol exercise yard, either here or somewhere else. Thinking the words *somewhere else* brings him with a rush back to the present. If he is supposed to die somewhere else, then there has to be a way out of the exercise yard and the corridors and the Reception Hall…

But perhaps there is no *getting out*; perhaps this *is* where it ends. He finds it vaguely amusing, given the fact that he has spent so many years in places just like this one, but the amusement is stifled by the surge of anxiety that is taking over his body. He definitely does not want to draw his last breath in such a place; he does not want to think about last breaths. He wants to go on and on, drawing breath after breath after breath. Then he looks down at his wrinkled body, and he wonders just how many more breaths he might actually have left. The silence around him is pressing down on him; he slides down the wall to a sitting position, putting his head in his hands. He wonders what he has done to deserve this, and for the hundredth time, he wonders why he is where he is.

Fragment Twenty-Nine

For some minutes after the guards had passed by, Oswald remained where he was, his back pressed hard against the wall. He was grateful, relieved, ecstatic, but he was also confused. He had no idea what could have happened to Tilda. Perhaps her parallel reality, if such actually existed – and it must have, or otherwise the guards would have seen them – took a sharp turn and moved off on another trajectory, just at the moment the two men approached.

He pressed his hands against his head and moved away from the wall. His legs had turned to water and he was shivering all over. It was obvious that Tilda was nowhere to be seen, and, being completely practical, he knew that it would be impossible to look for her.

The shock of the two men walking past without noticing him was still thundering through his body. He had wanted it to happen, but he had not dared believe in the possibility. Not completely. As he attempted to steady himself, he became increasingly aware of the fact that parallel realities, in some form, must exist, otherwise he would not be standing where he was at that moment. Instead, he would have been on his way back into the building, escorted by the two guards. He really needed to sit down and pull himself and his thoughts into some kind of acceptable balance, but he decided, before the thought and the need had really taken hold, that it was probably better to get out of the tunnel as quickly as possible.

He could no longer hear footsteps in the tunnel beyond him, so he began to walk quietly in the same direction as the two men. As he walked, trying not to make any noise, his mind was attempting to find some order in the concept that time might be divided into many different layers, and that, within those layers, there could be many different realities. He decided that it really did not matter whether it was a question of parallel realities or universes or even separate realities. The theory had worked, but he had no idea how it had worked; it had only ever been a theory, an idea. He had not really thought it through, he had just taken the idea that one step further, and he had believed that it was possible.

He knew that, on some level, it fitted in with everything else that had been happening; he also knew that he had been right all along when he had been saying that everything that was happening had something to do with time.

But what if he was not where he thought he was? He remembered Tilda suggesting something about the corridors and the doors – in fact, the entire building – being part of a nightmare and that perhaps nothing of what anyone thought they were experiencing was actually happening.

If none of it had happened or was happening, then where was he? Oswald shook his head in an attempt to rid himself of all the questions to which there were no obvious answers. If he put out his hand, he could feel the cold, hard surface of the wall. It was a reality: it was not something that he could simply push his fist through.

Then he thought that if he was not where he thought he was – in a tunnel somewhere inside a hill – then where on earth was he?

He continued walking through the tunnel, and gradually the descent evened out, and soon he was walking on an almost even plane. He was thinking that if he were not really where he thought he was, then absolutely anything could happen, and it would be as though he were not actually part of it. His head was spinning with the events of the last few hours, and all he really wanted to do was to lie down in a comfortable bed and sleep for about a week.

Then, without warning, the tunnel suddenly came to an end. In front of him there was a door. It was an ordinary brown door with no panelling, and instead of a round door knob, there was an elongated brass handle. He pressed down on it and opened the door.

A very bright, clear light poured in, blinding him for a moment. He stepped out, not on to the side of a hill or on to some stretch of grassy wasteland, but into an enormous room.

He was back in the Reception Hall.

Fragment Thirty

Back in the building that was obviously somewhere completely disconnected from anything that had the slightest affinity with the outside, things were much the same as they had been for the past days or weeks or months: people were continuing to line up in the queue at Reception where they were being handed keys to new rooms, and the Receptionists who handed out these keys changed in accordance with their shifts. Those people who normally would have complained did not complain and later wondered why not. They obediently walked along the mazes of corridors and opened doors and ate small brown tablets when they were told. Some people were intent on trying to work out why they were there, but the answers were not forthcoming, and there was no one to ask. As the days and the weeks and the months marched on, they lost their motivation and accepted that there was nothing they could do to change the situation. As Oswald had already observed, everyone had turned into sheep.

Those who dared to complain aloud, while standing in the queue or while resting on one of the benches in the Hall, usually felt that their conversations were being closely monitored by someone dressed entirely in black, and, as a result, most complaints fizzled out, a little like a firework that begins to promise some kind of exciting experience and then simply dies. Some people complained to themselves while they walked along dreary, monotonous corridors, but no one was listening, and, quite often, they wondered whether perhaps everything around them was actually normal and that they were simply out of step with what was going on.

There were people who briefly contemplated the changes in their appearance as they moved between different points on their own timelines, while there were others who were experiencing things they had never before experienced: they were looking at what they may have imagined could be their future, if they were to have a future, while, at other times, they were completely confused by what they believed could well have been the past.

Most people had resigned themselves to the idea that this was probably the end of everything: many were trying to relate that which was happening now to how the end-of-time had been presented in the different holy books; others decided that it was the obvious and much-to-be-expected result of consumerism's global rampage with the resulting downward spiral of all things spiritual, but, when pushed for more information, they could not say why nor could they give any details. No one knew why they were all gathered together inside what appeared to be a building without any specific shape or form, but they all knew that there was no way out. There were no answers, there was no logic, there was no place where they could stand back and look at everything from some other normal perspective. Many were hoping that the end – whatever form it might take – might take place sooner rather than later. The tension and the anxiety and the confusion were just too much for some people. It would be far better to slip into a state of eternal sleep and not to have to worry about anything any more.

People did not need moments of sudden clarity to understand that the place where they were imprisoned was vast. Many, like Oswald, saw it as some huge undefinable building or structure which appeared to grow and spread itself in all directions, but they were unable to say exactly what it looked like because everyone was on the inside. If people were asked to link it to a colour, most of them would have said grey or perhaps black. It was a prison with long corridors, a hospital, a mountain, a building, a factory; it was like an enormous creature that had spread itself out over an infinitely large area, its inhaling and exhaling barely noticeable.

For many, it was death itself.

Milford in Room Eight was quite sure that this was where he was going to die. He was not trying to understand the nature of the building or why everyone had ended up there. He was far too confused and bewildered by everything that had been happening. He did keep thinking about Tilda, but he was not looking for answers, he simply wanted to get out. As he looked down at his blotched, wrinkled skin and felt the weakness in his legs and arms, he was beginning to believe that such a thing would not be possible.

He had often wondered about the *end*, especially during those times when he was confined in gaol. He wondered whether it would be painful or whether it would simply happen without his fully realizing what was happening. Now he believed that he knew what it would be like.

As he sat, his back against the wall, he thought that it would have been nice to have had someone else with him.

He really did not want to die on his own. There was something frightening about the thought: being about to be thrown into some unknown eternity without anyone there to hold his hand and tell him that everything would be all right. Nothing had been all right with his life, so he could hardly expect the end to be all right.

He sat and waited for that which would inevitably come, and, eventually, he fell asleep.

Fragment Thirty-One

Tilda was back in the Reception Hall, standing near one of the walls; her legs were shaking and she was terribly unsettled and bewildered. She could remember everything – the room, Oswald, the tunnel, the men – with complete clarity. Then she remembered a sudden blackness and a feeling as though she were being tumbled around in the surf, no longer knowing what was up or what was down. It was a feeling that went on and on while, somewhere in the back of her mind, she recalled wondering whether or not she was drowning or whether she had already drowned. Then there was a blinding light as she opened her eyes in the Hall.

She could not stop trembling. This was definitely not how it was supposed to end. She and Oswald had been so sure that they would find the exit, the way out. She looked around, but she could not see Oswald anywhere. She knew that he had been right next to her, squeezing her hand, and then there was just blackness. It was as though she had been dreaming and the dream had folded in at the edges and all the things in the dream, including herself, had fallen into some kind of vacuum. She wondered about the possibility of returning to the dream if she were to close her eyes, but, when she tried, nothing happened.

The Reception Hall looked exactly the same as before: there were people standing in the queue and people sitting on the benches. Tilda could even see the tea lady doing her rounds. She remained standing where she was for a few minutes, and then she walked to the closest bench and sat down. She looked down at herself and noticed that she had reverted to being twenty-five again. Although she may have felt strangely thankful, there were too many worrying thoughts and anxieties pressing in upon her. Did the two men in the tunnel actually see her? She did not believe that they did, but why then was she back in the Hall?

For Tilda, this is where the world would have to end, and she would now begin a descent into the uncharted waters beyond. She had reached the limit of what was humanly possible; she could not face another corridor, another room, another key. Twice now she had believed that she would actually escape and twice she had been bitterly disappointed. There was no logic in anything any longer, and she wanted to be removed from all the insanity. As she sat on the bench, looking out into the immense, but exceedingly sterile, space, the idea that she was not going to play the game any longer took form in her mind and gradually became clearer and clearer.

Her eyes wandered around the room and darted in and out of the queue. Some of the people she believed she had seen before, others were completely new faces or faces that she had probably seen and since forgotten. From where she was sitting, she could only vaguely distinguish the reception desk, but she could not see the Receptionist on duty. She returned to studying the people in the queue and her eyes rested on a man in his late thirties. He was of average height and quite good-looking. Her eyes noted his perfectly tailored dark grey trousers and matching sports jacket; she could even see a maroon – most probably silk – handkerchief peeping over the top of the jacket's upper pocket. He was wearing a cream shirt open at the neck and no tie. Tilda stared at him and then clamped her hands over her mouth to stop herself from screaming.

She stood up, and whether it was to run in his direction or as far away as possible, she would never know, because, at that very moment, she fell to the floor in a dead faint.

Fragment Thirty-Two

Milford could not work out why he was not dead. Then he decided that perhaps he actually had died and that this was what it was like after death. But, after some thought, he came to the conclusion that everything was exactly the same as it had been since he had first found himself surrounded by corridors and rooms – whenever that might have been – so perhaps he was not dead. On the other hand, he could have been dead for days, even weeks, and he had not even been aware of it.

He mused over the possibility of being dead and not being aware of it, but he was unable to formulate any kind of explanation.

He was sitting on a bench in the Reception Hall. When he looked down at his hands, he saw that the wrinkles and blotches had all disappeared and he was his normal fifty-year-old self again. A feeling of relief surged through his body, and he was even able to manage a slight smile. The experience in the gaol compound had been a bit too much for Milford. In a strange way, he felt as though he had suddenly been given an extra thirty years.

Deciding that he needed to celebrate, he took out a cigarette and lit it; he reasoned, seeing as he most probably was not dead, that he must have simply dreamt the whole thing. He decided that it was very possible: he was, after all, very afraid of growing old and dying. He tried not to think too much about the inevitable. He knew that there was only one way out of life and that was death. No one could live for ever. He had insulated himself against such thoughts, hoping, unreasonably, that the less his thoughts engaged with such a terrifying truth, the more likelihood there was of his somehow circumventing it and completely avoiding the end. He imagined himself moving along life's path to a point, close to the end, where he would step back a few paces and then remain in some safe, non-dead, zone.

It was an encouraging thought, but he knew that it was impossible: everyone had to die; there was simply no way around it.

The tea lady – he wondered why he insisted on thinking of her as the tea lady when she did not serve tea – came into view, and Milford gratefully took the drink she offered him. He could not say that he preferred the drink to any other drink he had ever tasted, but he was beginning to get used to it. At least it was hot, and, when there was no real food, it was the next best thing available.

He lit a second cigarette and drank his 'tea', deciding that he was glad that he had not died and that he was still alive; it definitely was not much of a life, being in a place full of corridors and rooms with no way out and no sky, but it was ever so much better than being dead.

Dead, after all, was the end of everything.

He finished his drink and his cigarette and placed the cup and the two cigarette butts in the rubbish slot; then he walked slowly to the end of the queue. He would have actually liked to have walked out of the Hall and kept walking until he found an exit, but he knew that there was no exit – only corridors and more corridors. Even if it was becoming more and more obvious that it was impossible to get out, Milford could not let go of his very great need to do just that. He was not sure how long he could remain in such an enclosed space without going completely mad.

When he was finally released from gaol, he headed north-west and picked up some work on a sheep property. He had an intense need to be outside, to feel the sun on his face, to smell the earth around him. He also needed to be able to get as far away as possible from people. The work suited him, but then the drought came, and, eventually, there was no work for him, and he was forced to return to the city.

But, once again, having become used to the solitude and the expanses of sky and earth, which were all so much part of who he was, and he found the city confining and noisy. Also, this time, there was no Tilda, and he tended to feel lonely in spite of the crowds of people all around him. He was not a person who easily made friends, and, resenting the daily routine of an uninteresting job and a small con-fined room in a boarding house, he was very soon slipping in and out of depression. With his thoughts constantly returning to Tilda and how things might have been, he decided to find out where she was living, wondering if perhaps there was a slight chance that the pain of the past could remain where it was while they resurrected and remoulded all the positive aspects of their time together. It did not occur to Milford that Tilda may have moved on and that there was no longer any room in her future for him – reformed or otherwise.

When the telephone directories gave him no answer to what he wanted to know, he took himself to the electoral office, where a woman with kind eyes and grey hair pulled back loosely in a badly-constructed bun helped him find the information for which he was looking.

A few days later, he took the bus to Balmain. He had bought himself a map of the area, and it was not difficult to find either the street or the house. Then he sat in a small café opposite the house, wondering whether or not he might be fortunate enough to see her and whether, if he did, he would have the courage to speak to her.

On his second trip to Balmain, he did see her, fleetingly: she stepped off the bus and, after standing for a moment, looking around at nothing in particular, she walked up the street and then into the house where she was living. He did not have the courage to make himself known to her, and resenting both his cowardice and his indecision, he took the next bus back to the city, and he never returned.

With the depression and frustration becoming worse, Milford's circle of bad luck and wrong decisions finally broke loose into a new spiral that was pointed downwards, and it was not long before he was back in gaol for six months. The pattern was established, and, although he hated the confinement and the raw emotions, he sometimes had to admit that he welcomed the routine – a routine where he did not have to think. Each time he was released, he was torn between the overwhelming sensation of freedom and the dread of once again having to face the world on his own.

After a few years, he jumped off the spiral before it hit rock bottom, and he moved back west. He was already in his thirties, and his life had been going nowhere ever since Tilda had left him. He found work in a medium-sized country town with a man who resurrected second-hand furniture. It was a small business: besides Milford and the owner, there was another carpenter, a driver, and Shelley, who worked in the office.

The queue was moving and, whether he liked it or not, Milford was moving with it. He looked around at the people closest to him; no one looked particularly happy, but no one was complaining. It was the passive compliance that Milford could not understand, but, even if he could not understand the complacency, he knew that he also was one of the submissive people. He was just one in a crowd of people obeying senseless regulations; he was not standing to one side, refusing to be part of the queue, refusing to take keys, refusing to walk down corridors. He wondered how it was possible to be so impassive and whether or not it had anything to do with the time he had spent in gaol where everything was regulated and where there was no freedom and where people moved, because they were told to, or ate because they were told to, or slept because...

But the more he thought about it, the more he decided that, in spite of any dubious connection with regulated establishments, there was still something weird about it all: in gaol, at least, there seemed to be some kind of reason behind the regulations – here there was no reason. Here, there was no reason behind anything.

He would have liked another cigarette, but even though he had replenished his supply, he knew that he had to be restrictive: he had no way of knowing how much longer he would be in this place. Also, he was quite certain that he would not be allowed to smoke in the queue. Milford briefly considered the possibility that the rooms and the corridors could all be part of some kind of punishment, but, if that were the case, he had absolutely no idea for what he was being punished.

The idea about punishment had not occurred to him

before, and he began to wonder if this was simply a different kind of prison system. He looked around him at the people in the queue and in the Hall; it was difficult to imagine that all those people needed to be punished – some of them perhaps, but definitely not all. His eyes rested on an elderly woman with soft white hair, and he tried to imagine what she could have done that would have possibly warranted such a punishment. He decided that the bad dream, or whatever it was, had nothing to do with punishment, but there still had to be a reason why all these people were here. Trying to locate that elusive reason, he could only relate everything back to himself – what had he done? why was he here? – but everything that had happened directly prior to his arrival in the building was a complete blur.

There were about six people in front of him, and it looked as though the Receptionist on duty was extremely efficient as he seemed to be processing everyone very quickly. Milford had seen this particular Receptionist before: he was the one with blonde wavy hair and the immaculate suit. He thought it extremely strange that all the Receptionists were men: so far, he had seen no women behind the very large desk in the middle of the Hall. He wondered what the Receptionists did when they were not working; he wondered what the men in black and even the tea lady did when they were not working.

There were only two people in front of him. He could feel the security of his cigarette pack in his trouser pocket. He was confident that he would get a chance to light up once he had left the Hall.

The Receptionist gave him a key and a brown tablet. Milford put both of them into his pocket, but, before pocketing the key, he saw that it was Number Nineteen.

The number appealed to him: it was the same number as his birthday. Perhaps it was an important coincidence. He half-listened while the man told him how to get to Room Nineteen, and then he walked towards the corridor that had been indicated.

Fragment Thirty-Three

Tilda wakes up. She is not lying on the floor where she fell; in fact, she is no longer in the Hall. She is lying on a couch in a pleasant room with cream walls and vanilla-coloured drapes. There is a heavy glass table near the couch, and she is vaguely conscious of the vase of roses in the middle of the table. The roses are pink and a couple of petals have fallen on to the glass. Tilda is aware of the pinkness and the softness and the contrast between the petals and the glass, but she is unable to put her awareness into anything that resembles logical thought.

For a few minutes, she does not move but continues looking at the walls and the petals. Even though the room is calming, her thoughts insist on returning to the Hall, trying to work out what had happened. She tries to remember why she fainted and then she remembers Gary: Gary who was killed so horribly all those years ago.

The dull awareness that she first felt when she woke up has changed a little, and she is beginning to feel anxious. She sits up and looks around her: there is no one else in the room. She wonders where she is and what will happen next and whether or not there is a way out. Always the same question: is there an exit? is there a way out?

She tries to work out how she got to the room. Of course, someone must have carried her, but she has no idea who it was; it was probably one of the men in black. It is not so difficult to understand why she was removed from the Hall; it could not be at all good for general morale to have people fainting all over the place. She swings her feet down to the floor and is about to stand up when the door opens and a man enters the room.

He is short and plump, dressed in an old-fashioned three-piece suit, and he is wearing highly polished black leather shoes.

Tilda cannot take her eyes from the shoes; she has never before seen such shiny shoes.

He walks over to where Tilda is still sitting on the couch and extends his hand. "The Administrator," he says.

Tilda does not know whether she should remain sitting or whether she should stand. She stands and takes his hand. She notices the thinning blonde-red hair and the tiny pencil moustache.

"Please remain seated." He smiles and walks to one of the armchairs on the opposite side of the table and sits down. "So you're Tilda," he says, the smile still settling around the corners of his mouth.

Tilda is thinking that she knows him. She nods. She is sure that Oswald mentioned something about someone called the 'Administrator'. She says, "To tell you the truth, I'm so dreadfully confused and exhausted and completely fed up. I have absolutely no idea what's going on or even why I'm here. Honestly, I don't think anyone knows why they are here."

For a moment the Administrator does not speak, but his eyes, which Tilda notes are very kind, remain fixed on her face. At length, he alters his position in the armchair and says, "Actually, I think you *do* know; it is just that you refuse to accept…"

"Refuse to accept? Refuse to accept what? This endless, meaningless round of corridors and rooms?" Tilda is both angry and bewildered. "What on earth are you talking about? Am I supposed to accept everything that's going on here?"

"But is there?" The Administrator has moved in his chair and is leaning forward again. There is an open, earnest expression on his face. "Is there actually something *going on*?"

Tilda looks at him; she has really no idea what to say. If the man who is administrating the nightmare has no idea that something is going on, then there is really no point with anything any longer.

"Are you trying to say that everything that's happening is in my imagination?" Tilda is so angry and upset, she can hardly speak. During all the days, weeks and possibly months that she has been part of the building with its corridors and its rooms, she has wondered occasionally if, perhaps, everything could simply be part of a dream, something that is wholly confined to her own mind. She is still not completely certain that this is not the case, but dreams always come to an end, quite often abruptly without any warning. Nothing here seems to be coming to an end, instead, as far as she can see, things are rapidly becoming more and more complicated.

She looks at him defiantly and repeats her question. "So the corridors, the rooms, you, everyone here, everything is simply in my mind?"

The man shakes his head slowly. "No, not quite. You said something about time…"

Tilda wonders how he knew, but she suddenly feels very

tired, and she finds that she really does not care what he knows or does not know. She ignores what he said and, instead, she asks, "How do I get out of here?"

The man laughs. It is a genuinely kind laugh, almost as though she has caught him by surprise, and he is not quite sure what to say. "But surely, Tilda, that is quite obvious?"

As far as Tilda is concerned, nothing is obvious at the moment, and she is irritated by the Administrator's nebulous suggestions that she should know more than she actually does – that she should actually be able to work it all out.

He stops laughing and says, "Are you feeling better now? We were really quite concerned for you."

Tilda suddenly remembers why she is in the room; her thoughts turn to Gary. She begins, "Gary…" She is not sure how to continue. "He's dead. He died years ago."

The Administrator looks at his fingers resting on his knee and nods. "Yes, that's correct. And…?"

Tilda is not sure how to proceed. "But I saw him," she says. "Here, wherever *here* is. He looked no different to when I saw him last." She is thinking that dead people cannot be joining queues and walking around corridors. It is one thing to *think* about dead people; it is a completely different thing to actually *see* them.

"Think about time. Think about the way you define the past and the present and the future. Now rethink all those thoughts, and it is very possible that you may have the answer."

"There is no past or future, not even a present. Is that the answer? Time is simply an illusion or some kind of hallucination?"

The man smiles.

Tilda is feeling irritated by the constant smiling, even though the man seems kind. She knows that she has met the Administrator before. Somewhere.

She says, "I know you, don't I?"

"That is actually quite possible; in fact, most things, or should I say, all things, are possible." He stands up and again offers Tilda his hand. "If you're feeling better then you probably need to be getting back to the Hall."

Everything is moving too quickly, a bit like the Big Dipper once someone has pushed the *on* switch. Tilda feels as though she has been left standing on the rails, unable to keep up, knowing that she needs to catch hold of the small carriage that is already racing down the first sharp incline, increasing the distance between what she needs to do and what is possible. Her head is filled with rails twisting and climbing as she shakes his hand and watches as he walks towards the door. A man in black appears out of nowhere, opens the door for the Administrator, then beckons Tilda to follow.

Fragment Thirty-Four

After abruptly arriving back in the Reception Hall, Oswald, spent some time trying to come to terms with the fact that he was actually back in the Hall and not on the side of a hill contemplating freedom. He had really believed that he would escape, and it was taking him some time to fully comprehend that it had not happened. No matter how he calculated or what he did, he kept running up against brick walls, and he was no longer sure if they were virtual or completely real.

He walked across to a bench and sat down. He closed his eyes, stretched out his legs and leaned back against the wall. He was irritated that he had failed, but he knew that he was even more irritated that he had still not found the answer. There *had* to be an answer. He saw the whole thing as some kind of enormous puzzle, and, if it was a puzzle, then there had to be a solution.

The tea lady came past; Oswald could hear the sound of her trolley as she made her way around the Hall. He would have given anything for a cup of strong, hot coffee, but he knew that such was not on offer. He had not realized that he was as tired as he was. Sitting on the bench, he could feel his body dropping through layer after layer of consciousness; very soon, he would undoubtedly be fast asleep. Hanging somewhere between sleep and wakefulness, Oswald decided that sleep could perhaps be the answer; perhaps the only way out was to turn off one's mind completely.

After about ten minutes, he forced himself into a more upright position, and, opening his eyes, he rubbed them several times before stretching. Even though he really wanted to succumb to sleep, he had a strong feeling that it would not be permitted – not here in the Hall. He stood up and did a few more stretches and then moved towards the end of the queue.

He desperately needed to solve the puzzle, but he was too tired and something inside his head kept telling him that he could put it off until tomorrow. It was almost as though the problem had been wrapped up in some kind of soft padding and had been neatly shelved with a tag saying, 'to be attended to tomorrow'. He sighed as he was pulled between what he felt he really needed to do immediately and the prospect of everything automatically falling into place tomorrow.

The queue was moving reasonably quickly towards the Reception Desk. He circled the bottom part of the Hall and joined the end of the queue; he did not recognize anyone in the queue, but that really did not mean anything: people were coming and going all the time; they were simply a conglomeration of shapes and faces; there was no way that he could remember them all – if any of them.

The Receptionist was someone he had never seen before: very thin with a thick shock of grey hair and rimless glasses. Oswald wanted to ask him why tunnels leading downwards end back up in the Hall, but he decided that the man would have absolutely no idea what he was talking about. He took the key with number Three Hundred and Four. He looked at the number and then at the Receptionist but said nothing. Oswald assumed that the Receptionist probably knew that he had not opened the door to Room Nineteen, and he was almost expecting some kind of rebuke, but there was nothing. The man behind the desk simply smiled at him and explained how to get to Room Three Hundred and Four. Oswald put the key into his pocket and moved off towards a corridor on the left-hand side of the Hall.

The ferry was already docking at a ferry wharf and Oswald could hear a mixture of sounds as the vessel strained heavily against the mooring ropes and as the timber gangways fell noisily into position between the ferry and the wharf. He could also hear gulls overhead and the irregular sound of water slapping against the side of the ferry. When he looked around him, he could see that people were already queuing up to leave the ferry, and he decided that he might as well do the same.

There were not a lot of passengers, and it did not take many minutes before he was standing on the wharf, wondering what he should do next. He had a strange feeling that he had been on that very same wharf once before, but he could not remember when. There was something about the place that kept nagging at his memory; even the weather, pleasantly warm and sunny with clouds cutting across the blue sky, was trying to remind him of something he had obviously forgotten. He tried to ignore all the nagging, troublesome thoughts and, instead, looked around at the people heading away from the wharf area; most of them in light summer clothing. There were also a lot of children. He liked seeing the children: there had been no children in the corridors or the Hall.

His mind spun back to the building and to Room Three Hundred and Four. It had taken him some time to reach the room, tucked away, as it was, on the third floor. The corridors had been exceptionally long, and, a couple of times, Oswald had begun to panic in case he may have misinterpreted the Receptionist's instructions. When he finally reached the last corridor, there was not another person in sight. It made him think of Room Nineteen, and he had an uneasy feeling that there might be some kind of connection.

He was extremely angry with himself; after all, he had decided not to be a sheep, and now he *was* one. Walking along the long, dismal corridors, he had tried to justify what he was doing by telling himself that he had no choice, but something inside of him was insisting that he *did* have a choice; he was simply choosing to ignore it.

It was when he finally opened the door to Room Three Hundred and Four that he had walked on to the ferry.

In spite of a strange recognition of déjà vu, he enjoyed being out in the open air and feeling the sun on his face. He noticed that he was back to being twenty-five again, complete with ponytail and duffel coat. He removed the coat and hung it over his arm, revelling in the sensation of bustling, happy people around him, people who most probably knew nothing about corridors and rooms. He followed the small crowd of people off the wharf and out into the main street; he recognized the street as he had also recognized the wharf: he was in one of Sydney's harbour suburbs.

He broke away from the crowd and followed the street up a small hill. As he did so, he knew that he had done exactly the same thing once before. Before when? He did not know, and he did not have the energy to delve into his mind. All around him was the harbour with sun glistening on blue water, and craft of different sizes making patterns across the blue. He found a bench overlooking the water and sat down. Although his mind was still struggling to find an answer to 'before when?', he was focusing his thoughts on all the people who had been on the ferry with him. He wondered whether he may have been wrong when he assumed that they knew nothing about rooms and keys and corridors; he was, after all, in a room at the moment – at least he believed that he was – but it certainly did not look like a room.

He put his face in his hands, blocking out the view. All he wanted was some kind of answer; he wanted to know what was going on and why. He sat up and ran his hands along the surface of the bench. The bench was real; the sea, with its soft, almost invisible clouds of spray, was also real: he could see it and he could smell it. Occasionally, when the spray blew in his direction, he could even feel it. He looked further along the street at the cars and the houses. He was not in the middle of a dream; he was quite sure about that.

He sighed and got up. If he was going to be on the outside, whether it were the real outside or not, he decided that he would make the best of it. His first priority was to have a decent meal and a cup of coffee.

He found a small restaurant further along the street skirting the harbour. Beyond the somewhat dark inside dining area of the restaurant, there was a small courtyard with a partial view of the harbour. There was a large purple bougainvillea covering two of the courtyard walls, and there were a number of large terracotta pots with green plants scattered between five or six lace metal tables. He sat down at a table facing the view, and, as soon as he was seated, he knew that he had been there before, in that same restaurant, at that very same table. He had a strong feeling that he had not been there alone.

It was shady with just sufficient sun to remind him that it was still summer. He noticed a young couple and a group of three women in the courtyard, but they were all far enough away from Oswald to make him feel that he was more or less on his own.

He felt it was strange that he should want to be on his own when that was really all he had been for the past weeks or months. He thought about it until the waiter arrived, deciding that there were probably different kinds of aloneness and that, just now, he needed to be physically on his own at a table in a restaurant with a view over the harbour.

Everything to do with the restaurant was a shadow of other memories that were somewhere in his mind but frustratingly out of reach. The purple flowers and the ice cubes clinking in glasses of water, and the sunlight dancing across the stones of the courtyard, while trying to avoid the shade shaped by green leaves and flower-filled branches, were all things that he had experienced before. Even the plates of food and the waiter's polite questions were not new. But, no matter how much he delved into his memory, he could find no answers; instead, he tried to analyse what it actually was to be free and how it was that he could appear to be free when, in actual fact, he was not. He knew that beyond the flowers and the water and the sunshine – whether he had actually experienced them before or not – there were more walls and more corridors and more rooms with doors that needed to be opened. At times, while he was sitting enjoying what must be some kind of virtual freedom, he wanted to rush up to the other people in the courtyard and ask them whether or not they were free and whether or not they knew anything about rooms and corridors.

He had no idea what he should do after he left the restaurant. He wondered momentarily about the possibility of seeking help, but he had absolutely no idea where he would even begin. His freedom was contained: everything looked normal, but he was quite sure that things were not at all normal. Even if he were to consider the possibility, he was quite sure that there was no point in going to the police or the newspapers as not only would no one believe him, but he would probably end up being sectioned.

He briefly wondered if, perhaps, it could be a good idea – at least there was a slight possibility that he might then be safe. But, the more he thought about it, weighing his need for complete freedom against the probability of his being confined to a room, the less certain he became. *Safe* was no longer a very reliable word, and, as far as he was concerned, there did not seem to be very many options left that could be called *safe*.

He had to keep focusing on the fact that he was actually *not* in a harbour-side suburb, enjoying the late summer sun: he was in a room somewhere in something that might be a building. Even though he assumed that this most probably was the case, and that, at some point, he would be removed from the room, and that the water and the sun and the feeling of freedom would all suddenly disappear, he still wanted to be able to believe otherwise. He tried to keep both scenarios at the forefront of his mind, knowing which one he wanted to be true.

But, perhaps that was what it was all about: making people believe that reality was not reality and that virtual worlds and experiences were real. Or was it the other way around? His head was beginning to ache. After leaving the restaurant, he had walked down some stone steps to a very small beach, and he was now sitting on the sand. There were a couple of children playing with a black dog further along the beach. The sounds of the children and the dog made him want to believe that this was reality and that everything else was simply a distorted kind of dream.

He was almost certain that this was not the first time he had seen the same children and the same dog.

He was quite sure that everything was relative, and he remembered telling Tilda that it was important not to let go of the relationship between things and that it was this relationship that held everything together. He knew that it was this relationship that was the reason he could be so certain that they would get out. He based everything on a sense of logic, like two sides of an equation; things had to add up, otherwise there would be chaos. If there was a beginning, then there was also an end; if there was an entrance, then there had to be an exit.

He thought back to his not wanting to be a sheep, and he felt that he had failed miserably. He began to wonder if it actually were possible to break out of the herd and be an individual. As he thought about his failure and his need to be an individual, the more it occurred to him that perhaps it was up to him to decide if the reality with which he was faced was virtual or real, but, in order to make such a decision, he had to be able to believe in himself.

If he were to believe that what was happening was real, and if he were then to act accordingly, perhaps that was all that was needed for him to physically and mentally break out from everything that was keeping him a prisoner. He had to move his mind into a space where there were no corridors or rooms and where he knew for certain that he would soon be boarding a new ferry and that he would then be returning home. He had to be able to believe that he would then open the door to his home, and he would enter his own house and sleep in his own bed... The thoughts were coming fast and strong, and Oswald felt that, perhaps, he had begun to move in a more positive direction.

The children were leaving the beach, the dog close behind them. Oswald stood up but, for some minutes, remained looking out across the water. He could see the city skyline in the distance, and, in the middle ground, there were all kinds of vessels, large and small. A couple of gulls landed on the sand, possibly hoping that he had food with him. When they realized that such was not the case, they flew off, sweeping low across the water.

Eventually, he walked back up the short flight of stone stairs. This was real: there were no corridors, no rooms, no keys. In a little while, he would return home. That was the reality; anything else was make-believe. The word *if* kept crossing his thoughts, which made it difficult for him to completely believe that everything was normal. He tried to ignore it, but it was difficult.

He smiled at the people he met and even exchanged a few words with a man waiting at a bus stop. He looked in shop windows and imagined going into a florist and buying some flowers. He was still unsure if he had anyone for whom he could buy flowers, but the idea of buying them appealed to him, and it helped to negate all the images of corridors.

He walked on, trying to remember anything at all from his past. There was a post office near a crossroad, and he pushed open the heavy timber door and went in. Over near the wall, he found a shelf with a number of telephone directories. Surely, *they* might be able to tell him something. He opened the first one and flicked over the pages, looking for his surname. It was not a common name, and he expected that it would be easy to find. There was no mention of him in the first two directories, but, in the third, he found four people with the same surname and his listing was the third. There was no other name connected with his name, but that told him nothing as to whether he was married or not.

On the desk in the corner, he found a piece of paper and a pen and wrote down the address and the telephone number. He put the paper in his pocket and returned the directory to its shelf, then he left the post office.

As he walked back towards the ferry terminal, he tried to think normal thoughts, but he could not stop thinking about what it had been like when he and Tilda had been in the tunnel, believing that they were about to escape. He wondered what had happened to Tilda; he had not seen her since she disappeared. While he was vaguely worried about Tilda, he could still remember the excitement he had felt when he reached the door at the end of the tunnel and believed that, on the other side, everything would be normal again. Now, surrounded by all the water and the sun, although he had made no effort to escape, he felt that, in some strange way, he actually had escaped, but part of him was terrified that he would very soon be back in the building. He really wanted to believe that he was free, but something was stopping him from believing.

Although Oswald could still not remember anything about his past beyond the fact that he was a mathematician and that he had had Eugene Turnbull as a maths teacher when he was in high school, he now knew where he lived. Whether he was married or not was a question he could still not answer.

He boarded the ferry bound for the city. He was early, and he found a seat outside, idly watching people on the wharf. He wondered whether it was genuinely possible to believe, without reservation, that his present reality was the one and only reality; he also wondered at what point he would be able to feel comfortable making decisions within that reality: decisions like returning home or taking a holiday or even finding out more about himself.

He wondered if there would be a point in time when he would know for sure that he was safe within that reality and that nothing was likely to happen that would send everything into a state of disarray. It was a bit like when the shark alarm went at the beach, and everyone scrambled up on to the sand to watch and wait. Later, when the all-clear was given, he had often wondered just how anyone could be absolutely sure that the shark was not still out there, lurking somewhere in the deep water, just beyond the furthest row of breakers. In both cases, there could be nothing signifying that everything had returned to normal, that the shark had moved on elsewhere or that the maze had miraculously disappeared and the people had been released. Not unless the story about the corridors hit the news-stands and the TV screens, which he knew was most unlikely.

He looked at his watch; it was an automatic reaction. He had not been able to look at his watch for what seemed like weeks, because there was absolutely nothing around him to which he could relate the reading on the dial. But now it was different. The time on his watch corresponded with the time on the large clock on the wharf; there were barely five minutes left before the ferry was to leave.

Oswald took a look at the sky and watched the clouds moving together, blocking out the blue sky. There was also a cold breeze that he had not noticed earlier. He stood up with the intention of moving inside the ferry. While he was standing up, he knew that it had all happened before: the sky, the clouds, the cold. He noticed a woman running. She had short fair hair, and she was wearing a long green embroidered skirt. The man who was about to pull up the gangway waited patiently until she was on board, and then he pulled up the gangway and released the mooring ropes.

Something inside Oswald told him that he knew the woman, and with absolute certainty he knew what would happen next. He pushed past passengers who had not yet found seats, excusing himself, wishing himself forward, wanting to change what he already knew, wondering if it was even possible.

As he reached the stairs leading down to the bottom deck, the woman was already standing on the top step. For a split second, she turned in his direction with a look of recognition – and, he would later believe, undisguised love – and then, catching the hem of her skirt beneath her foot, she plunged head first down the stairs.

The same feelings; the same dreadful, numbing sense of powerlessness; the same feelings of guilt.

Oswald ran down the stairs, taking them two at a time, just as he had done before, and, just as he had done before, he prayed for some sign of life. There were other people taking charge, moving the passengers away from the stairs. One of the ferry employees put his hand on Oswald's arm, telling him to move away.

"I can't… You don't understand." Oswald pushed away the man's hand and sank down beside the woman lying at the foot of the stairs. "Not even this time…" he whispered to no one in particular and buried his face in his hands.

Fragment Thirty-Five

The layers of time had reshuffled themselves, sweeping Oswald forwards into something that he did not recognize as the present but which he could not be completely sure was the future. The ferry was moving with a slight sway from side to side, and, sitting near a window on the bottom deck, Oswald was contemplating the many different colours in the water. The clouds had closed together and it had become darker; rain began to beat against the window, and people who had been sitting on the outside decks moved inside. From where he was sitting, he could see the stairs, but nothing was out of the ordinary, and no one was looking at him as though he should be given extra space or respect, having just lost his wife.

Had it happened or not? Oswald was not completely sure, but he knew that it *had* happened, a long time ago. The ponytail and the duffel coat were both gone; the beard was back. Oswald was becoming disorientated with all the sudden changes; he could no longer say who he actually was or how old he was, but at least he could now piece together some of his past.

Marianne fitted in next to university buildings and black-gowned lecturers and all-night parties. She was studying languages; he was doing science. They fell in love even though, or perhaps because, there were differences. Marianne was impulsive and she loved life; he was always intent on finding reasons for things being the way they were. But, after only a few months, they moved in with each other. The flat comprised one room and a tiny bathroom with a toilet that was flushed by pulling on a long thin chain. For three years, they both worked at part-time jobs, studied at odd hours, argued, made love, occasionally talked about the future and were anti anything that reeked of the Establishment. Then one day in summer, they took the ferry ride that drew a line under everything and boldly separated the past and the present from the future. Oswald remembered that the ferry ride had been a last-minute decision. They ate lunch at the restaurant, and they had argued over something trivial that Oswald could no longer remember. Marianne had gone off on her own, saying that she would might meet up with him on the ferry, and he had walked down to the beach to be by himself.

Marianne had meant everything to Oswald. After her death, he had moved from the flat with the chain-pulling flush. He rented a furnished room and threw himself into mathematics and the problem of stacking up numbers on either side of the equals sign. He did not actually forget Marianne; he simply placed her in that part of his mind where her presence could no longer hurt him.

Oswald had felt all along that the nightmare with the building and the corridors had something to do with individual perspectives. His way of remembering, or forgetting, Marianne was important, in the same way that his perspective on his present physical situation – the ferry, the window, the water, the encroaching storm – was also important. It made him who he was in that millisecond of time. In another millisecond the perspective might change and he would also change.

He suddenly thought of what the Administrator had said, about the essence of the thought not being what you believe it to be. He had spent a lot of time mulling over what Turnbull might have meant by that, but, as he sat near the window, the rain beating against the pane, he decided that he might finally be starting to understand.

The fact that what he could see or understand did not need to be the same as what anyone else might see or understand, was obvious, but it was also of the utmost importance. He held on to the idea and continued pushing it until he was quite certain that the way any person related to him or understood him had to be separate and quite different to the way that same person related to him- or herself. Consequently, it stood to reason that his under-standing of other people would rarely equate with how those other people understood themselves. While his mind was playing with the idea, Oswald knew that the thought was not new, and that he had definitely visited it before, but now he saw it as the opening to a whole line of thought that might finally explain what he was experiencing and why.

Accepting that his own personal understanding of any-one around him was never going to correlate completely with how others understood themselves, he could see that everyone is destined to live within the confines, not only of how they perceive themselves and how they perceive others, but also of their perception of things around them, including their own experiences. Change any one of the many perceptions just a fraction and everything will begin to spin out of control.

Being pulled along by his train of thought, Oswald decided that everything – both perception and experience – is real, but always only in relation to where we are at that particular point in time and in relation to what we are actually thinking at that moment. He began to feel excited, suddenly realizing that quite often what we *believe* we are thinking or experiencing might not be what we are *actually* thinking or experiencing.

He was now quite sure that the situation he had been grappling with for the past weeks was not a case of imagining things; it was all very real. The more he thought about it, the more he felt that, in its own particular place and in its own particular moment, every single experience was real, but if, for whatever reason, the place or the moment was moved just a little to the left or to the right, then everything could very easily change. If it were possible to reverse time a minute or propel it five minutes into the future, then suddenly, once again, everything would be completely different and the experience and even the place would most likely be completely different.

But if everything remained in the same time zone and simply moved just a little to one side or the other, then perhaps it would be possible to talk about parallel experiences or parallel perceptions. Or even parallel universes.

The rain had become much heavier, and it was difficult to see any differentiation between the sky and the water. It was only the roll of the vessel that anchored Oswald mentally on a ferry in the middle of the harbour. He could see nothing, but the constant heaving as the ferry cut through the rough sea gave Oswald no doubt as to where he was.

Although he felt that he may have made some kind of breakthrough, there were still many straggly ends. He may have stumbled on a solution of sorts, but he was not completely certain that it was the correct solution. His head was full of questions that he was still unable to answer, even if he felt that he was part of the way there. He stood up and, holding on to the seats around him, made his way cautiously to the opposite end of the ferry. He had no intention of going outside, but he had been sitting down for a while, and he needed to stretch his legs.

As he swayed along the aisle, grabbing hold of seats when necessary, he turned his head for no specific reason, and there, in the middle of a long row of empty seats, was a man who looked a lot like Eugene Turnbull. He was sitting with a folded newspaper on his lap, looking straight ahead.

Oswald inwardly gasped. It took him a few seconds to fully grasp that he was actually looking at the man who called himself the Administrator. He had not been expecting to see him, or anyone who had anything to do with him, here on the ferry. Then he recalled that he may have seen him that time on the beach, and he tried to force his mind back into that box with all the corridors and rooms; the box that he had labelled *building*. For a brief moment he had actually let himself be deceived by all the normal things around him; for a moment, he had actually believed that he was on the *outside*.

He tried to regain his sense of place and to retain his composure, and, ignoring the man with the newspaper, he continued walking back towards his seat, but when he had almost reached the place where he had been sitting earlier, he regretted that he had not confronted Eugene Turnbull – there were so many things he really needed to ask him – and he turned around and walked back. When he reached the place where he was completely certain he had seen the Administrator, Turnbull was nowhere to be seen, and there was another man sitting in exactly the same place with the same newspaper – or one that certainly seemed to be the same – on his lap; he was also looking straight ahead. Oswald was beginning to feel quite peculiar, as though he was part of something that was in no way linked to either the ferry or the other passengers, something that was completely confined to himself and the man sitting on the bench. He could see that the man was not Eugene Turnbull – he was not even someone he thought he knew – but the fact that he was sitting on the same bench, with possibly the same newspaper on his lap, made Oswald feel that, in some inexpressible way, they were actually connected.

All the seats faced the same way, so it was not possible for Oswald to find a seat from where he could easily study the man. The seats were arranged in three blocks: one wide block running along the middle of the ferry and two narrower blocks on each side. The seats on the sides had access to the windows; those in the middle had the advantage of two aisles. The Administrator was sitting on a bench in the middle aisle, and, behind him, there was a wall blocking off that section of the ferry from the stairs going up to the next level. Oswald found a spare seat near a window but also at the back of the section. From where he sat, he could easily see the man with the newspaper.

He was in a quandary: he really did not know what to do. Initially, he had intended to talk with Eugene Turnbull, but this was obviously not Turnbull, so Oswald was undecided. While he was wondering what course of action he should take, he was also trying to understand why the Administrator, or Eugene Turnbull or whoever it was, was actually on the ferry. Perhaps everywhere and everyone had been sucked up by the corridors. Perhaps there was no longer an *outside* or *inside*; perhaps everything was *inside*.

The man sitting in the middle block of seats placed his newspaper under his arm, stood up and walked across to where Oswald was sitting.

"No one sitting here?" he asked politely, indicating the seat next to Oswald while lowering himself into the seat.

Oswald shook his head. "I know you, don't I? Or, at least, I thought…" It all sounded too ridiculous; Oswald stopped mid-sentence and looked at the man; then he began again. "You *are* the Administrator, aren't you?"

The man had moved his newspaper on to his knee. He smiled at Oswald. "I believe I am."

"But I was so sure that the Administrator was Eugene Turnbull and that you were Eugene Turnbull…"

"Eugene Turnbull?" The man was holding on to his folded newspaper. He said, "That depends."

Oswald frowned. He could not see on what it would have to depend: either the man was Eugene Turnbull, or he was not.

"It depends on how you decide to perceive me." The Administrator moved one of his hands from the newspaper and placed it on his knee, and then he looked directly at Oswald. "If you believe that I am Eugene Turnbull, then, as far as you are concerned, I *am* Eugene Turnbull. Someone else might see me as a neighbour, the President of the United States, the captain of the football team or even some kind of god-figure. As the Administrator, I am part of the collective memory, but I am also part of what we all call the present. Depending on who is doing the perceiving, I can be anyone at all…"

He stopped talking for a moment. The hand on the knee moved a little and brushed away a small fleck of white from his trouser leg. Oswald waited patiently, hoping that they had not reached the end of the conversation. Much of what the Administrator was saying made sense; it pulled together many of the fragments into a *something* that Oswald was beginning to understand.

The man looked back at Oswald and continued, "Memory and perception are the two most important factors here. I suppose that it is all mathematical to a point, but it is also philosophical, even religious. In many ways, it has to do with each person's own perception of time."

Oswald nodded. "But for me, you were Eugene Turnbull, and now you're not…"

The Administrator smiled. "Memory is illusive. Just now you are in another space, and Eugene Turnbull is no longer as important."

"But I don't think I know you at all; I mean, you're not part of what I remember."

The man shrugged. "There are lots of things and people that we don't consciously remember, but they are still part of our memory. I can assure you that we have met somewhere, sometime, either in the past or in the future."

"And the rooms, the building – or whatever it is – and the corridors?" Oswald was excited. Perhaps he would finally get a definite answer to everything that had been going on.

"Just keep thinking about the fact that the essence of the thought is not necessarily what you might believe it to be." The man looked at his watch and picked up his newspaper. "It's been nice to talk with you, but I really must be going now." He stretched out his hand, and Oswald took it, then he stood up and walked towards the stairs leading to the upper deck.

Oswald was too amazed to wonder where the man might be going – after all, they were still at sea – and he remained sitting by the window, looking at his hazy reflection in the now dark pane, while he unsuccessfully attempted to tie together all the fragments into something that made some kind of sense, and where the essence was the complete opposite of his own understanding.

Fragment Thirty-Six

U nlike Oswald, Milford did not hesitate at Room Nineteen. He had no reason for not opening the door; he had opened all the other doors for which he had been given keys, and there was nothing about door Nineteen that indicated that it should not be opened. Admittedly, he found it strange that everyone, himself included, was obediently opening doors, but he did not feel that there was much he could do about it. Had he been aware of Oswald's theory – that people were turning into sheep – he doubtlessly would have agreed, but if anyone had accused him of being a sheep, he would have pointed his finger at all those years of being regimented within the prison system. They were years when he had had no other option – everyone was there to learn about being sheep – and, later, when he finally discovered that he was free, he also discovered that, in most things, it was easiest to keep his head down and follow the mob.

This is exactly what he did when he found himself standing outside Room Nineteen. There was nothing to indicate that someone called Oswald had been there but, at the very last moment, had decided not to open the door. Milford slipped the key into the lock and turned it. He put his hand on the rather large doorknob which was not smooth, as most doorknobs, but was covered with a strange relief pattern that resembled twisted ropes. Milford was not in the least artistic, but, as his fingers moved over the surface of the knob, he sensed a vague feeling of pleasure. His fingers tightened around the knob; he turned it slowly, and he opened the door.

Milford's dislike of confined spaces and his need to feel some contact with the outside were the two main things that made him Milford. He wanted to be able to see the sky and, if possible, to feel the outside air on his face. He was completely dependent on the feeling of freedom that was an important ingredient in being able to see further than a brick wall.

Although he liked and needed wide open spaces, he had never really liked the bush; he simply did not understand it. He found that it was too exacting – too compact and vast at the one and the same time. For Milford it was both the confinement of the room and the terror of there being no limits. Milford needed to be able to see the boundaries, and the further away they were the better. When he could look around him, as if on a small boat in the middle of some endless ocean, and see the line that defined the extent of what he could see, he felt strangely secure. The bush was incapable of giving Milford the security he needed; it made him feel lost and threatened.

He stepped into a thicket of heavy undergrowth, and, as he pushed his way through the tangled foliage, he saw that he was surrounded by trees and bushes stretching, probably for kilometres, in all directions. He looked at himself and understood that he was at least thirty years younger than when he had opened the door, and, whether he liked it or not, he was in the bush.

Through a small break between the trees, he was able to see that the ground dropped away into some kind of deep gully, and, beyond that tree-filled gully, it rose again in the distance to a line of tree-covered hills. All he could see between himself and the hills were trees and bushes.

Above him, the sun blazed down from a cobalt blue sky. He could hear the loud, monotonous singing of cicadas in the trees, a sound that went hand in hand with summer. Some large sulphur-crested cockatoos squawked overhead, and a rustle in the bushes nearby made him think of snakes. He had no idea what he was supposed to do: should he walk towards the hills or should he stay where he was? He looked around him, and he knew that, without any definite boundaries, it would not be at all difficult for him to get completely lost.

There was an indistinct track that Milford guessed probably led in the direction of the gully, so he decided to follow it: there was little point simply standing where he was. He wondered how far he would actually have to go, and whether he would have to walk as far as the hills beyond the gully.

Besides the many sounds of insects and birds and the sharp, short sounds of twigs breaking and small stones being dislodged as his feet navigated the rough track, there were no other noises. It was the silence between all the sounds that worried Milford the most. The silence was something that no one could control, and one never knew what might be hiding in it.

He lit a cigarette and, when it was finished and his anxiety had still not diminished, he lit a second one.

It was warm, and Milford began to feel thirsty. At first it was simply the recognition of a slight discomfort, but after about an hour, Milford was unable to focus on anything else. He was worried that there might not be any water anywhere, and, as the day wore on, the anxiety caused the recognition to treble in size and Milford became quite sure that he was going to die of thirst.

He hoped that there might be a creek further down in the gully, but the gully was still a long way off, and there was no guarantee, even if there were a creek, that there would be any water in it. He sat for a few moments at the side of the track under the shade of some very tall eucalyptus trees with mottled white bark. Despite the sun and the fresh air, he would have preferred to be back in the library, tearing pages out of books.

First it was a drink at the local pub, and then, a couple of weeks later, it was dinner at the town's only restaurant. By the end of the month, he had taken Shelley to a couple of movies, and, after work had finished for the day, he usually walked her home to the small flat she was renting on the main street of the town. By the end of the second month, he was staying over several times a week – his extra toothbrush and razor sitting expectantly in Shelley's bathroom – and, whenever he thought of her, which he often did, the word *girlfriend* flickered through his mind, simply underlining everything that Milford was hoping for just a little further down the track. But the track petered out before either of them got that far, and Milford's expectations receded to the back of his mind where they remained pushed together with all his other hopes and missed possibilities. Milford suspected that his ignominious past may have managed to stretch forward into his present, painting it with bleakness and retribution, but then he decided that some tracks just come to an inexplicable and unaccountable end.

He stayed on, repairing second-hand furniture; Shelley, on the other hand, having found an bank teller in a white shirt with a thin, dark tie, became Mrs Thin-Dark-Tie and moved on. For some time after Shelley's departure, a series of new girls replaced each other in the front office until one of them decided to remain, and things returned to some kind of neutral reflection of the past. Milford, not wanting to revisit the hopes he had dared associate with Shelley, chose to veer away from tracks offering any kind of vague promises, having decided that life was probably easier and less complicated when he was on his own.

It was much warmer, and the track was becoming exceedingly difficult to follow. In parts, it disappeared completely into the heavy undergrowth, forcing Milford to stand, sometimes for several minutes, debating with himself as to where it was likely to reappear.

Milford encountered yet another fallen, moss-covered tree, the enormous branches of which stuck out at strange angles, forcing him to make a quick decision as to which way to go and whether he should climb over or crawl under. In the process, he managed to scratch his hand and tear the sleeve of his shirt. He swore loudly while his eyes attempted to pick out the track in front of him. He could see that he was not that far from the edge of the ridge, and he was hoping that the track would continue downwards, but he knew that it was very possible that it might vanish completely, somewhere beyond the ridge ahead of him.

The parrots were becoming very raucous and the small black flies were sticky and irritating. Chasing away the flies with one hand, Milford checked the cigarettes he had left – there were not many. He was irritated that they had disappeared so quickly, and he tried to reassure himself that everything would be better when he got out of this room. Then he began wondering if he actually was in a room, or if the room had changed into something completely different. Perhaps he actually was in the bush, and perhaps the chance of him getting out was becoming slimmer by the minute.

He took out a cigarette and returned the packet to his pocket. Then he placed the cigarette between his lips, and, still chasing away flies, he took out his lighter. All this would soon come to an end, and he would then be back in the Hall; hopefully, he would get some more cigarettes. He inhaled deeply and tried to make himself think about other things. The only other thing he could think about was his thirst, so his mind wound around rocks and hard places and he decided that he was most definitely caught somewhere in between. He would have to be very careful with his few remaining cigarettes and keep them until things became really bad or, perhaps, until things became less bad than they were at the moment. He was not quite sure which was the more relevant, but he could imagine that in both cases he might be extremely grateful for a cigarette.

With the ridge not that far away, Milford's spirits rose a little, in spite of the fact that the track had not become any easier, covered as it was with small branches and leaf matter and even a long trailing form of grass that managed to twine itself around his ankles, causing him to trip several times.

The small, unexpected rustles in the thick undergrowth worried him a little, his mind filling with images of snakes book-ended between his desperate need for both water and a cigarette. He had a rough idea of what to do if he were bitten – apply a pressure bandage, begin at the bite area and work up the limb – but he did not want to end up in such a situation, having absolutely nothing on him that even vaguely resembled any kind of pressure bandage, and he attempted to push the probability of being bitten to the back of his mind. He felt that he had more than sufficient to worry about without mixing snakes into the equation. Still the images remained, and he walked even more carefully and listened even more intently.

When he finally reached the top of the ridge, the landscape opened up a little, and he was able to look across the very wide gully below towards the line of small hills rising in the distance. He had no idea what lay beyond the hills, but he could see no other option than to keep heading for them. It was possible that everything would become obvious once he reached the top of the hills, but he also knew that there was a very strong possibility that it would simply be more of the same: trees and more trees.

He sat for a few minutes looking down into the gully; it was not large enough to call a valley, but he knew that it was going to take him several hours to climb down to the bottom and then up on the other side. He could glimpse a rough track winding downwards, but he guessed that it was not going to be an easy descent. In parts the ground seemed to fall away vertically, and Milford's stomach clenched when, after scrutinizing the side of the drop, he saw that there was obviously no other way down.

His need for water was screaming at him from every cell in his body, and it was only the possibility of finding water at the bottom of the gully that was pushing him onwards. He was so focused on his need for water that all other worries seemed to have dissipated entirely. He stood up and brushed away the few twigs and leaves that had fastened to his shirt and trousers. Very slowly, he began following the track downwards.

It twisted past small and large trees and boulders of different sizes. In some places, it dropped vertically through dense vegetation or, in others, it meandered past stretches of sand and stones and exposed roots. Several times, it seemed to fall away completely, and Milford grabbed frantically at whatever branch or even clump of grass that happened to be close by, hoping to be able to break the fall that he knew was likely to be imminent. Occasionally, a few dislodged stones would continue rolling downwards unhindered, and Milford would imagine that he was one of the stones and that it was he and not the stone that would soon come to rest somewhere completely out of sight.

Out of sight. He could not help but wonder just how far out of sight he actually was and whether or not anyone was watching him. It was the feeling that someone could be watching him that really upset Milford. In gaol, there had always been someone watching him: he had lived with that feeling for years, but, once he was on the outside, he wanted to feel that his life was his own, that he could do what he wanted, when he wanted, without anyone's knowing. He wanted to be, and remain, anonymous, but he was not sure that he was anonymous at the moment, not even in this vast, terrifying place.

He stood for a moment, supporting himself against the side of an immense outcrop of orange-brown rock. There was a drop below him of at least two metres, and the track had disappeared. He lowered himself into a sitting position and tentatively launched himself over the edge, sliding rapidly over sand and stones until he came to a sudden stop at the bottom. Beyond him, he could see the vague outline of the track, and, looking back the way he had come, he realized that he was more than halfway down the cliff face.

The track now continued at a relatively easy angle. The vegetation was denser and there was a definite feeling of moisture in the air. Milford felt that it was as though he had broken through some kind of ceiling and that he was now in an enormous glasshouse with tropical plants. Huge ferns and large-leafed plants fell across the track, and, in other places, small rivulets of water broke from rocks to snake their way in long thin lines across the ground. If he stood still and listened, he could hear definite sounds of water further down the incline.

Water.

He put his hand against one of the rocks in an effort to collect some of the water, but the rewards were meagre, and he decided to push on. The small rivulets became greater in number and many of them, although not much more than a film of water over the rocks, were quite wide. Milford was forced to carefully choose his steps, fully aware of just how easy it would be to slip on the wet, and often mossy, rocks. As he reached what he felt had to be the bottom, he rounded a small bend formed by a high rock face and there in front of him was a fast-moving creek.

He stood for a moment, revelling in both the sight and the sounds, and then he bent down and scooped up the water with both hands, delighting in its freshness and its coldness. After drinking several handfuls, he splashed it over his face and arms, and then he drank some more. He was not going to die of thirst after all.

He lay down on one of the flat rocks near the creek and looked upwards through the broken net of undergrowth. Above him, he could see the freckled sky and the sun. Perhaps things would be all right after all. He took out one of his few remaining cigarettes and lit it, pulling himself up into a sitting position on the rock. The cold water and the tobacco were chasing away the worst of his anxieties. Hopefully, the hill rising up from the other side of the creek would not be quite as difficult, and, perhaps, on the other side of the hill, he would find the way out.

Fragment Thirty-Seven

Tilda had been given a small bronze key with a large wooden tag, and she noticed that the tag had the words *Room Two Hundred and Twenty-Five* written in a beautiful cursive script. The Receptionist told her that the room was on the same floor but at the other end of the building. She reacted mentally to the word *building,* but she said nothing.

It was a long walk. Although the key would have easily fitted into her pocket, the tag would not, so she had to hold it in her hand. She held the key by its tag, letting the key itself swing erratically at her side. The door, which was flanked on one side by Room Nine and, on the other, by Room One Hundred, was black timber and, instead of the number being painted directly on to the door, there was a plate which, like the key, was made from bronze.

She was thinking about what the Administrator had told her about reassessing her thoughts and possibly finding the answer. She was almost positive that it all had to do with the combination of past, present and future, but she was unable to break through and find the answer. She was fifty again, but she was becoming used to being flung from one age to another; as far as she was concerned, it was the least of her worries. While she was thinking about time and reassessing thought patterns and the fact that she was being thrown back and forth between one age and another, she was also thinking about the Administrator. She could not completely let go of the certainty that she had seen him somewhere before.

On the other side of the door, she found herself standing on a busy street. There were people everywhere, and, for some strange reason, she was overwhelmed, not only by the people, but by the noise of the traffic. There were crowds of people in the Hall and in the corridors, but there was also a silence. She had adjusted to the silence, and now she found all the noise both threatening and disturbing.

She moved back against the wall of the building closest to her so as not to be in the way of people pushing past her on the street. Everyone seemed to be in a dreadful hurry, and Tilda could but wonder why. She was curious as to where they were all going and whether, when they finally arrived, they would be able to stop hurrying. Somehow she doubted it. Many of the people were talking on mobile phones. The people were all part of the street scene, but, in reality, they were all somewhere else.

She looked around to identify the building where she was standing, and she saw that it was a police station. This recognition shook her a little; she found it quite strange that, given her present situation, she should be standing outside a police station. Was she supposed to go in and make a complaint? Against the Administrator? Against the Administrator's organization? Against his building? She laughed to herself, wondering what she would say to the officer on duty. No, she did not know where the building was, how big it was, who owned it, and, no, she had no idea what the Administrator was called other than Administrator…

She knew that it would be completely impossible to make any kind of complaint, and then she thought about the need to rethink what she thought was true. She knew that the police would think that she was insane, but, on the other hand, they might be able to give her some kind of protection. Even though she could see that there were a few advantages in talking to the police, she was still very dubious. How could she explain to people on the *outside* about the corridors and rooms on the *inside*? How could she make them understand something that not even *she* could understand? And what if the outside and the inside were actually the one and the same? If that were the case, then there would be nowhere to run to, and definitely no one who would be able to help her.

There was a bench outside the Police Station, and on it, Tilda saw a discarded newspaper. She picked it up, eager to know what had been happening, but also to get some idea of dates and whether or not there was any mention of anything that in any way resembled what she had been experiencing these last weeks or months.

With the newspaper in her hand, she breathed in deeply, telling herself that everything was going to be all right. She pushed open the door to the police station, hoping that there would be someone who might be able to understand, and, if that happened, then perhaps she might finally be able to break out of the nightmare.

Fragment Thirty-Eight

Milford had reluctantly left the creek behind him and was pushing his way up from the gully. He had wasted a good half an hour trying to find the track on the other side of the creek, but now he felt that he knew where he was going. The sun was not as high in the sky, and Milford guessed that it was already mid-afternoon; he did not want to think about what he would do once night fell. He tried to push away such thoughts by telling himself that he would soon be at the top of the hill and from there he would have a much better view of everything around him.

The initial climb from the creek was relatively steep, but then the ground began to flatten out into a very gradual ascent. Milford did not doubt that he was still moving upwards, though he did feel that the track was making long, unnecessary loops around itself. However, he dared not cut through the bush; more than anything he did not want to get lost.

Thinking about getting lost, he laughed loudly, the sound disappearing quickly into the bush around him. In effect he *was* already lost: he had no idea where he was or what was likely to be on the other side of the hill. He did not know if there was anyone else nearby or if he was the only person for hundreds of kilometres. He could no longer be sure that he was still in a room, or if the *inside* had changed places with the *outside*. No matter how he chose to look at his present situation, it was more than difficult: it was disastrous. He tried to concentrate on what might be on the other side of the hill; he tried to push his thoughts in other directions.

As he walked through a stand of large eucalyptus trees drawing long late-afternoon shadows across the path, he heard another sound. By now, he was used to the bird noises and the sounds of things rustling through the bushes, but this noise was different.

It sounded like someone or something pushing its way through the bush.

Milford stopped walking and listened. He listened beyond all the noises that he had been hearing for the last few hours. He could still hear the other sound, and it was definitely something moving through the bush. From the direction of the sound, Milford gathered that whatever it was, was higher up, further along the track, and it was coming towards him.

While he was trying to pinpoint the sound, he was also trying to work out what, in only a matter of moments, would be bursting out of the bush in front of him. There was no doubt that whatever or whoever was ahead of him was definitely coming towards him and, whatever it was, was moving fairly quickly. While reason was telling him that it had to be a bushwalker, Milford was well aware that the situation he was in was not normal – nothing had been the least bit normal for weeks – and whatever was coming along the track in his direction need not necessarily be normal either.

In any other situation, Milford would not have been especially concerned: he was used to taking care of himself. But his present situation was one that he was unable to get a grip on. Was he in a room, or was he somewhere in the bush with trees both hiding and extending the boundaries? Was he within four secure walls or was he completely lost? Was the thing that was rapidly moving into his space something that he could contend with or was it, like everything else that had been happening to him of late, without any kind of normality or logic?

Milford could not be sure, and he hesitated for a moment while he considered whether he should stay on the track or whether he should keep out of sight. He did not have much time to make up his mind; he decided to stay where he was. Perhaps, if it were a bushwalker or a ranger, there might be a possibility that what he was fearing might actually turn out to be his salvation.

The sounds were becoming louder, and Milford could even hear whistling. Animals did not whistle, so it had to be a person.

Was this a glimpse of eternity? He was not sure. It seemed like an eternity, but then eternity was supposed to go on for ever, and the steps were coming closer. Milford felt that everything around him was holding its breath. Even the birds were silent.

From his spot on the track, Milford saw the figure of a man appear between the trees. He was coming directly towards Milford, and Milford doubted that he was a bushwalker. In fact, the man seemed to be a little unsure of where he was going, and, like Milford, he was not dressed for walking in the bush.

Milford peered along the track, not sure whether he

should call out some greeting or whether he should wait until the man had come closer. There was something about the man, about his gait and even his clothing, that insisted on rattling Milford's memory. He noted the ponytail, and then he remembered that he had seen the man before.

In the queue.

He stepped out into the middle of the track, calling out a greeting. He felt relief, almost exhilaration, knowing that he was no longer alone. They might be in a room, or they might be in the bush, but at least they were now two. He began to walk along the track to meet the man who was not more than ten metres from him.

It was obvious that the man had seen Milford; he returned the greeting but did not quicken his pace.

Milford waved both hands in the air and smiled. Perhaps now they would be able to work together to find an exit. He said, "I'm Milford…" and, as he drew closer, he added, "I think we may have seen each other before, in there." He stretched out his hand.

As Oswald came level with Milford, he took the outstretched hand.

"Oswald," he said. He was not sure whether or not he had seen Milford before; the name certainly did not ring any bells, but if Milford said that they had seen each other, then perhaps they had. Perhaps Milford had been much older or even younger; Oswald was not sure, but he nodded anyway.

The strangeness of meeting up with someone from the building, especially someone who actually recognized him, was not of sufficient consequence to break into Oswald's other thoughts. He was still thinking about the ferry and the storm and the heavy rain. He could recall seeing Eugene

247

Turnbull and then someone who was not Turnbull but who had said he was the Administrator, and then how he had simply disappeared. Oswald was almost sure, after the Administrator had left, that he had remained sitting, trying to piece together all the things that had been happening. He had been hoping, when and if everything came together, that he might suddenly find the answer, not only in regards to Turnbull's disappearance, but also in regards to everything else that had been happening. Then there was a moment when he had placed his head in his hands, and when he next looked up, he was standing on the bush track. The ferry had gone, the rain had gone, and all he could see were trees.

Oswald was now even more confused. The fact that he had actually moved from one room to another without going via the Hall and the Receptionist threw everything that he knew, or thought he knew, into disarray. Then the thought occurred to him that he might not even be in a room.

He turned to Milford and asked him which room he had entered. "You *did* enter a room, or…?" he asked.

Milford told him, and Oswald remained quiet for a moment, his mind isolating and examining a plethora of possibilities. So he was actually in Room Nineteen, even though he had not entered of his own free will. When he thought back, he felt that things had been very disrupted since he had stepped out of the queue, and especially since he refused to enter Room Nineteen. Perhaps this is what Turnbull meant when he said that it was dangerous to step out of the queue. There was probably a sequence to the way things happened, even if it were possible to move in and out of experiences. The experiences could be from the past or the future, and, at first glance, they could seem very haphazard, but there was an order, and it was important not to change the order in which they happened but, by moving out of the queue, that was exactly what he had done. There had to be some kind of order to prevent chaos, and, at the moment, he was balancing on the edge of chaos. Perhaps he would never get back to the right place.

He was trying to define *right* place when he noticed that Milford was looking at him curiously, probably waiting for some kind of comment or reply.

Oswald was thinking how strange it was that the two of them should be in the same experience or memory or… Obviously it was an unexpected situation caused by the disruption to the natural order of things. He tried to disengage himself from his thoughts, and he asked: "So, where have you come from?"

Milford pointed back across the gully to the other line of hills. "Way over there." He paused for a moment before asking, "Did you happen to see something, anything, that might be a kind of exit? The way out?" It was obvious that he desperately wanted a positive answer.

Oswald shook his head, but his thoughts were still elsewhere. There was so much that he needed to sift through and analyse; he would have preferred to have been on his own. He really did not need Milford at the moment.

It was obvious that Milford sensed Oswald's reluctance, but it was also apparent that he wanted answers. "What's it like back there, over the hill?" he asked.

Oswald shrugged. "Much the same as here: trees and more trees."

He was thinking of the almost impenetrable undergrowth that he had pushed his way through before finding the track, and, when he looked down at his hands and forearms, he noticed the long red scratches and angry welts.

Then his thoughts, bundled together into a loose ball that was rapidly disintegrating, reached back to what he had been thinking about order and chaos and the definition of *right* place and why he was where he thought he was and not where he wanted to be.

Milford was extremely disappointed; he had been hoping for something else, but he was not sure what: a door marked *Exit*? A sign on the track saying *Way Out*? A small town with houses and a decent pub?

He was also disappointed with Oswald: he had definitely been hoping for a completely different response. He had expected that Oswald would have felt as he did about there being strength in numbers. He looked around at the darkening sky. "Perhaps we should find somewhere safe for the night," he suggested.

Oswald looked at him, almost as though he had not heard him, or, if he had, as though he was unable to comprehend what had been said. Then, without responding to Milford's suggestion, he said, "Do you know, I actually think I may have solved it. It all has to do with intention and the individual and focus and –"

Milford was not particularly interested in hearing about intention and focus. At the moment, standing in the middle of the bush with nightfall rushing towards them, Milford felt that there were many other things that ranked much higher on his scale of priorities. He interrupted him, "But now. What are we going to do now?"

Oswald laughed. "But that's the point: it's all up to you, and me. How stupid of me not to have understood it before. It's all so simple really."

The essence of the thought. That was what it was all about.

Of course individual perspectives had something to do with it as well; after all, what he, Oswald, might be perceiving or understanding need not be at all similar to what Milford might be seeing or understanding. In fact, there was absolutely nothing to indicate that there had to be any form of similarity. Glancing quickly at Milford, Oswald was quite sure that they had two completely different inter-pretations of the situation; there was nothing to say that they were even seeing exactly the same things.

Oswald's mind was rapidly computing the diverse pieces of information he had been gathering over the past weeks or months. It occurred to him, as he was standing there in the middle of the track, that the connection bet-ween two human beings can never be more than super-ficial, because all people are limited by who they are and what they think. When people recognize similar patterns of limitation in others, there may be some feeling of con-nection, but usually people live parallel to each other, each of them tightly cocooned within the essence of who they are.

He was looking at Milford, but his thoughts were filled with the building: the Administrator, the rooms and the whole maze of corridors. He also thought of Room Nine-teen and how he had refused to open the door. And then he thought how the corridors and the doors were simply part of someone else's perception, and that they need not be part of his perception at all. That was why the Administrator had told him he was so close to solving the puzzle when he had talked about *getting out* being at the centre.

Of course! It was all making so much sense now. His thoughts were racing in many different directions, trying desperately to pick up all the ends of his ideas and knot them together into something that made sense. He fastened on to Eugene Turbull's comment about the essence of the thought. *The essence of the thought.* What was it at this moment? Apart from trying to make some kind of sense of what was happening, there was frustration and there was also anxiety for Milford. But Milford was not actually part of his reality.

Oswald noticed that Milford was staring at him.

He said, "It's so blindingly obvious. We don't have to be here if we don't want to, and really, I don't fancy the idea of spending a night anywhere in the open." He offered his hand to Milford. "I doubt I'll be seeing you again; at least, I won't if I'm right about all this."

He knew that it sounded heartless, but he really did not know what else he could do. He could not take Milford with him, because Milford had not reached a point where he understood what was actually going on. It had suddenly become very apparent to Oswald that understanding was the key, and it was impossible to hand this understanding on to someone else: everyone had to work it out for themselves.

Milford was looking devastated. "Please take me with you; I…"

Oswald, feeling strangely elated and despondent at the same time, looked at Milford and said, "Sorry, I would really like to be able to help you, but it's impossible; your getting out has absolutely nothing to do with me and everything to do with you. I wish I could explain it better… Just keep thinking about what you want – what you *really* want. I know you'll work it out." He paused for a moment, wrestling with a deluge of emotions, and then, having weighed all the options against each other and having reached a conclusion, he repeated, "I'd definitely help you if it were even slightly possible, but it's not."

It was obvious that Milford wanted to say something more, but Oswald was already walking very quickly back along the path.

Fragment Thirty-Nine

She pushed open the door to the Police Station as two police constables were on their way out. The younger of the two smiled at her, holding the door open to let her enter. She thanked him, vaguely considering her next move and what she should do and what she should say.

On the other side of the door – to her surprise and consternation – there was no busy reception area, no one in uniform and no posters telling people what was expected and what was forbidden; in fact, there was not one single thing about the room that even remotely resembled a police station, and there was not a person to be seen anywhere.

Tilda immediately turned and attempted to leave through the same door by which she had entered, but the door would not open. She grabbed the handle and shook the door, calling out at the top of her voice. She had seen the police constables pass through the door; there had to be other people somewhere.

No one opened the door and no one came to her rescue. The room was completely quiet. A clammy coldness slowly began to fill every part of her body, pushing its way into her fingertips, winding itself around her intestines, replacing the blood that was pumping through her veins. Her head was beginning to ache and she felt nauseous; no matter what she did, she always seemed to end up in the same situation. There did not seem to be any escape. She lifted her hands to her head and slowly sank to the floor, her back against the door.

The newspaper she was holding spread out around her, painting the floor with meaningless letters and words, but Tilda was not looking at the sheets of paper; she was not looking at anything. Her eyes were tightly shut, and her whole body was shaking with sobs. She had reached the limit of what she could manage. Up until the moment she entered the space that was supposed to be a police station, she had tried to remain restrained, but she had now crossed that very tenuous line between being in control or not, and she knew, without even verbalizing it for herself, that she was no longer in charge. She really did not care what happened now; she was far too tired to continue fighting against something that was obviously so much stronger than she was. It did not matter what she did, she always ended up back at the same point.

She opened her eyes, the tears still wet on her face, and made a half-hearted attempt to gather together the pieces of newspaper. She almost laughed in spite of her frustration and exasperation. How could a collection of mundane news items in any way compare with what she was experiencing?

When she had roughly bundled the pages into something resembling a newspaper, she folded it and then stood up. The room she was in appeared to be a sizeable hallway to a flat or a unit. There was a wardrobe on her right, and she assumed that, if she were to open it, it would be filled with coats and possibly an umbrella or two. Behind her was the door and in front of her there was another door which led into another room. The door opened easily and she saw that she was in a very large living room and, opposite the door, there were several large windows. The windows were all covered with full-length drapes, and she walked over and pulled them aside.

She was looking out over the harbour. To her right loomed the Bridge and, almost in front of her, she could see the Sydney Opera House, the sun playing on its white tiles. The blue water, broken here and there by short erratic lines of white and, in other places, swathes of darker blue and even green, was patterned with a variety of craft, both large and small. She could see the ferries at the Quay, while, at the overseas terminal, an enormous luxury liner dwarfed everything around it. The sails on the many small sailing boats were full of a wind that Tilda was unable to feel behind the glass of the doors leading on to the wide balcony. She tried the handle of the balcony door and found, to her amazement, that it actually opened.

Out on the balcony, she could not only feel the breeze, but she could also feel the warm sun against her face, and she was able to hear the sounds of boats and traffic and people below. It was all so very normal and sane, and it lifted her mood a little. After standing on the balcony for a few minutes, she returned inside.

It was obvious that there had been a party in the flat: there were empty and partly-empty glasses everywhere. Tilda thought that whatever caused the party to end must have been very abrupt.

She walked through to the kitchen, noticing the platters of food and a variety of drinks. Many of the bottles were already opened; the food was fresh and the heated dishes were still warm – it was as though the people had walked out of the flat at the same time as she had walked in.

She took a sandwich from a plate and ate it, and then she took another. She opened the refrigerator; it was well stocked, and she took out a bottle of beer. Walking to the white sofa facing the balcony, she sat down and opened the bottle.

If she had to be here then she might as well make the best of it.

There was absolutely nothing about the flat that stirred up any memory: she knew for sure that she had never been here before. She speculated as to who might actually own the flat, and then she fantasized a little about why there had been a party and who might have been there. Obviously, the party had broken up very suddenly, and she wondered what had happened and where everyone was now.

Then she remembered that the man called Oswald had talked about a party, and how it had been broken up by men in black. She acknowledged that there could be a connection, but then she decided that it was absurd to even contemplate the possibility of walking into someone else's experience. It would not even be the actual experience, simply some kind of weird aftermath.

She shook her head, wanting to rid herself of such thoughts, and finished the sandwiches and the beer. Then she walked around the flat, which was quite large, looking into the three beautifully furnished bedrooms and the bathroom with the large sunken marble bath. There was a small office adjacent to one of the bedrooms, but she found nothing that told her anything about the people who owned the flat. After a quick look around, she returned to the lounge room and, once again, settled herself on the sofa.

She was thinking again of the owners and what might happen if they were suddenly to return home: somehow she did not believe that her story – about walking into the

Police Station and finding herself in the flat – would carry very much weight. She understood completely that they would either assume she was lying or else they would be convinced that she was raving mad.

Tilda asked herself whether it could actually be possible that she *were* mad and that everything she had been experiencing was simply a result of her madness. It made sense, but then she did not feel mad; the more she thought about it, Tilda had really no idea how it would feel to be mad, so she had nothing with which she could compare.

That the door was locked could simply mean that she was locked in for her own safety, but, if that were the case, then there should be people around, people who would be looking in occasionally to see how she was. There should be people enticing her to take small coloured pills and people telling her that everything was going to be all right…

No, she decided, she probably was not mad, and she was not locked up in the room because of any perceived madness. At the same time, what was happening was definitely not simply some wild figment of her imagination: she was able to see everything on the harbour and hear all the noises. She could feel the breeze, she could taste the food, and there were now crumbs on the table after her sandwich. She stood up and walked across to the light switch: she was able to turn the lights on and off. In the kitchen she turned on the tap and felt the cold water wash over her hands. She picked up a knife and slid the point along the back of her hand. She could feel the sharpness of the metal, and she knew that were she to push just a little harder, she would break the skin.

No, she was not dreaming. She was not imagining things. This was real. But the reality stopped at the door –

she was not sure on which side. In a normal world, it was possible to open doors, and, she argued with herself, if one entered a Police Station, then one did not end up in a luxury flat overlooking the harbour.

In the kitchen, on the bench, she saw a box of matches and an insanely desperate idea occurred to her. If she were to set the flat on fire then someone from outside would have to react, that is if there were some connection with the outside. If no one reacted, then there was a chance that the fire, although real in one sense, would not be real in the general sense. She would probably find herself somewhere else. In other words, there was a strong possibility that she would either be rescued or else her time in this particular room – because it had to be a kind of room – would suddenly come to an end, and she would find herself back in the Reception Hall.

She was completely aware that it was an insane and possibly very dangerous idea, but she was running out of ideas, and she had to break free from whatever or whoever was ruining her life. If the worst were to happen, and she died, then, she thought: so be it. Being dead would be a lot better than being flung from room to room with no one anywhere offering any explanations.

She walked back into the lounge room with the pile of newspaper and the box of matches. Her hands were shaking, and she tried not to think of what she was about to do. Apart from the fact that she might kill herself, she was also about to destroy someone else's property. Or was she? She really was not sure.

She decided to set the drapes alight; after all, a fire against the windows might be seen from the water, and that was all she was hoping for: that someone would see the fire and send help.

She sat down again on the lounge and did some deep breathing. The box of matches and the newspaper were on the table in front of her; through the glass doors to the balcony, she could see the water. Everything looked normal. It was the normality that terrified her: imagine if she had got it all wrong, and there were no rooms, no corridors, no strange building. Perhaps she was simply delusional and now she was about to destroy a luxury unit and probably kill herself. She stood up, picking up a few sheets of the newspaper. She twisted them into a rough wand, and then she picked up the box of matches.

She tried to strike a match, but her hands were trembling so much that it flared and then extinguished almost at the same time. She struck a second and a third match, and finally managed to get a flame. Scarcely breathing, she held the flame to the paper and then held the burning paper to the bottom of the drape.

The flame seemed at first undecided as to whether or not it would unite with the drape; then, all of a sudden, it caught on and flared, growing bigger as it moved up the middle drape, its eyes already fixed on the drapes on either side.

Tilda was almost frozen to the spot at the sheer madness of what she had done. Something inside her head clicked into action, and, dropping the paper and the matches, she rushed out of the lounge room into the hall area. She closed the door to the lounge room, the noise of the fire behind her gathering momentum.

Once again she tried the front door, but it refused to yield, and then she slipped down on to the floor, trying to calculate just how long it would take before she was completely overcome by smoke or worse.

As she lay on the floor, speculating on just how many

minutes she had left to live, she remembered who it was the Administrator reminded her of: it was the accountant who had cared for her after her grandmother's death. She was thinking that perhaps it was not a question of *reminding,* but more a question of *was*, but then the smoke finally overcame her, and there was nothing more to remember.

Fragment Forty

Milford made himself breathe slowly, in and out. He knew that his breathing could hardly change the situation, but it did calm him a little. He had watched Oswald disappear along the track, and, shortly afterwards, he heard the kookaburras, and he knew that it would be dark in fifteen minutes or even less. He began subconsciously counting off the minutes, wondering what he would do once it became dark. The darkness would come without warning; it would descend swiftly, removing all the colours and most of the shapes. Things that were recognizable by their shape and colour would suddenly be reduced to tonal patterns of grey, and it would not take long until everything was simply dark grey or black, and then Milford knew that he would not be able to see any-thing at all. Once that happened, the noises in the undergrowth would become even more disturbing.

When he thought of the darkness descending, he knew that he could not stay where he was, but there did not seem to be anywhere to camp. Thinking of the word *camp* made him laugh ironically; all he wanted was a safe place where he could spend the night. As far as he knew there were no such places along the track, and he definitely did not want to plunge into the bush, especially now when everything was balancing on the edge of darkness. Even the noises around him were becoming more alienated and strange.

He decided to continue along the track; he could always lie down on the ground, though he really doubted that he would be able to sleep much, no matter where he ended up spending the night. Then he thought again about snakes, and he tried to remember if they came out in the night-time, or if they remained tucked up in their holes until the sun came up.

There was a sharp cry from some animal and a flock of birds flew past, preparing to roost for the night. Milford was trying to work out what Oswald may have meant when he said that getting out had everything to do with him and nothing to do with anyone else. He was still upset that Oswald had not taken him with him. He assumed that Oswald must have been correct in his thinking and that he must have worked out where the exit was, because he had not come back. He gathered that he had most probably escaped, and, if that was the case, Milford felt that it was dreadfully unfair, but then life had always been unfair as far as Milford was concerned.

He tried to stop his thoughts from going in such a direction. Thinking about how unfair everything was would hardly help him, even if such were the case. Instead, he put all his energy into concentrating on the track which was winding upwards. Milford hoped that when he reached the crest of the hill he might have a better idea as to what to do, but with the darkness and the shadows and the grey tones all enveloping him at such a rate, he was unsure that he would reach the crest while there was still sufficient light available.

By now, Milford was feeling both physically and mentally exhausted. With his eye on the crest of the hill, he tried to hurry, but then the track became much narrower and more difficult to follow, and Milford missed his step. Throwing his arms out to catch hold of anything at all, he felt the ground slipping away from under him as he slid, through the darkness and the shadows, down the side of the hill.

Fragment Forty-One

Oswald was sitting in his study. His cat, large and ginger, was purring in the armchair, and Oswald was watching the evening descend as he tried to make up his mind what he would prepare for dinner. Not that it was a very big problem: there was only himself and the cat, and the cat had her own food in tins neatly arranged on a shelf in the pantry.

Finally he stood up and stretched. He had spent the entire afternoon sitting in front of the computer, writing a paper on Tegmark's mathematical universe hypothesis – the link between external physical realities and mathematical structure – and he felt stiff and not quite himself. The thought occurred to him that he really needed to get out of the house and do something physical, but instead, he walked to the kitchen and opened a bottle of wine. The cat followed him, expecting something else. He left the wine on the table while he took out a tin of cat food and emptied it into a red plastic bowl on the floor.

He poured himself a glass of wine and stood at the window, looking out on the very end of the daylight. Of late, he had been having some very strange dreams, almost daydreams. They seemed to be tied to some kind of undefined building or structure with corridors or tunnels that criss-crossed it like fractures in a broken glass window or like deep, irregular fissures in parched soil. Beyond the corridors there were countless rooms, and he believed that the rooms somehow equated with experiences, though whether they were actual experiences or simply dream experiences, Oswald could not be sure.

He sighed with a profound sense of satisfaction and took another sip of wine. Perhaps there was some kind of logic in his dreams; after all, we are constantly moving between experiences, and perhaps it was possible to see each experience as a separate room.

Oswald opened the refrigerator and took out some left-over soup. He tipped it into a saucepan which he then placed on the stove. The dreams, if they were dreams, had been very clear. He wondered where the line went, not only between the divisions of time but also between dream and reality. Perhaps dreams were more real than we believed them to be.

He turned down the heat under the saucepan and fetched a spoon to stir the soup. He was thinking about the possibility of experiences crossing over and interlocking with other people's experiences. He felt like he did when he was trying to remember a dream and only small fragments let themselves be caught. For some reason, he remembered the name Turnbull; yes, Eugene Turnbull, his maths teacher. Now why would he have been dreaming about Turnbull?

The cat had finished eating and was carefully licking herself clean. Oswald turned off the stove and moved the saucepan to the table. He took out a bowl from the cupboard and a spoon from the drawer. He poured some of the soup into the bowl and then sat down at the table. The cat, who had now finished washing herself, looked at him critically for a moment, and then sauntered off to the lounge room, her tail held in the air like a flag. Oswald assumed that she would be aiming for the most comfortable sofa where she would curl up for the rest of the evening.

He began to eat the soup, still trying to work out why he should have been thinking of Turnbull. He had not seen him since he left school, and he had not thought of him for years, but, when he thought about it, Turnbull *did* have an important influence on his life.

Small pieces of memory were swirling back to him, joining with other pieces, making something much bigger; he could not help thinking of gravity and the creation of the earth. He drank some more wine. It was dark outside now. He stood up and pulled the curtains across the window and then sat down again. The soup was the same as it had been the day before; in fact, it reminded him of the day before. His thoughts went off at a tangent, while he thought about what he had done yesterday, and then, for absolutely no reason at all, some things became startlingly clear.

He believed that he had been in a building, but, from what he could remember, the building had no form. He had not seen the building from the outside, so he had no real idea of its actual appearance. He had a feeling that it may have contained a great many corridors and stairways and rooms, so he assumed that it must have been rather large. He vaguely remembered some kind of central hall, a kind of reception hall or lobby, and there was someone there, or perhaps there were several people – Oswald really could not remember – and the *someone* was handing out keys. He tried to remember why, but, at that point, his memory hit a wall.

He took another mouthful of wine, worrying about the keys. Obviously the keys must have been to rooms in the building, and perhaps that accounted for the corridors and the stairways. He wondered what the rooms were for and why people were supposed to enter them. He was quite sure that it was not a hotel; from what he could remember, he had the strange feeling that the rooms had something to do with experiences from one's past or future.

He stood up again and moved the remnants of his meal to the sink in the kitchen, then he collected his wine glass and walked into the lounge room. The cat was lying curled up in the middle of the sofa and barely acknowledged Oswald as he sat down in one of the armchairs. He was still trying to interpret the meaning of the rooms; he had the feeling that, sometimes, they were not just concerned with one person's experiences but seemed to be caught up with other people's thoughts and experiences as well.

The cat uncurled herself, stretched and then delicately stepped down from the sofa and walked over to Oswald, where she arched her back and sidled around his leg. He leant down absent-mindedly and stroked her until, tiring of being sociable, she returned to the sofa.

The name, Eugene Turnbull, seemed to be mixed up with everything about the building, but Oswald could not work out why. Turnbull had been his maths teacher, but that was years ago, and he had not had anything to do with Turnbull after leaving school. Brilliant man, he thought, trying to tie together all the fractured memories he had of Turnbull – a bit eccentric but brilliant all the same. He had no idea why Turnbull should be part of what he was trying to remember.

His mind was picking over the assorted bits and pieces

he could remember about the rooms. Some of the fragments had actually begun to gravitate together, and he had
the feeling that there may have been a room that he was
supposed to enter but did not enter. He wondered why.

The cat was snoring very softly. Oswald looked at the
wine glass, but it was empty, and he did not feel like walking back to the kitchen.

If the rooms had something to do with experiences, and
he was still not completely sure that this was the case, then
perhaps there was some connection between these
experiences and his overriding need to get out of the building, away from the experiences. Oswald's logical mind
needed things to fall equally on either side of the equals
sign. He wondered if the overriding need to escape had
anything to do with feelings of being confined by certain
experiences, then he moved on to the thought that if we
believe there is no way out, then there *is* no way out.

There were phrases running around in his head: *there is
no past and no future* and *the essence of the thought may
not be what you believe it to be.* Then he remembered
telling someone that *getting out* was at the centre of everything.

Of course it was.

He could not remember everything about the building;
in fact, he could remember very little, but the bits that he
could remember seemed to be telling him that everything is
up to us as individuals, and he could certainly accept that.
He knew that it was necessary to make resolute decisions
to change situations; it was never sufficient simply to say
that we want to get out. The *getting out* is always up to us.
Perhaps it was this understanding that had something to do
with his not entering one of the rooms, but perhaps, even
though he had decided not to follow the flock, he had still

been tied to the *idea* of getting out. The most important thing about getting out or being free is to be able to accept that one actually *is* free.

He found the thought quite liberating, and whether the thought had been motivated by a dream or an actual experience, Oswald was quite prepared to accept the logic of being able to believe in himself and in his desire to be free. The exit from the building would have been all around him; it would never have been a matter of looking for it or finding it. It was as simple as *believing*.

His belief in parallel universes and parallel experiences came back to him with a rush as he looked at the red scratches and welts on his hands. He had absolutely no idea where they could have come from.

Fragment Forty-Two

Tilda was lying on her back, and she felt that there was someone leaning over her. The face seemed pleasant enough, but Tilda could not make out the features. She concentrated on the two small things that looked like eyes and the mouth that was moving. Tilda tried to understand why the mouth was moving and whether or not it had any significance for herself. She felt completely disassociated from everything around her and even from her own body. She was simply a thought floating in… she was not sure of the medium in which she was floating. There was something though that she really had to remember. It kept nudging at her consciousness, telling her that it was important.

She closed her eyes again; it was easier that way. There were sounds all around her, but everything seemed so muted and far away. Nothing was really her concern, except the nagging thought. It had something to do with where she was, but there was a gap and she could not bridge the gap.

All at once, she was concerned that the sounds may have been directed at her, and she opened her eyes again. She had been so sure that a face had been hovering above her, but, as she became more aware of her surroundings, she saw that there was no face and that she was back in the Reception Hall, lying on one of the benches.

She swung her legs down to the ground and sat up. She could vaguely remember something about a fire. Obviously, she must have survived; as far as she could see, she was still alive. Unless, of course, she had been right about this place all along, and she was actually dead.

She wondered why she had been imagining someone hovering over her; perhaps it had just been wishful thinking. She looked at her arms and hands: no burn marks. So, if she were dead, it was not because of the fire. Or perhaps it was. She began to think about smoke inhalation and suffocation, but her thoughts simply petered out into some kind of vacuum.

Small irregular fragments of images were beginning to float together into something that was vaguely beginning to resemble a definite image. She remembered the smoke and the noise of the fire. The noise was like a wind roaring in the room behind her. She could also remember the heat, and, before the heat and the noise and the fire, she could remember being in the unit overlooking the harbour and setting light to the drapes.

But why was she back here in the Reception Hall? She was not sure whether she should be screaming or whether she should be grateful that she was still alive. She wondered about the fire. She knew that she had lit it: she had seen it, smelt it, heard it. It must have been real, but perhaps it had not been real.

She rested her head in her hands. She believed that she could remember someone saying something about parallel experiences. Was it possible to be in one place and to be in another place at the same time, and, if such a thing were actually possible, what about the fire? Perhaps she was able to escape into another time configuration, but there may have been other people in that building, people who did not escape.

Things were becoming far too complicated. She lifted her head and looked around the Hall. She watched the people in the queue, none of them objecting, all of them obediently standing in line. As she had done on countless other occasions, she wondered why. There were so many ideas running through her head. She was sure someone had told her that *getting out* was central, so it must be possible to get out.

She remembered the plump little man who called himself Administrator and who might very well have been the accountant from all those years ago. She also remembered his telling her that it was necessary for her to rethink everything that she may have previously thought about the past, future and present. He told her that when she could do that, then she might have the answer.

He had made it sound so simple and perhaps it was. Perhaps she had been making things more complicated than they actually were. She was thinking about what he had said: *Rethink everything.* Then, though she knew that she was supposed to get up and join the queue, she also knew that she was not going to. If she had to rethink what she was doing, then this was where she would start. She would start by doing exactly what she wanted to do, and not what she was being told to do. She was tired of doing inane things simply because someone was telling her to do them.

Fragment Forty-Three

When Milford's foot slipped and he felt himself sliding over the edge, he had first clung on to the rocks at the top, and then, as the rocks slowly gave way, one after the other, he had fallen, at first slowly and then much faster. The small branches and prickly bushes that attempted to stop his fall scratched at his arms and legs, and the dislodged rocks and stones tumbled alongside him and then below him, making him sickeningly aware of the extent of the drop.

Then it all came to a stop. He could still hear some rocks tumbling further down the drop, so he understood that something must have stopped his fall. He felt strangely disconnected from his body, and yet, at the same time, he was acutely aware of intense pain. He tried to move his left arm to pull himself around into a slightly more comfortable position, but the pain was extreme, and he could feel tears welling up behind his eyes.

After a few minutes of lying very still, he put all his weight on to his right arm and pulled himself up into a sitting position. His fall had been broken by a very large boulder, and, beyond it, he calculated that the drop continued for at least another twenty metres. Although

Milford was relieved that he had not continued all the way down, he felt that, given his present situation, it probably would not have made a lot of difference. His upper left arm was probably broken – he guessed that it had happened when he had been flung against the boulder – and he was halfway down a steep drop. It was almost dark, but he could see that the ground above and below him simply dropped away in perpendicular lines of rock face or sandy ground. There was no track or anything that even resembled one: all he had was the boulder.

Although he doubted very much that there would be anyone around who would be likely to hear him, he tried calling for help several times. His voice seeped out into the grey darkness, sounding ineffectual and feeble; he had known even before he had called out that it would be a waste of breath. While he lay there, wondering what to do next, a night bird flew overhead, its sharp, lamenting cry cutting through the darkness. The cry merely emphasized his anxiety; he really did not want to remain where he was, but, as far as he could ascertain, there was really not much he could do about it.

As he expected, there was no answer to his calls, and he had to accept that beyond the night birds and all the things in the darkness which he was unable to see, he was completely and utterly on his own.

Later, Milford decided that it was probably the most dreadful night he had ever experienced in all his life. He was in dreadful pain; he was uncomfortable; he was even terrified that the boulder he was leaning against might give way, which would doubtlessly cause him to slip all the way down the drop. And he was on constant alert in case some wild animal should want to tear him to bits. He thought a

275

lot about the wild animals and decided that the idea of their tearing him to bits was probably a little exaggerated, but he knew that there could well be snakes, and though they would most probably not tear him to bits, the end result would still be the same.

The boulder afforded him a certain amount of support, but it was hard and unrelenting, and, after some time, his body was screaming out for something soft to counter the hardness between his body and the rock. He thought again of Oswald and how unfair he had been to leave him in such a place. If Oswald had taken him with him, or even if he had stayed, then he most probably would not have fallen, and, if he had, then there would have been someone who could have helped him. While he was feeling sorry for himself, he tried not to dwell too much on what Oswald had said about his getting out having absolutely nothing to do with him, and that it all had to do solely with Milford.

He tried to sleep, but the pain and the discomfort and his fear of snakes kept him awake. For hours, he could not really see very much, just a variation in shapes painted in different tones of black and grey, but, then, very gradually, he noticed the slightest lightening of the sky in the east, and the forms around him took on more definite shapes and then colours, like a painting coming to life. Gradually the warmth returned. The night had gone; it was finally day.

Milford could now see exactly where he was. He could see where he had slid from the top, and, when he turned his head, he could see just how far the drop continued down beyond the boulder. If the boulder had not been there, he would have fallen all the way down to the bottom. Milford was already feeling uncomfortably cold, but, underneath the coldness, there was a growing clamminess that was mirroring his growing anxiety. Although not one to pray, he did pray that the boulder would remain where it was and not suddenly lurch into the void below him.

To his right, he noticed that there was the semblance of a narrow track running along the edge of the drop. In all probability it had once continued past where he was now sitting, but a landslide, possibly caused by heavy rain, had wiped away any indication of a track. He found it sobering that he fell at just that place; if he had fallen only a little further to the left or to the right, there would have been no boulder to have stopped his fall.

The effort of simply trying to find out where he was had exhausted him, and he leant back against the boulder, weighing up his options. Except for the birds beginning to stir in the many different levels of the vegetation around him, everything was very still and quiet. Then, as he sat there, trying to decide what he should do, he became aware of the sound of water a long way below him. It was most probably the same creek that he had crossed the previous day, and it was very possible that the small track running off to his right might actually connect with the creek further down the hill.

His options were minimal: he could either stay where he was and die, or he could try moving along the track and possibly survive; for how long that might be, Milford was not sure. There was no saying that the track would ensure his survival, but Milford felt that anywhere would have to be better than where he was at the moment. He did not fancy the idea of having to leave the spot where he was – the pain in his arm became worse with every movement he made – but at least he would be doing something constructive. He tried to avoid thinking about the narrowness of the track and the steepness of the drop; instead he attempted to visualize a rescue party with a stretcher and some kind of very strong pain relief that would immediately remove all the pain and transport him to an enviable state of unconsciousness.

There really was no other option, so he decided to follow the track.

Pulling himself to a standing position took some time: his body was stiff and the smallest movement exaggerated the pain in his arm. The break had not cut through the skin; though he was not sure whether that was a good thing or not. After some thought, he decided that it had to be positive. He could not avoid noticing that the arm had swollen considerably, and there were signs of bruising extending down his arm towards his elbow. As long as he could keep himself and his arm completely still, there was just a heavy dull ache – an ache that he would definitely prefer to do without but which, at least for the moment, was within the limitations of what he could manage.

However, as he began to move slowly along the track, he was very aware that there was no way he would be able to keep the pain contained, and he sincerely doubted that it was going to remain within the limits of what he believed was manageable. Added to his concerns about the pain, there was an acute awareness of the drop on his left. Without actually looking, Milford knew that the ground fell away in a perpendicular line until it disappeared beneath the treetops metres below.

He tried to push his thoughts away from his pain and the perpendicular lines reaching down into the treetops, and concentrated instead on reaching the point where the track would finally veer away from the drop. He pressed himself as close as possible to the cliff face looming above him on his right-hand side, thankful that it was his left arm that had been injured and not his right. He had no way of supporting his injured arm, and every footstep and every movement of his body sent pain speeding along his arm like a line of wildfire. He could do nothing about the pain, but he knew that he had to get past the drop: all he had to do was to focus on each step – a step closer to the end of the track, a step further away from the boulder. He gritted his teeth, ignoring the waves of pain and an overwhelming sense of weakness that made him both dizzy and nauseous. Only a few more steps…

The sun was now well above the trees, and he could feel the heat beginning to beat down on him. Initially, he had welcomed the warmth after the cold of the night, but it was quickly becoming an added source of discomfort. Also, he was dreadfully thirsty: he had not drunk anything since crossing the creek the previous day. The images in his mind kept changing between a wide, safe, easy-to-manoeuvre track away from the drop and a fast-running creek filled with clear, cold water.

At the point where the track widened and finally swung away from the edge of the drop, Milford slid to the ground under some trees. He was thankful for the shade, but he was even more thankful that he could remain completely still. The sharp knife-like pain in his arm gradually receded to a heavy, dull throbbing, and he leant back and closed his eyes, wanting only to sink into some kind of pain-free unconsciousness.

More than half an hour passed before he woke from an unsettled and disturbed sleep. The sun had moved, pushing aside the shade, and Milford was feeling both hot and uncomfortable. From where he sat, he could see a much wider track moving downwards to where he assumed it would connect with the creek, and, with the taste of ice-cold creek water hanging in front of him like some invisible carrot, he slowly got to his feet and began walking down the track.

His assumption was correct as the creek at the bottom of the track did not look very different from where Milford had crossed it the previous day. It was fast running but not very deep, and there were many flat rocks which provided an easy crossing and which also broke the creek up into several largish pools. Although the dense vegetation hindered access along much of the creek's course, there was, just where the track dipped down to the water, a flat, sandy area where it was possible to reach the water without any problem.

When Milford arrived at the creek, he lowered himself carefully on to the wide finger of sandy ground and, with some difficulty, scooped up handfuls of water with his right hand. As the cold water trickled down his throat, and even down his neck, his mind wandered around different interpretations of heaven. He could feel his body filling with a definite sense of satisfaction in spite of the pain in his arm. He could never remember appreciating water as much as he did at that moment.

For some time he sat, his right hand trailing in the water, watching the movement of the water over the flat rocks, then he removed his hand from the water and, with the help of an overhanging branch, pulled himself up. Further back from the creek there was an open, sandy area under a couple of large trees that he felt would probably be a good place to sit and wait. Wait for what? Milford was not sure, but he did know that he would not be moving from the creek. He no longer had any intention of trying to reach the other side of the hill; he knew for sure that he would never make it.

He rested his arm across his chest, and, closing his eyes,

he attempted to sleep. All around him he could hear birds and insects interlaced between water-sounds as the creek rushed over stones and fell into sunlit pools. Finally, the relief of having reached the creek, together with the warm sun and the monotonous sounds, lulled him into a restless sleep where, very occasionally, the pain drifted off else-where, and he was able to believe that perhaps everything was going to be all right.

When he woke, it was already mid-afternoon, and he felt feverish and his arm was throbbing. The sense of well-being that had occasionally filled his dreams while he slept had been short-lived, and, as the reality of his situation once again became worryingly obvious, Milford's thoughts circled around Oswald and how inconsiderate he had been. If Oswald had taken him with him then none of this would have happened: he would not have fallen down the drop; he would not have broken his arm and he would definitely not be now lying next to a creek waiting for a rescue that might not even eventuate. If he died, which he probably would, then it would be entirely Oswald's fault.

As he leant against the tree trunk, trying not to concentrate on the pain that was demanding all his attention and, all the while, feeling extremely sorry for himself, he thought again about what Oswald had said to him: *Your getting out has nothing to do with me, and everything to do with you.* Milford wondered how that was possible; after all, Oswald had obviously worked out how to find the exit, and it would have been so easy for him to have shared what he had discovered. Then he remembered Oswald's saying: *I'd help you if it were at all possible, but it's not.* It did not make any sense to Milford; he could not understand why it would not be possible. Surely it had just been a matter of letting him tag along.

He dozed off again, thinking that he really did not want to be where he was; he wondered if it were even possible to simply wish himself somewhere else. Oswald's words kept running around in his head while he contemplated just why Oswald could not help him. Halfway between wakefulness and sleep, the thought occurred to him that, somehow, it possibly did have something to do with him: with what he wanted and what he did not want, with where he was and where he did not want to be. He knew what he wanted, and he knew where he wanted to be. He was trying to pull it all together into something that made sense when everything went black and he fell sound asleep.

Fragment Forty-Four

Tilda is rethinking her present situation. She is in the Hall, and she knows that she is expected to join the queue, but then she makes the momentous decision that she will not join the queue. As the decision takes form in her mind, she knows that she is doing the right thing; all the anxiety that had been pushing down upon her since she first arrived in the building has suddenly vanished.

She stands up slowly and walks across the Hall towards the Reception Desk. She is not in the queue, she is simply walking by herself across the empty part of the Hall. It feels remarkably liberating. She is aware that many of the people in the queue are looking at her; many of them seem concerned and even worried. She smiles in their direction, and she continues walking. She is already about halfway across the Hall, and she can see that the Receptionist – the one with the smile and the wavy hair – is looking at her. She believes that he wants to say something, but he is attending to a client – or is it a customer? – and he is obviously split between what he is doing and what he would like to be doing. She smiles at him as well.

Somewhere on the extreme boundaries of her vision, she can see a couple of men in black, but they are not doing anything; they are simply standing near the wall, possibly waiting for orders. She is almost level with the Reception Desk, and everyone in the queue is looking at her. The Receptionist is looking at her; the men in black are also looking at her.

She walks up to the desk and, ignoring the person standing there, says in a very clear voice: "I don't want to be here any more; I'm going home. I have no intention of walking down any more corridors, and I'm not going into another room. You can keep all your keys; in fact, for all I care, you can drop them all into that hole marked *Rubbish*."

She half-turns to the people in the queue, but she does not say anything to them; there is really nothing to say. Tilda instinctively knows that if anyone follows her it will only be those people who have already understood: people who have been able to rethink everything and who have come to the same understanding as she has done.

A few people begin to take tentative steps out of the queue. Tilda can see that some of them are really quite nervous, and several quickly change their minds and return to the queue.

Tilda begins to walk towards one of the walls; there is no door, but she is walking as though she knows that there is an exit in front of her. Those few people who stepped out of the queue have now joined her. Tilda is calm and con-fident; she knows that this is the way out.

As Tilda and the handful of people with her walk into the wall, it drops away before them; indeed the entire building collapses. Yet, when Tilda momentarily turns to look behind her, she can still see the queue and the people moving slowly towards the Reception Desk; she can even see the Receptionist, and he is not even looking in her direction any longer. It is as though everything behind her is completely disassociated from what she is experiencing and from where she is. For all those people still in the queue, the building, the corridors and the rooms continue to exist. There is no collapsing building and no obvious exit; everything is as it has always been. Most of them are still focused on their need to get out; none of them have understood that it is actually possible.

The sensation of the building's collapse is akin to a dream: there are no dangerous falling objects, just an amazing sense of things breaking up. Tilda feels as though she is in the centre of a whirlwind.

Then, without warning, everything becomes still.

She is sitting at her kitchen table. There is a cup of freshly-brewed coffee and a newspaper in front of her. Outside, there is the sound of a pneumatic drill and men's voices, and she guesses that the council is fixing the footpath: she remembers hearing that someone had complained about it a few weeks ago. Or perhaps it was much longer ago. She is feeling jet-lagged and somewhat out of sorts; she is trying to decide whether she needs to go back to bed, or whether she should do something physical. The idea of taking a walk occurs to her, but then her mind starts to throw up images of long corridors going nowhere. She cannot understand why she should be thinking about corridors, and she tries to remember when she last walked along any kind of corridor. Eventually, she gives up and takes her now empty cup to the kitchen to fetch more coffee. The men outside on the footpath must have stopped work, because she can no longer hear the drill or the voices.

She walks into the front room with her coffee cup and looks out of the window. The bright yellow bands are still in place, indicating men at work, but there are no men, just a few tools strewn around next to the now silent drill. Tilda looks at her watch and gathers that it is morning teatime. Back in the kitchen, she puts her cup on the table and opens the newspaper, wondering just how long she will be able to remain awake.

Fragment Forty-Five

Tilda stepped out of the modest sandstone building on Kent Street where she worked. The lobby's interior was dimly lit, so, coming out into bright sunshine, she was momentarily blinded. She put her hand up to her face, but it was too late for her to see the man walking along the footpath.

"I'm so dreadfully sorry," she apologized, feeling both embarrassed and flustered about having bumped into him.

He was kind and even sympathetic. He obviously understood completely about dim lobbies and sunny streets. He told her that he had done the same thing himself, several times.

They were standing on the street near the building, and people were hurrying past them in both directions. Without wanting to appear curious, Tilda attempted to look at the man more closely. He was about the same age as she was, and he had a friendly face; while she looked at him, she was trying to work out whether or not she had seen him before.

Then he said: "Have I seen you before? Recently?"

Tilda shook her head. "I really doubt it. I only just got back here on Tuesday after a month in England, so, unless you have been in England… " She laughed and then added, "But, you're right – about possibly knowing each other – I actually felt the same way about you."

"Perhaps it is some kind of psychic connection, or perhaps we did see each other somewhere – the train station or perhaps the coffee shop…" He paused for a moment, looking at her closely. "Look, talking about coffee, I was just on my way to have one now; there's a reasonable place in the next block, and it would be lovely if you could join me. By the way, my name's Oswald," he said, offering her his hand.

"That would be lovely," she replied, taking the offered hand and adding, "Tilda. My name's Tilda."

In the café, they found a table close to a back wall; it was somewhat secluded and relatively quiet. They gave their orders to a young waitress with purple hair and a nose piercing, and then they sat back, waiting for their coffees to arrive.

Tilda said: "It is strange, isn't it? The feeling that we've met before…"

From a glass bowl on the table, she removed one of the small paper packets of sugar and tipped it first one way and then the other, enjoying the very soft rustle of the sugar inside and the almost imperceptible movement of the grains between her fingers.

Oswald was looking at her, thinking that, for a woman in her fifties – at least, that was what he assumed – she was particularly good-looking. He agreed about the strangeness but added that, according to what he had heard, it was quite common to experience such feelings of recognition when, in fact, there should not be any.

"As I said, it's very possible that we may have seen each

other somewhere before; you know, in a crowd or even on the street. Passing strangers, you could say." He moved his chair back from the table and crossed his legs. "Though I sometimes wonder if there is not much more to these déjà vu experiences than we fully understand."

There was a large television screen towards the front of the café, and, from where they were sitting, they were aware of the sound, and though Tilda could see the images flickering across the screen, Oswald had his back turned to it and could not see anything.

Tilda was more interested in what Oswald had to say than in the television, but, parallel to what Oswald was saying, she could hear that a politician was talking about plans for a new irrigation scheme, while images of fruit-trees and vegetable crops flashed past on the screen. She was wondering if Oswald was right about the experience being reasonably common. She put the sugar packet on the table and was about to say something when a large banner appeared across the screen with the words *Breaking News;* there was also a snippet of appropriate music as a serious-looking reporter replaced the fruit trees and the politician.

"My goodness!" she said, "I wonder what has happened?"

Oswald was obviously aware that she was looking at the screen, so he turned his chair so that he also could see.

The serious-looking reporter was still speaking: "… man found in thick bush not far from Mount Victoria was safely helicoptered out late this morning." A number of images from the area were moving across the screen, focusing on emergency personnel in their bright yellow uniforms. A man on a stretcher could be seen being transferred from an emergency helicopter to a waiting ambulance. "According to the two young bushwalkers who found the man early this morning, it was nothing short of a miracle…"

The camera switched to the bushwalkers, both of them standing to one side, their packs on the ground beside them. One of them picked up where the reporter had left off. "It's really thick bush where we found him, and he was nowhere near the main track. We were on our way to Mount Victoria; we'd camped out last night, then Colin here thought he saw a wombat, and we left our packs on the track and did some bush-bashing. He was so lucky; we'd never have found him otherwise…"

The reporter was once again commanding the screen. He said that the man had a broken arm and was being treated for hypothermia but that otherwise he seemed to be in reasonably good health. So far, they had no other details: the man had not been reported missing and it was not clear why he was in the bush on his own. At the moment, the only name they had for him was Milford.

Tilda turned to Oswald and said: "That's not a very common name, *Milford*." She picked up the sugar packet again. "You know, I used to be married to a *Milford* a very long time ago."

"No, I guess it's not a name that one hears every day, although, come to think of it, I believe that I may have heard it quite recently, but I can't remember where." Oswald moved his chair back opposite Tilda. "He's a lucky bastard, though. Imagine being lost up there! From what I've heard, the bush is really thick, and it just goes on and on…"

The coffee arrived and Oswald thanked the waitress while Tilda emptied the contents of the sugar packet into her cup.

When the waitress had left, Oswald continued, "I don't think I'd like to be up there on my own. I wonder why he was there…?"

Tilda smiled at him and took a sip of the hot coffee. When she put down the cup, she said: "*Oswald*. That's also a very unusual name."

Oswald smiled at her. "It has something to do with German woods."

He was wondering whether the cat would have anything against sharing the sofa, and though he knew that it was a question the cat would not need to contend with immediately, he was quite sure that eventually she might have to accept the inevitable.

Tilda was rethinking everything about what she had perceived as her future, and, as she took another sip of coffee, she decided that life had definitely taken a distinct turn for the better.

Acknowledgements

My sincere thanks to Monica, Ruth, Signe and Andris for their invaluable assistance reading and/or proofreading and editing the manuscript, as well as for their encouragement and advice. I am also extremely thankful to Annette, who not only created the wonderful cover design but also helped with the text conversion.